SILK
SADDLES

WOMEN
OF THE
OLD WEST

BY
PHYLLIS DE LA GARZA

Silk Label Books

Unionville, New York

To Jeanne Williams,
Trailblazer and Friend

Silk Label Books
First Avenue, PO Box 700
Unionville, NY 10988-0700
(845) 726-3434
FAX: (845) 726-3824
email: slb@rfwp.com; website: rfwp.com

ISBN: 1-928767-19-2

Printed and bound in the United States of America on recycled, acid-free
paper using vegetable based inks and environmentally-friendly cover
coatings by Royal Fireworks Printing Co., of Unionville, New York.

FOREWORD

Apache May died in the arms of John Slaughter. Janette Riker spent the long Montana winter of 1848 stranded in the mountains after her father and brothers disappeared. Ella Eweing was a gentle giantess, who, from the time she was a young girl, earned her living in a Ringling Brothers, Barnum & Bailey circus sideshow.

These girls women, and others in this collection of 19 biographies, were real people who made their mark on our Old West. I have fictionalized these stories by inventing some secondary characters. However, the leading characters, dates, places and general events are historical fact.

Phyllis de la Garza
Willcox, Arizona

TABLE OF CONTENTS

MRS. MO-CHO-ROOK

No woman—unfortunate enough to become a wife, or captive, of Mo-cho-rook—lived to tell about it. Mo-cho-rook was born in Mexico in the late 1820s. While still a baby, he was taken captive by a Comanche war party, and raised as a Comanche. Mo-cho-rook grew into a warrior more fierce than the Indians themselves, his name meant "so cruel he makes Commanche's blood run cold." During his many years of raiding with the Comanches, he was never known to take a captive alive. Mo-cho-rook was notorious for carrying a prized lariat plaited from his female victims' hair. It measured more than thirty feet in length—and nobody dared question him about it.

The year was 1915. Mo-cho-rook was my brother-in-law. We lived in the Indian camp near West Cache Creek. Many members of our tribe were camped there, for it was our place to live, confined by white man's rules.

Mo-cho-rook loved to race on his chestnut stallion, and he usually won. I watched him that day in July from the safety of the white man's boardwalk in Faxton, Oklahoma. The horse was gigantic, very tall and fast. Half-wild, nobody else had ever ridden him. But Mo-cho-rook, dangerous and determined himself, was more than a match for the unruly animal.

Mo-cho-rook was a short man, five foot two, weighing slightly more than one hundred pounds. He was smaller in stature than most Comanches, but then he was not Comanche. He had been a Mexican captive, taken from a Mexican village when he was one year old. His whole family was killed by Comanches. He remembered nothing of his life in Mexico; he was trained and raised Comanche. But something sinister lurked in his soul, setting him apart from the rest of our people.

1

Now he was nearly seventy-five years old, older than anybody else in our village. He had outlived all the men he was raised with years ago. The young men of a newer generation shunned him, feared him; his temper was well-known.

My sister, Little Fawn, stood beside me watching the race begin. She was a tall, strong girl with a one-year-old child in her arms. Of all of Mo-cho-rook's wives, my sister Little Fawn was the only one ever to conceive and bear a child by him.

I looked at her. Holding the baby in her arms, she had the stone-face of one living in constant fear, like an ill-treated dog waiting for a kick. Despair pooled in her dark eyes. I remembered her as a happy girl tattling and giggling with the rest of our sisters before her marriage. Mo-cho-rook had married our eldest sister first, and when she died he returned to our father and asked for the next sister. After she died, he came for the next.

My sister Little Fawn was the third sister in our family married to Mo-cho-rook. Two already dead from beatings and overwork, Little Fawn was third in line. I cringed, knowing if something happened to her, I could be next. At sixteen I was one year younger than she. Lately I'd been noticing the way Mo-cho-rook stared at me as if he had plans. I think the young men in our village had noticed it too. None made advances toward me about marriage; it was as if they were afraid. Mo-cho-rook with one cruel glance had made his intentions known.

A group of young men jostled their horses in a circle in front of the General Store. Mo-cho-rook prepared to mount his plunging stallion. He vaulted easily onto the horse's back. Riding with smooth confidence, he controlled the horse while swaying with its movements. In seconds the riders shot away at full gallop. Mo-cho-rook rode furiously in the center of the pack. His unique, high-pitched, frightening scream was meant to drive his horse forward. And it worked.

I looked at Little Fawn. "I will go inside the store to buy some sugar our mother wants."

Little Fawn merely shrugged. She could not move from her place at the hitching post. Mo-cho-rook had tied her to the railing by his thirty-foot long rope woven from women's hair. I looked down at the hated thing. He had been carrying it for as long as anybody could remember. Each captive woman he killed, each wife who died, her hair was woven into his rope. It was known that each new wife, or captive, was sentenced by Mo-cho-rook to braid her own hair into the rope. He taught them how to do it tight. No slipping. They were beaten until they did it right. After that he dragged them around, or tied them up, doing whatever pleased him.

With morbid fascination I looked at the different colors—black, brown, gray, blonde, red, and more black. The last strands were woven directly into my sister's own hair. She was attached to it, Mo-cho-rook's possession.

I went into the store and bought the sugar. Returning to the street, I saw the galloping horses suddenly come into view on the road. A cloud of dust circled the shouting riders. Mo-cho-rook plunged across the finish line first, finally pulling his horse to a jarring halt far down the street.

Returning the victor, his dark eyes glinted. He put his hand out to receive the money owed him by everbody who raced against him. The younger men sneered—but they paid. Anybody who owed him paid. Nobody dared refuse Mo-cho-rook.

After nodding to Little Fawn, I hurried back to my spotted pony. I rode the three miles to West Cache Creek where the teepees of our people were spread along the bank. I tethered my pony. Still living with my parents, I slipped into our teepee. My mother sat in front of the fire, as usual, cooking. The aroma of roasting bobwhite mingled with herbs.

"Thank you for the sugar." She smiled at me. A good and friendly woman, I loved her dearly.

"Where is father?" I asked, sitting beside her. I tucked my buckskin skirt between my knees.

"He went hunting for prairie dog."

I nodded, asking for hot coffee. My parents had learned to brew the white man's coffee. I liked it. I poured in some of the new sugar. "I saw the horse race in town. Mo-cho-rook won."

My mother merely shrugged. "I know you do not like him, but he is a good provider."

I looked at her. "He has killed two of your daughters, and now Little Fawn is ailing."

My mother stiffened. "There is no choice in the matter. You know that. It is the way."

"Father should do something about him," I complained.

My mother took a sip of her own coffee. She fanned the charcoals with a stiff piece of tanned bull hide. "Mo-cho-rook has been with this clan since before your father was born. He is an elder to be respected."

"He is a cruel man everybody fears. Perhaps he was a great warrior a long time ago. But our people are no longer at war. And Mo-cho-rook is no longer in need of a wife—

4

he merely wants a slave. Father accepted four horses for Dove, and six horses for Shining Leaf. Then eight for Little Fawn."

Mother looked at me. "Including the pony you ride. Don't forget where it came from. Besides, you and I have no say in the matter. We are only women. It is between the men."

I choked on the coffee. It suddenly tasted bitter. "I suppose if something happens to Little Fawn, I will be next."

Mother merely turned back to her cooking pot.

"Doesn't it bother you Mo-cho-rook ties your daughters up like dogs? Attaching them to that hair rope of his? That hair came from countless women he's killed from the old days when he was on the war trail. White women—Indian women—Mexican women—including his own wives. How many?"

"No more talk!" Mother said, just as father entered our teepee with a grin on his face. He held up three fat prairie dogs. My parents then got into a big discussion about the hunt. I left, using the excuse that I wanted to tether my pony in a place where there was more grass.

I stalked away, untied my horse, and mounted. I rode away from the village to a sunny slope where I allowed my horse to eat grass while I brooded. Sitting there chewing a long green twig, I listened to the gentle sounds of my horse cropping grass. Below me, many teepees were spread along the peaceful hillside. Life was good. Except for Mo-cho-rook.

In the distance I could see some of the young men returning from the horse race. They rode together in pairs and small groups. I could see them laughing, and poking one another in fun. Behind them, alone on the chestnut stallion, rode Mo-cho-rook. Sullen and aloof, he seldom spoke to anybody unless it had to do with some harsh command. Tagging behind him, my sister Little Fawn followed on foot. She carried her baby in a cradleboard on her back. In her arms she lugged a bundle of trade items Mo-cho-rook must have bought at the store after winning the race. The long end of that hair rope was held tightly in his fist. He jerked Little Fawn when she lagged or stumbled so that she walked sideways trying to keep up.

I watched them arrive at their own teepee where Mo-cho-rook dismounted. He walked with his stallion, tying it in a large pole corral he had built for his horses. My sister waited like an obedient dog, arms laden, child hanging on her back. After Mo-cho-rook took his time caring for his horse, he marched into the tent, dragging Little Fawn behind him.

Once a month Mo-cho-rook hitched two of his horses to a spring wagon, and set out into the countryside. He always returned late in the afternoon with a slain deer. It was my sister's duty to skin and clean it. Mo-cho-rook took the meat to town the following day to sell.

On those days when he left early with the horses and wagon to hunt, I always sneaked over to my sister's teepee to visit with her. That was the only time he left her unattended, although she had strict orders not to leave the teepee.

"He does not take me when he hunts because he hates the whining of the child when he stalks game," she once told me. Mo-cho-rook, at the age of seventy-five, was not used to children. It had been a great surprise to everybody that my sister even got pregnant. But of course nobody dared say anything about that in front of Mo-cho-rook.

Little Fawn had the dreaded hair rope wrapped around her waist. Braided into her own hair the way it was, there was no other way she could move around unless it was coiled around her body. Her child momentarily slept on the white man's cot—Mo-cho-rook's bed. Usually she and the baby were required to sleep on the floor.

"It is a beautiful sunny day," I told her, standing in the door of her teepee. "Come with me, let's go for a ride." Mo-cho-rook had many horses inside his corral she could choose from. Apart from the chestnut stallion, there were six mares, two geldings, and a young black stallion. What with his hunting, meat-selling, and winning horse races, Mo-cho-rook was the richest among us.

"I don't dare go outside," Little Fawn muttered. Her hands worked a rabbit hide she tanned.

"You cannot live like some mole the rest of your life!"

"Blue Water," she said to me. "Don't you understand? Somebody will tell him if I am seen outside. He beats me at the slightest excuse." She looked hollow-eyed, listless, spent.

"Little Fawn, is there nothing I can do for you?" I asked.

She looked down, a dry and wrinkled woman only seventeen years old. Her eyes were full of fear. Dark bruises showed around her cheekbones, and I suspected where they had come from.

Suddenly a swishing noise over my shoulder caused me to jump. "Ih?"

Mo-cho-rook stood behind me. "What are you doing here?" he raved. The teepee filled with his ghostly smell of sweat and old saddle leather.

"Nothing…I…came only to visit my sister," I stammered.

"Get out!" he screamed. "No busybody visiting! She has work to do!"

Little Fawn jumped to her feet, cringing, quickly gathering her baby off Mo-cho-rook's bed; another sin.

Mo-cho-rook took a step toward me. "Come here again, and I will make you eat your boots!"

The baby cried. My sister tried to hush him, holding him in her arms, offering protection to the child while Mo-cho-rook raised the leather quirt dangling from his wrist. Grabbing Little Fawn's hair, he yanked her around and lashed her thighs and knees with the quirt—the only thing saving her chest and belly was the baby in her arms.

Furious, I ran from the teepee. I heard Little Fawn's shrieks each time the quirt met her flesh. Running into my own parent's teepee, I stood over my mother who busied herself at the fire again. She heard the cries coming from Little Fawn, but sat tight-lipped, flinching, silent.

"Do something!" I gasped, glaring at her. My own fists were clenched. "You listened to these same sounds from Dove and Shining Leaf, and now Little Fawn. When will it end?" My father had never beaten any of us, not even when he was drunk. I could not understand why our family had to put up with this.

My mother turned her eyes to me. "Be quiet. Stop complaining. Enjoy being young while you can. If something happens to Little Fawn, you may very well be next."

"Next! For horses, I suppose. How many horses?" I cried. I had never spoken to my mother like that before. I knew it was up to my father to decide what was appropriate payment for a daughter when a young man came

8

around with intentions about marriage. I accepted that. I understood that. But Mo-cho-rook was no ordinary young man. Everybody knew about Mo-cho-rook. Mo-cho-rook made Comanches' blood run cold.

That afternoon I saw Little Fawn working over the deer, skinning off the hide. Later she cut the meat into chunks. In the morning, Mo-cho-rook hooked his team of horses to the spring wagon. He loaded meat into the back, and shoved my sister and the baby onto the seat. Then he marched to our teepee and without looking at me, addressed my father who sat in front of the campfire.

"I need Blue Water to help me today," Mo-cho-rook said in that thin, raspy voice of his.

My father shrunk. "Help you? Blue Water?"

"I don't want to help him!" I cried.

"Quiet," my father said. "You are just a woman."

Paying no attention to my protests, Mo-cho-rook continued, "I go to Faxton to sell meat to the white people. I need her to help me. Because of her I had to beat Little Fawn yesterday. Now Little Fawn is unable to work because of the bruises." He stood over my father, hands on his hips, quirt dangling from his wrist.

While my father mulled the situation, Mo-cho-rook plunked two coins onto the ground beside my father's feet. White man's coins, money to buy many things at the store in Faxton.

My father quickly picked up the coins, pretending to examine them as if he could not make up his mind. But Mo-cho-rook knew he would keep them. Mo-cho-rook signalled me. Before I could run away, he pointed to his spring wagon. I was told to ride in the back with the meat.

9

Little Fawn did not meet my gaze. Her face was not marked, but I could tell by the way she shifted slowly on the wagon seat her lower body was hurt. Mo-cho-rook whipped up his team. I clung sullenly to the sides of the wagon, flagging my hand at the cloud of flies hovering over the meat.

Mo-cho-rook turned to me. "In town you will help cut the meat. It is time you learned."

I looked up at him. I felt my mouth dry with a combination of anger and fear. His orders told me I had defied him, and now I was in for it. Little Fawn merely kept her eyes on the road. She was no help. Back home my father had taken the coins, not meeting my gaze. Guilty and afraid, Father had given in to Mo-cho-rook as he had always done. My mother was no better.

While gripping the sides of the wagon I was filled with disgust for all of them. Fearful as slinking coyotes, allowing a cruel and relentless man like Mo-cho-rook to do what he pleased with our family. He was destroying all of us one by one with his cruelty...and his money.

In Faxton he forced me to watch while he set about slicing meat. The white people gathered around the wagon. Fresh meat was scarce, and Mo-cho-rook gave them good bargains. First he made customers show how much money they were willing to spend for meat. Next, he cut a chunk with his sharp hunting knife with the eight-inch blade. He had no way to wrap the meat. People took it raw in their hands unless they were smart enough to bring pots to carry it in.

The sun was hot. Dogs and flies circled the wagon. Little Fawn and her restless baby did not move from their place on the wagon seat. I stood beside Mo-cho-rook as he commanded. His knife sliced quickly, with ominous precision. By early afternoon most of the meat was sold. The leftovers had to be taken back to camp where Little Fawn would cut it into strips to make jerky.

Using some of his newly-earned money, Mo-cho-rook visited the General Store for tobacco, sugar, and a new knife. Afterwards we turned toward our camp. This time he made Little Fawn and the baby ride in the back of the wagon. I was ordered to ride beside him on the seat.

I cringed, sitting as far away from him as possible. How I hated him. He never laughed, or even smiled. The closest he ever came to enjoyment was causing discomfort or pain, then his eyes glinted like coals being fed bits of withered buffalo grass.

"I will teach you how to braid hair," he said suddenly. "It must be tight—no slipping."

My brain buzzed. I thought he would not ask for me as a wife unless my sister was dead. He had always been too stingy to take more than one woman to feed. Was he hinting Little Fawn would soon be dead? In the old days he took captives and made wives out of some. The long hair rope was proof of how many he had killed. But that was the old days—we lived on a reservation now, raiding and taking captives was no longer permitted. My eyes slithered to my sister whose body was tied to the wagon seat by the hair lariat. The different colors showed clearly in sections, where each victim's hair had been added to the rope. My eyes searched for the hair of Dove, and Shining Leaf.

Seething, I did not answer Mo-cho-rook. I knew it would lead to more trouble. Burning, I was angry with myself. There I was, keeping silent to avoid his wrath—I was already behaving like my parents, and three older sisters; cowering.

Looking at me he squinted, old and smart, knowing he had me cornered. I imagined I bothered him because I had shown resistance to him in the past.

"You don't scare me," I squeaked, swallowing hard, mouth dry.

He squinted when he looked at me. "Learn to do as I tell you, or you will have no time to practice getting old.

In the days to follow I noticed how thin and listless Little Fawn was becoming. Her sunken eyes turned away from mine when I tried to speak to her. Only on the days Mo-cho-rook went hunting was she left alone. But after getting caught last time, I was reluctant to visit her on the sly. She was the one who got the beating that time. I did not want to be responsible for her getting hurt again.

Life around my own family circle went on as if nothing unusual was happening. My father visited with his friends. Sometimes they went hunting for small game. More often than not he sat around the fire at night gossiping nonsense with my mother. I was the only one who seemed worried about Little Fawn's bedraggled appearance.

Then one morning I heard a terrible commotion coming from Mo-cho-rook's horse corral. He usually tied the two stallions apart from one another. Somehow the chestnut got loose and attacked the black stallion in that small space. The kicking and screaming and pounding brought our whole camp running from the teepees.

Mo-cho-rook rushed to his corral, jumping between the animals with his lashing quirt, grabbing the halter ropes, yanking the horses apart. But fighting stallions paid little attention to him in their fury. The black lashed out with its hind hooves, catching Mo-cho-rook in the hip. He collapsed in the middle of the corral with a scream.

Only then the other men entered the fray, two of them pulling the horses apart. My own father held the corral gate open while Mo-cho-rook waved everybody away from himself. The arrogant fool would not allow anybody to touch him, even in his pain. He crawled to the gate, pulled himself up, then ordered my sister to join him so that she could steady him. Like that he hopped toward his teepee— Little Fawn staggering under his weight. His face was drained of its color.

Our medicine man visited him, but came rushing away after Mo-cho-rook threatened to kill him. Later in the afternoon my father dared visit Mo-cho-rook's teepee. He soon came out, saying Mo-cho-rook had agreed to allow my father to ride to town to look for the white doctor. By now Mo-cho-rook was in great pain, unable to stand up.

That night a white doctor from Faxton came in a buggy. Some of us hung around the teepee, hoping to hear what was going on. He put something called a cast on Mo-cho-rook's right leg, high around his hip. The doctor left, saying he would be back in a few days.

That night a cold rain began to fall. Thunder and lightning lashed our village. I looked outside when I heard whimpering noises. Poor Little Fawn and her baby were huddled outside in the rain!

Slogging across the yard, wrapped in my own blanket, I stood over her. "Why are you out here in the rain?" Water ran down my chin.

"My husband does not want me inside. He says his leg hurts. The baby is annoying him."

"You will catch your death in the cold rain," I told her. "Come to our teepee where it is warm. Let Mo-cho-rook stay alone if he likes it that way."

"I can't," she said, pointing to her hair. I could see it strung out behind her through the entrance of the teepee.

"He has the other end tied around the ankle of his injured leg," she whispered. "He said the pain is so horrible he feels the slightest twitch. If I go farther, he will know it and haul me back...and beat me. It is no use."

The rain came down harder. I saw her anguished face, the sorrow in her eyes. She clutched the baby in front of herself trying to shield it from the rain. But the water gushed inside her blanket. It ran down the sides of her face and arms. She was huddled in the mud like an animal without a den.

"You will die out here," I told her.

"Good. Then let me die," she said. "Anything is better than this. Except...what will happen to my poor baby?" She looked at me as if I might take it from her arms. "You take him to our parent's teepee for the night. Keep him warm for me. If I die here tonight, perhaps he will be yours anyway."

The hair stood up on the back of my neck. Little Fawn! My own sister! Resigned to her own death because of Mo-cho-rook—even suggesting I would take her place. And thinking nothing of it? Sentenced to the wrath of Mo-cho-rook! Our whole family destroyed by him because we lacked courage. Our father accepting his money and horses while looking the other way!

I slogged back to our teepee and grabbed my mother's little knife she used to pare herbs and vegetables. Walking back to Little Fawn, I cut her hair loose from the hated rope.

"Uh!" she cried, reaching for her chopped hair. "What have you done? You have caused trouble. We are just women!"

I grabbed her by her arm, lifting her and dragging her to warmth and safety at our family teepee. Shoving her inside, I glared down at our parents, waiting for some response. But they were sound asleep, hidden under their blankets, lulled by the sound of falling rain.

I marched to Mo-cho-rook's horse corral. The chestnut stallion stood with its head lowered, rain dripping from its soggy hide. I led him from the corral to Mo-cho-rook's teepee. There I picked up the end of Mo-cho-rook's hair rope where I had cut it from Little Fawn. Working the ends quickly into the strands of horse's tail, I braided with great care. The thing must be tight, well put together... no slipping.... Isn't that what Mo-cho-rook said?

Thunder rumbled—wind came up. I turned the horse's head away from the teepee. I picked up a stout piece of firewood and smacked him across the rump.

The horse jumped forward in surprise, feeling the unusual sensation of his tail tied to something. He bucked, throwing his head, lunging forward after another whack from my club.

Inside Mo-cho-rook's teepee a howl rent the air. Next came a crash when the cot tipped over, followed by rattling cooking pots. Seconds later a billow of smoke erupted—the campfire sparked, spreading embers—flames shot up the teepee poles.

The terrified stallion streaked away, galloping headlong out of camp. Behind him, bouncing and rolling, Mo-cho-rook screamed.

In the morning we found the stallion grazing on a slope overlooking the creek. The horse was only slightly nervous when my father and some young men from the village caught him. By now the big chestnut had gotten used to the corpse dragging from his tail.

I stayed out of things while the men cut the tattered body loose. After all, I was just a woman.

FANNY STENHOUSE

Joseph Smith, Jr., founder and first president of the Mormon Church, perfected his Doctrine of Plural Marriage after claiming that he had received a Revelation from the Lord. In 1841 polygamy became a common practice in the church. The doctrine called for male members of the Mormon faith, in the name of religious duty, to take to themselves as many wives as they could. In 1862, President Abraham Lincoln signed into law an Act of Congress making the practice of polygamy illegal in United States territories. However, it was not until 1874, at the urging of President U. S. Grant with the enactment of the Poland Bill, that polygamists were threatened with imprisonment. The Mormon Church itself finally outlawed the practice in 1890.

In January 1860, Josephine became the second wife of Thomas Stenhouse. Josephine took it for granted that Fanny Stenhouse, his first wife, would give her blessing. Fanny attended the wedding, which was her duty. Brigham Young, the Prophet, officiated. Everybody felt it was only right for a successful farmer like Thomas Stenhouse to add another wife to his household. Fanny had not provided him with children... Josephine's own mother suggested Fanny would make a good helper when Josephine's children came into the world.

Josephine had been raised in a good, sheltered Mormon home. Her own father had four wives. She grew up knowing it was natural for a man to have as many wives as he could provide for. There happened to be an over-abundance of women in the church, and it was a man's solemn obligation to see to it few of them wound up old maids. Josephine had not been surprised when Thomas asked her father for her hand in marriage. Josephine had admired this rugged, good-natured Thomas Stenhouse since she was twelve years old.

On their way home from church that cold winter afternoon, Fanny sat rigid-backed in the seat behind Thomas and Josephine. Fanny's eyes, like two blue bullets, squinted straight ahead. She refused to speak. Meanwhile, Josephine leaned warmly against Thomas for support. She suppressed the urge to crawl up on his lap and worm her way inside his woolen coat. She giggled at the thought, but Fanny's icy presence prohibited carrying out the deed.

The big dun draft horses pulled into their collars. Harness leather squeaked, and the team snorted softly, blowing breath vapor in white billows. Hawks banked high overhead in a cloudless Utah sky.

Josephine turned in her seat to speak with Fanny, for she was trying to be polite. But Fanny would not look into Josephine's eyes. Josephine sighed, then shifted her own gaze to the trail of hoofprints and sleigh tracks being left behind in the newly fallen snow.

Thomas put Josephine's hand through the crook of his arm, and squeezed her fingers tightly against his side. They spoke in low whispers. He was wise in his thirty-eight years, strong, with a determined jaw and full black beard. His penetrating blue eyes told Josephine he was a contented man.

Thomas drove the team into the orderly Stenhouse yard. The big, two-story, white frame house stood squarely amid outbuildings, barn and corrals. Before a word was spoken, Fanny leapt down from the sleigh and hurried up the snow covered steps. She disappeared into the house with a door-slam.

Thomas patted Josephine's knee through her long skirts and heavy coat. He advised her to help Fanny with supper. Alone with him, Josephine was relieved, for she had felt

Fanny's deadly stare boring through her back since they'd left town.

"I hope that Fanny and I will become good friends," Josephine told Thomas, anxious to show him how mature she was for her sixteen years.

"She will be all right, Josephine," he said. "Fanny has been the only woman in this house for eight years. It will take time for her to get used to sharing."

But Josephine could do nothing right. As the months wore on, Fanny remained cool and uncompromising. Everything in the house belonged to her, from the spinning wheel to the guns in a rack on the parlor wall. Fanny could not bear for Josephine to touch the dishes or furniture. Each cup, each spoon, each doily represented some sentiment for her. With a grimace or squint, Fanny continually reminded Josephine of her territorial rights.

Besides, Josephine did not dust or sweep properly. She did not cook right. Fanny did not like Josephine's cheese-making, or the way she milked the cow. Fanny accused the girl of abandoning tools around the yard and garden. According to Fanny, Josephine needed correcting and scolding at every turn. When Josephine complained privately to Thomas, he simply reminded her that patience was a virtue. If there was trouble inside the house, he placed some of the blame on Josephine.

When Fanny's resentment toward Josephine became unbearable, Josephine tried discussing it with her mother one day when visiting in town. Surprisingly, Josephine's mother was indifferent to her daughter's concerns, strangely quiet with frozenness on the subject of plural marriage. Josephine discovered a bitterness hidden within her mother that she had not revealed when Josephine was a child still living at home. Her only advice was that Josephine learn to cope. It was her duty.

And then there was the question of children. It had been seven months since Josephine's wedding day, and still there was no sign she was with child. She had some suspicion that it was Thomas Stenhouse, and not Fanny, who was to blame for their childless home. When Josephine voiced this opinion privately to Thomas, he simply scratched his ear.

Thomas took to the fields each day, plowing or haying with the team as the seasons required—the farm brimmed with production. And while there were no children, everything else bloomed. The garden abounded with potatoes, carrots, beets and turnips. More than one hundred heads of cabbage neared harvest time. Thriving vegetable crops stood thick and green in perfectly tended rows. Stands of tall corn waved golden tassels in the wind. Fruit trees laden with apples, pears, cherries, and apricots drooped with luscious bounty.

Chickens and turkeys roamed the yard. A white pig grunted inside her pen. The milk cow produced so much milk that Josephine and Fanny were kept busy almost daily making cheese, and crocks of buttermilk, and butter.

Each evening after dinner, Thomas and Josephine strolled through the garden, or sat together in the parlor. After all, they were still newlyweds. Fanny remained grim and tight-lipped. Usually she excused herself and disappeared into her bedroom after the dishes were done. In time, Thomas spent an occasional night with Fanny, which was only right. But then Josephine's room seemed cold and lonely as she lay tossing miserably in the big featherbed, pressing the pillows against her ears—imagining sounds from Fanny's bedroom that she never really heard—nights full of jealousy bordering on humiliation. Josephine told herself that Thomas had his duty to perform. But when mornings after those nights revealed nothing but deepening hostility from Fanny, Josephine was not surprised.

Tension at mealtime became so unbearable that Josephine was not hungry anymore. Her body grew thin and blotchy-skinned under prairie dresses that hung like old sacks from her pointed bones. As she skinnied and weakened, Thomas frowned and grew somewhat distant, but he did not say exactly what was on his mind.

One hot morning in late August, Josephine and Fanny bent over their laundry tubs. Scrubbing, rinsing, wringing—back aching, arms weary—Josephine's hands burned from sun, lye soap and hot water. She scanned the clothesline swaying with drying blankets and bedding. Suddenly she heard the odd sound of vibrating drones coming from the fields. She stopped scrubbing to listen, then looked at Fanny who had stopped scrubbing, too.

"Inside!" Fanny shrieked. "Don't let them into the house!"

Locusts!

Both women dashed up the steps and slammed the door. Some locusts had already gotten inside and were hopping, flying, crawling; Josephine and Fanny tromped the creature's long bodies that squished and crunched, exuding brown liquid resembling horrid tobacco juice. Short antennae trembling, angular hind legs kicking spasmodically...the locusts' big round black eyes stared with fixed indifference while both women killed...and killed.

Josephine stomped and crushed. Fanny stuffed a rug under the door where the creatures crawled into the house. Josephine slammed windows while locusts beat against the glass like hail. She saw huge numbers settle on the blankets and laundry still swaying from the clothesline. She watched helplessly while the hungry hordes moved methodically over the garden and trees, devouring limbs, bark, leaves, flowers, stems, and each blade of grass.

Thunderous kicking sounds amid frantic groans came from inside the barn.

"The cow!" Fanny cried "She will kill herself!"

Looking at Fanny, Josephine was amazed. Fanny, who had been quietly controlled all these past months, was now exploding with energy. Her gestures were grotesque as she stomped and squished, killing...killing. Fanny ripped a broom from the closet and flailed with such passion Josephine thought it best to get out of the way. Then Fanny's blazing eyes fixed on Josephine! The girl shuddered when the broom came down so hard across her shoulders with a CRACK the handle broke.

"Kill!" Fanny panted, murdering Josephine with her eyes. Locusts crawled up Fanny's legs and over her arms and across her face. "Invader! Interloper! You creature inside my house!" she screamed, waving the broken broomstick.

Filled with terror, Josephine bolted outside and ran for the barn. She thought she might let the poor cow loose. Staggering across the yard, Josephine put her arms in front of her face while the darting, chewing insects flew against her body. Gasping, she sucked in breath only to have a locust fly into her mouth. Choking and gagging, she spit the foul thing into wind. It left a streak of brown juice running down the girl's chin, and a taste like raw spinach on her lips.

Swirling and slipping, Josephine fought against the buzzing, vibrating fog settling on everything in sight—the garden looked like one huge, brown undulating blanket.

Nearing the pigsty, she stopped briefly, fascinated with the pig. The animal seemed content wiggling her flappy pink ears, grunting with satisfaction. Methodically, the pig munched great hunks of locusts; wings, heads and legs mixed with brown liquid trickled from the corners of her grinning mouth.

From inside the barn, noises made by the berserk cow grew louder. Josephine pulled the door open in time to see the cow bucking and plunging crazily while kicking tools, buckets and equipment in profusion. Seeing the open door, the cow charged outside and galloped awkwardly across the yard and disappeared.

Josephine shrank from the creeping, chewing, crawling hard-backed bodies hopping and fluttering into each nook and cranny of the barn. Too disgusted to stay inside the building, yet unwilling to face Fanny again, the girl plowed across the yard in the general direction of a neighbor's farm, hoping to find Thomas.

Josephine scraped locusts from her skin and hair. She gagged—suffocating, pressing her hands in front of her mouth and nose. She stepped on thick, two-inch long crusty bodies covering the ground in waves. Her dress was in tatters from the creatures investigating everything—even pinching her skin raw with their rough mandibles until they realized the taste of human flesh was not what they craved. Flying off, others took their place.

Suddenly, Josephine heard the roar of a shotgun mingling with eerie howls. "Kill! Invader!" Fanny's voice carried in the darkness. More shots were fired...blasts continued as Josephine swam frantically away through the flicking, sticking, jabbing legs and wings. Wherever her shoe touched the ground, she tread upon mounds of rough-edged insects; brownish bodies crunched and twisted underfoot.

Thomas found Josephine later, after the great cloud had passed. He carried her, shivering and disoriented, into the yard. They gaped at what was left of the place—shreds dangling from the clothesline—the decimated garden—bare trunks where fruit trees had flourished. The locusts left such desolation, the farm seemed stripped to the bare earth.

"Merciful heavens!" Thomas gasped, dropping Josephine so that he could rush to the pigsty. The lovely big pig was dead in a pool of blood—the top of her head shot off. Her jaws still gaped with mangled locusts. The yard was full of dead chickens and turkeys, too. White and gray feathers fluttered like fallen leaves where the fowls sprawled bloody with buckshot. And down in the ditch beside the house where the flower bed once boasted white, orange, and purple rose mallow, the cow was shot dead, too.

Fanny, still holding the shotgun across her arms, stood on the porch looking at the ghastly scene. She did not say anything to Thomas or Josephine, but her gaze was venomous. After threatening them with her scowl, she marched back into the house.

The next morning at breakfast, Thomas made an announcement that caused all three people great relief. He had decided to build another, smaller house on the farm as soon as possible. It would be Josephine's house, filled with her own possessions.

In a month the new place was finished, and for the first time since her wedding day, Josephine felt she had a home. Happy beyond words, she thrived among her own furniture and dishes. A thing as simple as rinsing her own teapot caused the greatest joy. When Thomas made his overnight visits to Fanny's house, Josephine simply found ways to block out visions of the two people together. At least now Josephine could roam her own house, finding ways to distract her thoughts.

In the springtime Thomas began making visits to town; neither Fanny nor Josephine were invited to join him. In the days that followed, Josephine could tell that he was somewhat distracted because conversations between them had become awkward. However, she was not allowed to inquire about his business. And then one evening at the supper table he announced that he had decided to take another bride. His reasoning included it had been a year and a half since he and Josephine married, and she had not shown signs of pregnancy. So, he would have to try again. He was nearly forty years of age...he went on and on about how he needed a family...besides, it was his duty.

Dumbfounded, Josephine listened.

Two weeks later, in mid-August, Josephine and Fanny sat side by side in the stuffy church while Thomas exchanged vows with his new bride. Josephine felt faint from the stifling presence of a packed congregation. Her heart raced with fury. She sat, ignored; all attention was on Thomas's new bride.

Eliza June, a freckle-faced fifteen-year-old, whom Josephine had hardly noticed up until now, became the new wife. On the way home after the ceremony, Eliza June sat primly beside Thomas on the wagon seat. Josephine and Fanny sat behind. The horses gave off sweet-acrid horse aroma in the stifling air while straining against their collars. Josephine noticed Eliza June's plump little hand stuck in the crook of Thomas's elbow while the couple laughed softly as if they were alone in the wagon, sharing some private joke.

For the first time ever, Fanny gave Josephine a mildly understanding look. Josephine was still pondering this turn of events when they drove into the yard. Thomas pulled the team to a halt, saying over his shoulder, "Josephine, you will live with Fanny from now on. Eliza June is taking over your house."

Josephine's heart quivered with such fury and disappointment she felt the blood drain from her face. Eliza June! Inside Josephine's house! Numb, Josephine slid down from the wagon seat to follow silent Fanny up the steps and into Fanny's house. Thomas slapped the lines across the horses' backs. The wagon rattled away while Josephine gagged on a mind full of dust.

She ran to her old room she once occupied with Thomas. Furiously, she slammed the door. Kneeling at the side of the bed, weeping, Josephine wanted to die. Full of loathing and indignation, she could only think of blushing Eliza June taking over her house...her possessions! And Thomas! Josephine wanted to scream thinking of him with that dimpled brat in his arms!

While Josephine agonized, Fanny knocked softly on the bedroom door. "Josephine? Come and have a cup of warm milk. Nothing lasts forever. You will see."

Josephine joined her in the parlor for a cup of milk. No conversation passed between them. Only expressions of sadness and resignation crossed Fanny's face. Josephine was consumed with new understanding.

The next morning they did laundry together, for it seemed the best thing to do even though they did not speak. They had no desire to exchange words. They scrubbed side by side. Silently, Josephine admired the distant fields that had, except for the fruit trees, recovered from last summer's devastation. The new trees recently planted were still twigs. But the garden was richly burdened; hay in the fields was high. Two young pigs rooted in the sty. A spotted heifer in the corral promised to be as good as the old cow had been. Fat young chickens and turkeys scratched as they inspected about the yard and woodpile.

Josephine and Fanny could not help but notice Thomas and his bride had not yet appeared—neither woman had seen anything of the honeymooners since arriving home yesterday afternoon. Josephine boiled with uncharitable thoughts while glaring at the little house that used to be her own. Fanny only glanced occasionally at the house while wearing her customary slit-eyed look.

And then they heard a dreadful humming sound. The hair stood up on the back of Josephine's neck! A stealthy black cloud boiled up from the east. Josephine dropped her bar of laundry soap and staggered to her feet. She wiped soapsuds off her hands down the front of her white apron.

Fanny quit scrubbing, too. Then Josephine saw Fanny look at the honeymoon house. She heard Fanny whisper, "Invader! Interloper!" She turned to Josephine, eyes flat as anvils. "Will you help me, Josephine?"

Moments later the women were surrounded by semi-darkness from the insect-cloud blocking out the sun. Without hesitation, Josephine followed Fanny into the house where locusts had already entered the parlor. The women crushed insects under their shoes until the rug was matted with wings and twisted heads and gobs of brown juice; the killing had begun.

Fanny's gaze slithering out the window toward the honeymoon house. Panting, she yanked a shotgun from the rack on the wall. "Invader, interloper," she whispered. "Will you help me, Josephine?"

Without hesitation, Josephine reached for a gun.

BELLE STARR

Myra Maybelle Shirley, better known as Belle Starr, was born February 5, 1848 in Jasper County, Missouri. She is remembered in history as a bony, hatchet-faced woman handy with horses and guns, who had a series of ruffian husbands and lovers. Belle was a companion to desperados, spent time in jail for horse theft, bore two children, and met a violent death herself just a few days short of her 41st birthday. Her killer was never brought to justice. Belle Starr was buried outside her cabin near Eufair Lake, Oklahoma. A horse is engraved on her tombstone.

Amy Carpenter never forgot the day she met Belle Starr. Belle and her gang rode up to the Carpenter cabin in the twilight, Belle sizing up the yard with eyes full of suspicion. Looking grim, Belle rode tall in her saddle. She had two heavy gunbelts crisscrossed around her hourglass waist. A sharp spur stuck out from under the hem of her long black sidesaddle dress. She flipped her rein back and forth with confidence.

"It's Belle Starr and the Youngers!" Pa Carpenter said, peeking out the window. Amy ran for a look, craning her neck.

Outside, Belle shoved her flat-brimmed hat back on her head. Her face was young looking, but Amy figured Belle had to be at least thirty. Amy had seen Belle's picture on a WANTED poster at Fort Smith, Arkansas when she went all the way to town one time with her Pa—more than fifty miles from their farm.

Amy remembered her father standing there on the boardwalk that day in Fort Smith, staring up at the poster. There was a five-hundred dollar reward for Belle, for stealing horses. Belle was called "The Petticoat of the Plains." That was real romantic sounding to Amy. The girl just stared and stared and wanted to be just like Belle. Everybody knew that Belle had already spent nine months in the Detroit House of Corrections for stealing a colt.

Amy did not like the idea of going to jail, but riding with a gang and rustling horses and wearing a beautiful black fancy sidesaddle dress is what she thought about.

And besides, Amy thought to herself, Belle wasn't just a rustler—she had plenty of nerve. The whole territory talked about Belle last summer when she picked up the editor of the local newspaper with a wild swoop from her saddle during a rough-riding exhibition. Amy reckoned Belle did not like something he wrote about her in his paper.

Standing on the boardwalk that day in Fort Smith, Pa noticed the look on Amy's face because he poked her arm and said something about how twelve-year-old girls ought to be learning homemaking, not swooning over pictures of outlaws. But Amy noticed how he kind of ogled Belle's picture too, before he walked away. Pa Carpenter had a long-legged, stooped, weary gait—the way farmers walk on account of doing hard chores and following a team of mules and a plow all day.

The night Belle showed up at the Carpenter place, Pa was the first to step outside the cabin and stand in front of the gang. Cole and Jim Younger sat on their horses next to Belle. Another man was lying over his horse's shoulder, arms wrapped around his horse's neck—bleeding. Amy could not tell who the injured man was, but she'd seen the Youngers on WANTED posters.

Belle looked at Pa Carpenter. "Can you put us up for the night? We have a man hurt...shot himself...accidental."

Amy could see her Pa mulling things over. Amy herself suspected that the man had been shot by the law, but it did not pay to press the issue. The Youngers were nobody to mess with, and Belle could part a man's hair with a six-shooter if she took a notion.

Amy squirmed out the door to stand behind her Pa, even though her mother tried to make a grab for her arm. Amy knew they would not want her in on this, but she was getting old enough to defy them once in a while.

"All right," Pa said. "But you will have to put him inside the barn. No room in the house. Me and the wife have two kids—one of em's sick."

Belle nodded. Her black eyes swept the porch, Pa, Amy, and the woods behind the house. Belle signalled the men to head for the barn. They turned their horses around, crossing the hard-packed yard still deep with wagon ruts after the last rain.

Amy and her Pa walked back into the kitchen where Ma made noise with the dishes like she did when something was bothering her. She walked flat-heeled around the wooden floor, too. It was another way to let Pa know when she disapproved of something. But she hardly ever said anything.

After closing the door, Pa looked at her. "I know you don't like this, Myra. I don't either. But we have no choice. They have guns, and they'll use 'em to take what they want if we don't give it. They are looking for shelter one night. Besides, they have never bothered us before."

Pa kept rubbing his hands together, making guilty excuses, but Amy could see the bad spot he was in. Standing up to Belle Starr and the Youngers would likely get the family killed. Anyhow, Pa didn't have anything but an old squirrel gun that did not work half the time. It was hidden under Homer's mattress.

"The law must be after them," Ma said. "Belle Starr! Running with the Youngers, and taking up with Jim Reed, Blue Duck, and Jim July! At least Sam Starr married her! Can you imagine? That woman has got the morals of a skunk."

Pa rolled his eyes at Ma, signalling her that she should not be talking about certain things in front of Amy. But Ma was stirred up, saying, "Oh, pshaw! I'm worried that a posse will find them here. We'll be accused of harboring that woman and her gang. Or even caught in a big crossfire. Ever think of that?"

Pa lit the kerosene lamp, then looked at Amy. "Amelia, help your mother fix supper." He called her "Amelia" when he meant business, otherwise it was "Amy." She got right to it, spooning quail stew out of the big iron kettle hanging inside the stone fireplace. Pa promised to buy his wife a wood stove, but he had not been able to afford one yet.

"See your brother gets fed," Ma told Amy. Ma still had that stiff-necked look.

Amy did as she was told, and filled a plate of stew out of the pot. She figured Ma was trying to get rid of her so she and Pa could talk. Amy and her mother usually did not feed Homer till the family finished eating. That way they could take their time with the boy. At first Ma tried feeding Homer at the table with the family, but it made Pa sick.

Amy carried the stew into the little add-on bedroom with its rough plank walls. It had a cot with a wooden fence built around it so Homer could not fall out of bed. He'd been kicked in the head by a mule when he was two years old. The doctor said he was not going to live. But that was almost three years ago, and Homer was still breathing and able to eat. Sometimes he'd even give Amy a little lopsided grin when she spoon-fed him.

Amy liked Homer a lot. He was so gentle and helpless. Ma changed his diapers and washed his clothes. Amy did not like that part of things. Otherwise, Homer was all right. Sometimes she'd sit and talk to him and pet his blonde hair. He'd coo like a dove and act like he knew her. But it was Ma who really spent the time with him. Amy knew how broken-hearted her mother was to think that Homer would never grow up. Even so, she was always patient with him.

"Homer!" Amy said. She opened the wooden gate, and reached for him. Rolling him over, she smiled when he opened his blue eyes and grinned at her. "Time to eat," she whispered, "and boy do I have news to tell you!" She sat him up, leaning him in the corner against a pillow. Of course he did not understand a word she said. But that was all right, she figured that way she could tell him all sorts of crazy things that she'd never share with Ma or Pa.

Homer gulped. Gurgled. Swallowed.

"Belle Starr is here! Right inside our barn. I reckon it ain't just anybody's barn she'd stay in," Amy told him.

Homer sucked a big chunk of cooked carrot.

"I'm going to be like her someday, Homer. Pretty, and not looking old like Ma. I want to ride sidesaddle with a gang of my own. And I'll learn how to shoot a gun and get me a dandy saddle horse—like Venus. That's her mare's name. Did you know that? I bet Belle Starr don't have to do chores."

Homer jerked his head and rolled his eyes, telling Amy he wanted another bite of stew.

She ran the spoon up his chin, catching what he slobbered. "And I bet Belle comes and goes, free as a lark, never having to wear long old cotton dresses and sun bonnets like the ones Ma makes for me. I want a hat with a feather stuck in it. And leather riding gloves! So my hands won't get so dirty."

Homer sighed. He'd eaten enough. He slipped back into a dreamy sleep; corners of his mouth twitching. Amy watched him in the darkness; the outline of his fine little nose looked like a smooth white mushroom against the pillow. His silky eyelashes quivered.

Standing, Amy pushed the gate back up. She left Homer when she heard the front door bang open. A man's voice shouted. "We need water and some clean rags. Quick!"

Amy peeked around the door. It was Jim Younger giving the orders. Pa sat at the table. Ma was just lowering a bowl of stew in front of him. She wiped her bony hands down the front of her calico apron.

"Go ahead," Pa said to her.

Ma stomped to the sideboard, long dress swirling around her booted ankles. She grabbed a handful of rags and picked up the white enamel dishwashing pan. After that she followed Jim Younger out to the barn.

Amy joined Pa at the table. "Why do you reckon they need rags and a pan of water?" she asked.

"I expect they're taking the bullet out of that poor fellow," Pa said. "You better get something to eat, Amy. This is liable to be a long night."

They finally moved the wounded man into the house where it was warmer than the barn, with better light. It was Ma who insisted. Besides that, she gave the injured man the family's best blanket. Ma was the one who washed out the first wound, then burned the tip of the sharpest kitchen knife before digging around in the injured outlaw's chest just under his collarbone. She fished out a big slug, and he seemed somewhat relieved. But there was another bullet wound lower, in his stomach, and Ma refused to touch that one. She said it needed a lot more doctoring than she was able to do.

Belle and the Youngers watched, then ate up all of the family's stew. After that everybody got real quiet.

Ma checked on Homer. Later, she went to lie down in the bedroom beside Pa. Amy curled up on her own little cot in Homer's room and fell asleep listening to crickets chirping and coyotes singing. From the time Amy was little, Ma always referred to night sounds as the "Ozark Medley," so Amy was never afraid.

At first light, Pa sent Amy out to the well to fetch a bucket of clean water. When she got back to the house Ma was busy fixing breakfast for everybody, even though she was still keeping a tight lip. Belle and the Youngers drank a couple of pots of hot coffee, all the while keeping an eye on the injured man, who looked mighty pale lying there on the floor. His lips had turned blue.

"Will he live?" Belle asked suddenly, looking at Ma.

"He's lost too much blood," Ma answered, turning eggs over in the big iron skillet. "I expect some parts of his stomach are all mushy in there. He needed a doctor."

Belle looked at Pa and said, "Ain't you got something to do this morning? Like chores? Sodbuster! You make me nervous. I don't need you hanging around here gawking. Just don't go far from the house. If I see a head bobbing in the gully, I'll shoot!" She gave him a hard-eyed look that told him not to answer back.

Red-faced, Pa clumped out of the house. Amy knew he was embarrassed by the way Belle ordered him around. Ma never talked to him like that. Amy felt sorry for her father, but she guessed he was going along with things to avoid a fight that might hurt one of the family.

Belle looked at Amy. "What's your name, sis?"

"Amelia," she muttered, embarrassed. She could feel her face heat up. She looked at Ma to see if she was doing all right, but Ma minded her business at the sideboard.

Belle looked at Ma. "Nice little girl you have. I have a daughter, too. Her name is Pearl. She tried to marry a man I don't like, so I ran him out of the territory." She patted her six-gun and laughed. "Purtin-neer shot his ass off. Want some good advice? Don't ever accept a son-in-law you don't like."

Ma did not look up from her pot-scraping. "When the time comes for Amelia to take a husband, she can make her own choice. I won't interfere. She's the one has to live with him."

Belle squinted.

"We have to get out of here," Cole Younger said to Belle. "There's sure to be a posse on us."

"Posse!" Ma whirled at them. "You people getting my family in trouble with the law?"

Cole looked at her like she was a pesky fly. "Don't start frettin'. We'll be out of here soon."

A loud moan came from the man on the floor. He kicked out straight. His fists clenched. He relaxed. His head rolled to one side.

Ma rushed over to him and listened to his heart by placing her ear over his chest. "He's dead, poor man," she whispered.

Belle stared at the body, then shrugged. "He had it coming for not following orders. Too bad it took him so long to die."

"We better go," Cole said.

Jim Younger gobbled up the last of his eggs and bread, washing it down with hot coffee. He wiped his mouth on his sleeve.

Belle turned to Ma. "We're obliged to you." She pulled a small leather sack out of the folds of her riding skirt and plunked several coins down on the table.

Ma stood right up to her. "We don't take money that ain't honestly made."

Belle stared hard for a moment, and Amy thought she was going to hit Ma. But then Belle grabbed the money and put it back into the leather pouch. She nodded to the Youngers who started rolling the dead man up in the blanket. In a few minutes they had him loaded onto his horse and the gang trotted away.

Ma put her arm around Amy while they stood watching from the porch. Amy thought her mother's hand felt good and solid on her shoulder.

CARRY NATION

Carry Amelia Moore Gloyd Nation was born November 25, 1846. She lived first in Texas, and later moved to Kansas. She was the sister of Tom Moore, who became a popular Army pack-master during the Indian Wars in Arizona. Carry first married Dr. Charlie Gloyd, a drunkard whom she soon divorced. Her second husband, David Nation, was a newspaperman and teetotaler. Carry was convinced that "demon rum" should be stamped out. She smashed her first saloon at Kiowa, Kansas in 1889. After her divorce from David Nation in 1901, Carry took up a relentless crusade against liquor. She once chased John L. Sullivan, the champion boxer, into a men's room after he threatened to shove her into a sewer if she dared bother his saloon. Carry became the object of jokes, newspaper cartoons, and magazine illustrations. Eccentricity ran in her family; Carry's own mother, who died in a Missouri insane asylum, believed that she was Queen Victoria. Carry died in Kansas in 1911.

I had no way of knowing on that cloudy Friday afternoon in Butte, Montana that I was about to witness the last time Carry Nation ever smashed a saloon.

I worked as a dance-hall girl for May Maloy at May's Saloon in the old cow town. Word circulated that Carry Nation was making a cross-country tour from her home in Kansas. The year was 1909, and of course any woman who dared go around smashing saloons, preaching temperance and talking about something called "woman's suffrage" was bound to make headlines. Everybody knew about Carry Nation's Kansas adventures from all the newspaper stories. Mostly we treated it as a joke. But Carry had arrived here in Butte yesterday, and now things were not so funny anymore.

I was eighteen years old, and had spent the last two years working for May Maloy. And what can I say? Except it was a roof over my head, and May was good to me. My job included encouraging men to buy more drinks and whatever else they cared to spend their money on. It was not an easy life, but since when was life easy? I was born in a soddy. My folks died by the time I was twelve years old. After that I spent four years in an orphanage which conjures up memories of lice and stale bread. At sixteen I was released, and had my choice between drudgery on another homestead with a widower who already had seven kids, or working for May Maloy.

So here I was wearing pink powder on my face, dressed in a shiny yellow dress and gaudy red feathers. Nothing special. I learned early on that my eyes were too squinty, my lips too thin, and my shape awfully flat. While in the orphanage I had developed a cough that came from deep inside my lungs. It hurt to breathe when the air was cold, but I kept smiling and listening to drunks and braggarts because that was my job.

One man leaning against the bar said suddenly with a laugh, "May! What are you going to do if Carry Nation shows up here?"

May was behind the bar drying glasses with a white towel. Her blue-black hair coiled up on her head was kept in place with rhinestone combs. She wore a modest, high-collared blue silk dress over her full figure. Her mouth was painted bright red and she wore lots of perfume. She was nearly fifty years old, I guessed, but she would not admit her age. She was not the sort of woman you would question about things she wanted kept secret. She looked at her half-drunk customer, saying softly, "Don't you worry about Carry Nation."

Poke, the cowboy standing next to me, let out a snort not unlike the horses he rode. He had leather chaps over his Levis and wore a battered felt hat. His spurs jangled when he rested his boot on the brass rail in front of the bar. "I'm glad you think you can handle her, May, because I lived in Medicine Lodge, Kansas when Carry Nation began smashing saloons. It was not a pretty sight!" He shook his head, finishing the last of his beer. "In a month she had run every saloonkeeper out of town, and was last seen headed for Kiowa in a fast-moving buggy."

"She was chasing Kiowas?" somebody asked.

"Kiowa, Kansas!" Poke grumbled. "And after that it was on to Wichita! She carried a hatchet, a cane, rocks, and anything else dangerous you can think of. She smashed up every bar in town. There was no stopping her! She even went to jail a few times, but she'd sing that old church song of hers... something about 'WHO HATH SORROW? WHO HATH WOE'... I can't recall the rest of it. I was too busy getting out of her way."

The saloon was filling up by now. As I have already explained, it was Friday afternoon, our busiest time. When the conversation got around to Carry Nation, it seemed like everybody's ears perked up. Most tried to say something funny about her, but Poke had actually seen Carry Nation in action, and we could tell it was something he would not easily forget.

The rancher, Joel Baker sat at a poker table. He took the cigar out of his mouth and blew smoke in slow gray clouds. "It seems to me you are making a big thing out of one old woman. The men in Medicine Lodge, Kansas should have stopped her the first time she did her mischief. And that would have been the end of it. Imagine allowing an old woman to scare you!"

Poke turned to look at the cigar-smoking Joel. "Getting chased by a six-foot woman with an axe ain't as funny as it sounds."

"Six feet tall!" somebody whistled. "My God, she sounds like a tree!"

Poke nodded. "And with a face like the worst kind of sour toad, all screwed up with fire shootin' out of those glazed eyes of hers. You have never seen anything like it. That old bat thinks she is on a mission of God. Claims to have had heavenly visions. Thinks nothing can stop her." Poke slid his hand slowly onto my shoulder while nodding at May for another beer.

An elderly man, Mr. Larkin, who owned the feed store in town, came in for his Friday evening drink. He looked up at Poke from his position at the far end of the bar. "What is that woman doing here in Montana? She's a long way from Kansas, ain't she?"

May Maloy answered before Poke had the chance. "When you are on a mission of God, there are no limits to how far you can travel." May filled another glass of beer, sliding it across the bar toward a tall, heavy-set stranger who had just come in. He pushed his money across the bar to May, then swallowed the beer in one long guzzle.

"You new in town?" May asked him, being cordial like she always tried to be with newcomers.

He glowered a little before answering, "Yes, ma'am."

"Let me know when you're ready for another," she said, eyeing his empty glass.

"This is all I have time for," he said, wiping foam from the corners of his mouth on his sleeve. "I just left the Red Horse Saloon on account of trouble over there, and I reckon disaster will be here next."

Just then smashing noises like glass shattering against bricks were heard coming from down the street. Everybody

41

in May's got real quiet. Even the card players held their hands still, straining to listen.

SMASH! THUD! We heard sounds of running boots on the boardwalk, like people in a stampede. Horses whinnied; bridle reins popped at the hitching rail. "WHO HATH SORROW? WHO HATH WOE? THEY WHO DARE NOT ANSWER NO! THEY WHOSE FEET TO SIN INCLINE...." The words were sung by a deep voice.

"It's her!" Poke shouted suddenly. "How can I be unlucky enough to face that woman twice in one lifetime!"

Mr. Larkin looked quickly around the room. "There's enough of us here! She won't dare come inside and bother us...will she?"

Poke scoffed. "The bigger the audience, the better she likes it. She says she is on a crusade, even her God-given name, Carry A. Nation proves it. She hauls rocks wrapped in newspapers, and what she don't whomp with that, she crushes with her hatchet. When she starts swinging and singing, brother, I guarantee you won't want to be in her way!"

Joel Baker chewed thoughtfully on his cigar. "No woman is going to ruin my evening. If I'd wanted to be pestered by a female, I'd have stayed home with my wife."

"That's right," somebody else shouted. "Women are trouble. We come here to get away from them. I won't put up with Carry Nation's antics. A seventy-year-old crone ought to be home rocking her grandchildren, not destroying people's property."

"A woman's place is in the kitchen," somebody else chimed in. "You let them get away with closing saloons, and the next thing you know they will want the vote! No sir! Females ought to be kept in their place."

I looked at May Maloy and wondered what she was thinking. These men apparently forgot this place, where they were having so much fun, was owned by a woman. They talked back and forth like May and I were not there... as if we were not important enough to have feelings in the matter. May's face remained a cool, expressionless mask.

Looking at her, I guessed she must have been caught in the middle of a lot of emotional turmoil. She once told me how her stepfather abused her when she was a girl, and how she had no qualms now about getting as much money as she could out of men. She was a tough business woman, and I respected her. But I could see she was in a tight spot right now.

More ripping, smashing sounds came from down the street. The Red Horse Saloon was next door to the Double Shot Palace, and this place would be next.

"Sounds like she's at the Double Shot," Poke said.

CRASH!

Shouting, faces flushed, refugees from the other two saloons dashed into May's. "It's her! That old buffalo, Carry Nation! My God, ain't she a sight? If you're smart, May, you'll lock up. Don't let her inside if you value that mirror behind the bar!"

May just smiled and kept polishing glasses.

My eyes travelled to the two big oil paintings hanging on either side of the mirror behind the bar. Both pictures showed nude women lounging on fancy red couches. I imagined what Carry Nation would think of that.

Men continued drinking and talking while the card games resumed. But I noticed a definite pall now hung over the room, like nobody wanted to admit we were worried or afraid. In the back of our minds we knew something sensational was about to happen.

CRASH! CLINK! "THEY WHO TARRY AT THE WINE CUP, THEY HAVE SORROW, THEY HAVE WOE," drifted to our ears amid the thumping and cracking sounds coming from across the street.

"By gaw!" Mr. Larkin yelled. "Where's the sheriff when you need him?"

A tall cowboy named Woody dared a peek outside over the top of the swinging doors. "By golly, the Double Shot and the Red Horse look like they been hit by a cannon! Glass all over the street. The swinging doors have been pulled right off their hinges! And there goes Elmer Snoody running away with his bartender apron tied up around his neck! His face is red as a radish!"

"Shut up and sit down, Woody." Poke said. "We don't need you making it any worse than it is. Give me another beer, May."

Poke must have felt me shiver because he gripped my shoulder tighter. "Don't worry, Emmy Lou," he said under his breath. "When things get to flying around here, you can duck behind the bar."

That did not make me feel better.

Smoky Ahrens, the muscular blacksmith who had his shop down the street, dashed into May's—leather apron flapping around his knees. "By Jove! You will be smart to run for it, May. The Red Horse and the Double Shot are done for, and this place is next! A crowd of townswomen have gathered at the end of the street...Mrs. McCarthy's working the damned hand organ she plays in church. The rest of them are encouraging that Nation lunatic to put you out of business, May."

May only raised a dark eyebrow and kept polishing glasses. The women in Butte had been itching for a long time to make trouble for her. They did not seem to dislike The Red Horse or The Double Shot half as much as they disliked May's, and it was because May's was owned by a woman.

We were talking over a cup of coffee in the kitchen one time when I first came to work for May, and she said, "It's this female thing. Woman have trouble getting along with each other. Secretly, they'd all like to have some freedom, but when one of us acts different or gets independent, the others don't know how to handle that, so they gossip and criticize each other. I think in time that will change. We have to learn how to stick together. Meanwhile, I have my own life to lead, so I don't let their tattling bother me."

But I knew it did bother her. It bothered me, too. I was a victim of poverty and losing my family. There was no place for a girl to turn when she was tossed unprepared into the world, especially if she had no schooling. I could barely read and write. Getting pawed in a saloon was not what I had dreamed of when I was a child, but I had nothing to say about what life had doled out to me. At least it was May Maloy, a saloon woman, who offered me a chance.

I began coughing again. My lungs felt like cut glass. I noticed the room had gotten quiet. Out on the street a hand organ ground its tinny, flute-like melody while women's voices chanted *Bringing In The Sheaves*.

Suddenly the saloon doors swung open with a bang. And a terrible silence fell over the room. Poke gripped my shoulder so hard it hurt. The biggest, ugliest woman in the world stood in the doorway holding a long wooden cane in her left fist, and a hatchet in her right. Carry Nation stood six feet tall, weighed 185 pounds, wore metal-rimmed glasses, big black bonnet over her stringy gray hair, and a long black dress. Her surprisingly slim ankles were covered with black cotton stockings showing above her square-toed leather shoes.

Everybody in the place stared in awe—even Smoky the blacksmith was small compared to Carry Nation. The man who said she looked like a tree was not joking.

The corners of her chalky mouth turned down with disdain while her black eyes darted accusingly at everybody in the room. Carry's gaze lit on the paintings of those naked women behind the bar. With a bellow she raised her hatchet straight up in the air, roaring, "I MAKE ALL HELL HOWL!"

I was so thunderstruck my heart skip a beat.

Carry Nation's eyes glittered at May Maloy as she boomed, "YOU ARE A DESTROYER OF MEN'S SOULS!"

May's head snapped up. Carry Nation's cane snaked wickedly, knocking the cigar out of Joel Baker's mouth. Every man in the place hit the sawdust floor.

May Maloy and I were the only ones still on our feet. I, because I was too stunned to move. And May Maloy, because she was full of defiance with a business to protect.

Carry Nation took three long strides forward, covering most of the room in a second on those huge legs of hers.

But before she could actually do any damage, May Maloy coolly pulled her Colt .45 out from behind the bar. Her first shot busted the hatchet handle with a CRACK! The second shot hit the cane close to Carry Nation's gloved hand; the cane kind of popped in two pieces, dangling by one sharp splinter.

Carry Nation stopped in her tracks. I'll never know if it was the sound of gunfire, or the fury radiating from May Maloy's eyes that pinned Carry Nation to the spot.

May Maloy said, "You'll not run me out of town, Carry Nation. I've got nowhere else to go. You are nothing but a swaggering bully hiding behind a skirt, which makes you no better than an abusive man! You take one more step in here, and my next shot will put a dent between your bulging frog eyes. Improving the world cannot be done with a hatchet! Now get out!"

Carry Nation suddenly looked ridiculous, standing there with her weapons splintered, and a purely shocked expression on her face. She knew May Maloy meant business. The men began stirring a little, getting to their feet, so Carry Nation raised her chin in the air and walked stoically out of the saloon.

A big cheer went up from the men who began laughing and slapping each other's backs. Drinks flowed while everybody thought it was a big joke how May stood right up to Carry Nation. They thought they won because for as long as she lived, Carry Nation did not attempt smashing saloons again.

The Arkansas Ozarks was a splendid place to get caught up on all the reading and writing I missed out on as a child. Carry Nation's stout cabin overlooked the woodsy rolling hills where deer grazed and other wild creatures entertained us with their chirping and chattering. I learned to write well enough to help Carry Nation with articles she published in her magazines, *The Hatchet,* and *The Smasher's Mail.* Sometimes she sent me to Kansas City to tend business at the place she had established out of her own money called "The Home For Drunkard's Wives."

The incident in Butte, Montana taught her the written word had more impact than her hatchet. I grew rather fond of Carry Nation, who, in her youth had been disappointed in love, mistreated by a drunken husband, and in her old age became determined to lead women out of bondage.

When she died in 1911, two years after I joined her, few people mourned her passing, but I had promised to keep up her work for as long as I could...my cough was getting worse.

BIG NOSE KATE

Mary Katherine Horony, "Big Nose Kate," was born in Budapest, Hungary, in 1850. While still a child, she emigrated to the United States with her family. She grew up fast, and turned to a life on the wild side. She worked in Kansas saloons, where she eventually met the love of her life, Doc Holliday. Together, Kate and Doc were involved in a tempestuous relationship that would take them all the way from Kansas to Tombstone, Arizona. Doc Holliday died of tuberculosis in Glenwood Springs, Colorado in 1887. History lost track of Kate for a while after that. But it has been determined she married a blacksmith named George Cummings. Kate eventually deserted Cummings, and took a job in 1899 as housekeeper at the Rath Hotel in tiny Cochise, Arizona. In 1900 she went to work as a "housekeeper" for a cantankerous miner named Jack Howard who lived on a ramshackle homestead near the little mining community of Dos Cabezas, Arizona. Big Nose Kate spent the next thirty years living in obscurity with Jack Howard. Her neighbors, unaware of her past, knew her as "Mrs. Cummings."

"Let's go home, it will be dark soon," Dolly nagged. She huddled beside the wood stove. Her older brother paced the floor inside Jack Howard's wooden shack. It had been a two-mile walk to Howard Canyon from their house in Dos Cabezas, Arizona. A raw October wind had bitten through Dolly's thin coat. Her arms were stiff from carrying two big jars of honey that their father, the Dos Cabezas beekeeper, traded Jack Howard each year for apples.

Will was two years older than Dolly. At twelve, he was tall and ruddy-faced with devilish blue eyes. Dolly liked to tag after him, and he did not mind as long as she went along with his schemes.

"There ain't no vegetables left," Will said, looking out the window at the brown vines and lifeless stalks tangled in rows behind a brush fence in the back yard. "Maybe there's nothing to trade."

"This is apple season, dummy!" Dolly scolded. "You know Jack Howard trades apples for our honey this time of year."

Dolly saw Will stuff his fists into his coat pockets while pursing his lips—the way he did when he was bored and looking for something to get into. Dolly perched on the edge of the wooden straight-backed chair, glad to be close to the stove. The long walk from their house had worn her out because Will poked and teased her and kept her running most of the way, warning her not to drop the jars.

Wiggling her nose like an inquisitive squirrel, Dolly said, "This house always smells like mothballs."

Will nodded. "Beats me why Mrs. Cummings is worried about moths eating up her old raggedy dresses. Ain't nothin' around here worth much."

The year was 1929. The Great Depression was something all the grown-ups talked about. The mines of the Central Copper Company of Dos Cabezas had been the mainstay of the community, but now even they had closed down. Nearly everybody was out of work. Luckily for Will and Dolly, their father had a job at the Dos Cabezas post office, and besides that, he had the bees. So they had a secure roof over their heads. But even so, poverty was all around them.

Still hugging the jars of honey on her lap, Dolly nervously kicked the chair rungs with her leather high top boots. Will hummed to himself. He circled around the room wrapped in his heavy wool jacket with a knitted green scarf tied around the collar—Dolly made it for him last Christmas.

"We better get home before dark," Dolly repeated.

50

"We can't leave till Jack Howard or Mrs. Cummings gives us the apples," Will reminded her. "Pa will be mad if we come home without the stuff we're supposed to trade for."

Dolly nodded. Their pa had a temper when the kids did not do things right. But the afternoon was wearing on, and Dolly did not especially look forward to walking back to Dos Cabezas on that dark and lonely road that wound through shadowy yuccas and stretches of wind-swept rangeland. Half-wild horses and cattle roamed out there, not to mention Will and his scary tricks.

Dolly looked around the cabin with its plank floor and poor sticks of homemade furniture. The wall near the stove had wooden shelves lined with canned goods. A threadbare brown and red Indian rug was on the floor. Curtains across the windows were made from flour sacks. Decorating the house must have been the handiwork of Mrs. Cummings, Dolly thought to herself, because Jack Howard was a miner. He was not the sort to worry about curtains. He spent most of his time at his mining claims somewhere in the hills. Except for Dolly's family, Jack Howard would take potshots at anybody coming around his house.

As for Mrs. Cummings, she was known as Jack Howard's "housekeeper." She seldom visited town. Mrs. Cummings was always polite when the children came up to trade the honey, even though she did not talk much.

Will prowled around the cabin until he stood in front of a long white blanket hanging from a dowel across the doorway to the only other room in the shack. Will had never been inside that room, and was naturally curious. Dolly could tell by the way Will hummed and circled around that he was getting ready to do something he shouldn't.

51

"You better not go in there," Dolly warned.

"Oh hush up, little bossy boots. Ain't you ever wondered what's inside there?"

"It must be the bedroom," she said, herself feeling all hot and squiggly because they did not have much to do for entertainment. The prospect of getting into somebody's personal belongings had her chewing on her lip with anticipation.

"You watch the front door," Will said. "Keep an eye out for old hunchback Mrs. Cummings. You see her hobbling up the walk you let me know. Hear?" He darted behind the curtain while Dolly's heart thumped so fast it hurt.

Dolly put the honey jars on the floor near the stove and ran shivering to the door. She was scared to death that Mrs. Cummings would come along and catch Will. Dolly knew they'd both get a good tanning for snooping around, not only from Mrs. Cummings, but probably from Pa, too, if he ever found out. And not to mention tough old Jack Howard who was such a crank. Dolly was scared of him.

"Hurry up!" Dolly cried. "Will? Get out of there."

"Wow!" Will gloated from behind the curtain.

"What?" She had all sorts of ideas going through her head. The sound of wooden dresser drawers grinding against complaining tracks filled the house.

"Dolly!" Will said. "Come and look at this!"

Dolly scanned the yard. Terror-stricken, she eyed the chicken coop, horse corral, privy and the brown evening-shadowed slopes surrounding Howard Canyon. Neither Jack Howard nor Mrs. Cummings was anywhere in sight.

52

The old gray swaybacked mare was missing from the corral, which meant Jack Howard was gone. But Dolly had never seen Mrs. Cummings out horseback riding, so she had to be around there.

"Dolly! Are you going to look at this?" Will demanded.

She dashed across the room, eagerly diving past the blanket, joining him. Disappointed at first, she saw nothing but wooden furniture covered with dust like most everybody's furniture around there. The houses in Dos Cabezas usually had more dust blowing into them through the cracks in the walls than was blowing around outside. The bed had a rough wooden headboard; a white, black and green crazy quilt covered the mattress.

"Whew!" Dolly said. "Mothballs!" She waved her hand in front of her nose. The whole room reeked.

Will pulled open the top dresser drawer, exposing hand-painted fans, a red feather boa, and silky black gloves that seemed long enough to cover a lady's arms from her fingers clear to her elbows. Dolly simply gawked. Next, Will opened a wooden round-topped trunk and dug through rustling dresses covered with black jet beads and glittery rhinestones. A blue velvet jewelry box was crammed to the top with bunches of gaudy rings and strands of glass baubles. Will held up a deck of cards while flashing a small, pearl-handled derringer. It fit right in his hand like a toy.

Giggling, Dolly draped the red feather boa around her own shoulders.

"Fancy, eh?" Will said, pulling a floppy lady's hat from the trunk. It was satiny pink, smothered with red silk flowers and black beaded lace. Will stuck it on his head, posing for Dolly, smirking and squinting snake-eyed.

Dolly knew they had discovered something they should not have. She had never seen such clothing. Their mother did not own anything like this. They'd been living in Dos Cabezas all their lives, where the fanciest duds they ever saw amounted to black Sunday-church clothing.

Squatting, Dolly pulled out the lower dresser drawer and was disappointed to find nothing but stacks of papers and a bundle of letters tied with a string. She opened a black leather scrapbook. Its pages contained faded, yellow news-paper articles.

"What have you got there?" Will asked, looking over his sister's shoulder.

"These are newspaper stories about the Earps," Dolly said, reading slowly. The print was worn thin, and besides, some words were new to her. "The gunfight at the O.K. Corral, and something about Doc Holliday. He killed a man in Kansas...." She kept reading stories that told of Doc's daring escape from vigilantes with his accomplice, a woman called Kate. There were more bits and paragraphs about Doc Holliday's part in the Tombstone trouble, and finally a story that said he died of tuberculosis in Glenwood Springs, Colorado in November of 1887.

That was the last article. After that the pages of the scrapbook were blank.

Dolly did not know what to make of this. She wondered why Mrs. Cummings was interested in Doc Holliday and the Earps. While she mulled, Will slipped a picture out of the dresser drawer. It showed Doc Holliday sitting in a chair. A haughty lady wearing the frilly hat and fancy dress the children had just found inside the trunk, stood behind him with her hand on his shoulder. The two people looked proud to be together. Even though it was just a picture,

Dolly felt the smoldering eyes of Doc Holliday boring through her.

Handwriting in the corner of the picture said, "Doc and Kate, Tombstone, 1880. Fly's Studio."

Will pressed his nose up against the picture. "Why, that's Mrs. Cummings when she was young!"

Dolly took a closer look. "By gum, you're right!" Dolly sometimes imitated the way the miners around there talked. "The date is 1880, almost fifty years ago. But that's Mrs. Cummings all right. See her big nose?"

"Mrs. Cummings is Big Nose Kate!" Will said. "Ma and Pa have talked about all that trouble in Tombstone, you know, the Earps and Doc Holliday, and Big Nose Kate. The gunfight at the O.K. Corral—most people around here don't think much of the Earps. And they say Doc Holliday was nothing but a killer. Himself dying of tuberculosis, he did not care who he shot or stuck a knife into. In fact, my teacher said Holliday did a lot of mean things because he wanted to get shot—which was better than dying slowly of...."

Before Will could finish his sentence, a terrible shriek filled the house. He and Dolly were so busy snooping, they did not hear the door open. Little old Mrs. Cummings charged across the bedroom floor. She jerked the scrapbook out of Dolly's hands, and the boa from her shoulders. At the same time she snatched her photograph and hat and derringer away from Will. Mrs. Cummings rolled everything in a bundle in her scraggly arms. Wisps of gray hair stuck out from under her wool bonnet.

"Little devils! Sneaking around where you don't belong! Digging into my business. Get out!" She gave one of Dolly's pigtails a hard yank.

Will and Dolly stampeded toward the front door when Jack Howard walked into the house. His face brightened when he saw the kids, because he knew they always brought the honey.

"Hello, you…" before he could say anything else, Mrs. Cummings flew out from behind the blanket, still clutching her belongings against her old but sturdy body. She hopped around in her long black dress looking like a witch with her humped back, long nose, and jutting chin. Her eyes glinted like two black marbles.

Jack Howard gaped at her. "What's wrong?"

"They got into my things! Wretched snooping brats. They'll talk and bring trouble on me." Mrs. Cummings was so agitated she gulped like a fish.

Jack Howard's squinty eyes darted over Will and Dolly. "Is that right? You two been snooping?"

Will and Dolly hung their heads.

"Hmm….," Jack Howard scratched his craggy chin, as if trying to figure out what to do about this. He took his hat off, rubbing his sleeve across his shiny forehead. Jack Howard was completely bald.

Mrs. Cummings staggered to the stove where she poured herself a cup of boiling black coffee. She sipped it quick and loud without waiting for it to cool. *Slurp. Slurp.*

"Now, Kate," Jack Howard said, while throwing the children a walleyed glance. "Er…, Mrs. Cummings, don't get yourself all worked up. Those things you worry about happened a long time ago. These kids can't be interested in talking about what don't concern anybody anymore."

Slurp. Slurp. "Everybody talks about everything that don't concern them. People are cruel when they gossip. I've lived up here for thirty years, minding my own business, not wanting to be bothered, and not bothering anybody."

"Sure you have." Jack Howard nodded, running his thumbs around the brim of his greasy felt hat. "These children know not to go saying things that would hurt you." He looked at Will and Dolly with eyes hard as bullets.

Mrs. Cummings' bony white hand trembled so hard that coffee sloshed over the rim of the cup, splattering in quick sizzles on the hot stove. "Doc and the Earps and all that happened a long time ago, but it's my life, and I got a right to my privacy." She walked slowly back into the bedroom still holding the scrapbook across her chest. One end of the red boa was pressed in the crook of her arm so that the rest of it dragged like a fat snake across the floor behind her. In a moment sobs and sniffles quavered from behind the blanket dividing the two rooms.

"Come with me to the woodshed," Jack Howard told Will and Dolly. He sounded like he meant business.

"Yes sir," Will said, acting a lot more humble than Dolly had ever seen him. "We left the honey jars by your stove." He pointed, as if that would help his cause. "It was a mighty long walk up here for me and my poor little sister in the cold, but we don't mind doing it," Will added.

Jack Howard's look told Will he was not being fooled. The three of them trudged outside. Dolly cringed, wondering if Jack Howard's woodshed had the same meaning the one at home sometimes did.

Late afternoon sundown caused big purplish shadows to move slowly across the Dos Cabezas hills. Dolly noticed that far in the distance broken rocks and patches of thorny mesquite gave a stark and lonely feel to the land. The bitter wind reminded her to pull her coat around herself as she tagged after Will and Jack Howard. She considered making a run for it while she still had the chance, but she knew there would be some tall explaining to do when she got home. So she decided to take her medicine now and get it over with.

Jack Howard opened the shed door. Slowly, he reached for a burlap sack already filled with apples. "You know," he began, "things can happen to people that is out of their control. Like the way a vinegarroon got into my hat one time when I was working in a mine. When that critter stung me, I lost all my hair."

Will and Dolly grinned. They knew that was just a story Jack Howard liked to tell about how he was made bald from the sting of a whip-tailed scorpion.

"And take that old gray mare of mine," Jack continued, nodding toward the bony creature nibbling weeds inside the pole corral. "She didn't ask to be swaybacked, but she got worked too hard when she was a filly, and her bones could not stand the weight. Now she's having to live out her life like a freak, you know. People laugh when they see her go by."

Dolly squirmed. She too had made fun when Jack Howard rode his gray mare through town. The joke was that Jack's mare was so swaybacked, when he rode her, the only thing a person could see was his hat bobbing up and down.

Dolly wiped her nose, still scared and wondering when Jack Howard was going to get to the point.

Being more outspoken than his sister, Will blurted, "You mean things happened to Mrs. Cumming when she was young? Things she did not have anything to say about?"

Jack Howard leaned against the corner of the sagging wooden building. "Her papa died when she wasn't much older than you are." He eyed Dolly. "And she had to fend for herself in the world just so she could have something to eat. Things you children wouldn't understand."

"Like wearing feathers?" Will stifled a grin.

Of course neither Will nor Dolly had ever seen women dressed in feathers, but there was a place called a "sporting house" in Dos Cabezas that the men laughed about. And the women in town whispered how the girls who lived there wore feathers and that children should stay away from the place. Dolly had not figured out why.

Jack Howard looked at Will for a few moments, as if trying to figure out what to say next. "I had two daughters a long time ago, but they were raised up by their mother. I have had no experience in dealing with youngins. But I reckon there is no harm in talking straight to you, as if you were all grown up already. Of course, if you two were older, I might be handling the situation different."

The way he looked at Dolly caused her to shiver. Everybody knew Jack Howard's temper when it came to protecting his mining claims. Now it appeared that it was not only his mining claims he was protecting from snoopers.

"We won't tell anybody that Mrs. Cummings is really Big Nose Kate," Will said.

"Good," Jack said. "Kate had a special life a long time ago with a man named Doc Holliday. When he died, she took up with a blacksmith named Cummings who abused

59

her. She had to leave him, and there was no place for her to turn until I took her in here. She has been a good friend and companion…I…er, housekeeper to me for nearly thirty years. She has never harmed anybody in these hills, and I would hate to see trouble come to her." His eyes looked sinister when he handed Will the apples; the conversation ended.

Dolly never dared go back to Howard Canyon again. She and Will kept Mrs. Cummings' secret. Not so much because she and Will were trustworthy, but they knew if their Pa found out they'd snooped through Mrs. Cummings' possessions, they'd have really been in for it. So Mrs. Cummings' secret, for personal reasons, was safe with them.

The following year, in January of 1930, on a cold and windy day, Mrs. Cummings knocked at their door in town. Dolly's parents were the only real friends that Jack Howard had in Dos Cabezas, so Mrs. Cummings came to their house when disaster struck.

When Dolly's mother opened the door, Mrs. Cummings was standing there holding her long black coat against the bitter wind. Tears ran down her wrinkled cheeks. "Jack died last night," she gulped, "and I stayed up with him all night."

Dolly's mother let Mrs. Cummings into the house to warm herself. Thus began a lot of suffering for the poor old lady. She walked back and forth every day for a couple of weeks from Howard Canyon to Dos Cabezas. First she had to make arrangements for Jack Howard's funeral. Then she tried to get what was coming to her since Jack Howard left her his homestead and his mining claims.

But in the end, the land was worth little more than five hundred dollars, which she needed for funeral expenses and probating the will. Meanwhile the director of the Riggs Bank in Willcox told her Jack Howard's mining claims were worthless. Old, ill, and alone, Mrs. Cummings disposed of the property. She got rid of her belongings except for her black shoes and dresses. She wrote to Governor Hunt asking permission to enter the Arizona Pioneers' Home in Prescott.

Those were Depression years. Few people were able to help the lonely old woman. Nearing her 80th birthday, she found herself practically penniless because Jack Howard had been "on the dole." That expression was used in those days for somebody receiving public assistance.

Dolly heard her parents talking about Mrs. Cummings' predicament. After that Dolly and Will were glad they never told their parents who Mrs. Cummings really was. Dolly and her brother didn't know if that information would have made a difference to her parents, who helped Mrs. Cummings in what little ways they could. But it made the children feel better knowing they hadn't caused the poor old lady any more trouble than she already had.

One year later, Mrs. Cummings left Dos Cabezas forever. She passed a physical examination in Willcox given her by Doctor B. E. Briscoe, stating she was feeble and hard of hearing, but without contagious disease. She entered the Arizona Pioneers' Home in Prescott on September 25, 1931, where she lived in obscurity until her death on November 2, 1940. Big Nose Kate was buried as Mary K. Cummings in the Arizona Pioneers' Cemetery in Prescott.

CRAY-GEE

The word "Apache" conjures up visions of strength, stealth, and bravery. The Apaches were finally forced from their land by overwhelming numbers of invaders. Apaches were a tough, determined, desert-bred people whose legends seem endless. And names like Cochise, Geronimo, Juh, Chato, Mangas Colorado, and Victorio are spoken of and written about time and again. But what of their women? What of the wives, mothers, daughters? What of the food-gathering, child-bearing, and sometimes warrior-women who lived, fought, and died without complaint beside their men?

They ate their meals running; wood rats and insects. Deen-dih and her sister Cray-gee, struggled behind the men up the slippery escarpment entangled with bushes and naked dry roots. Behind Geronimo, they were twenty-seven Apaches following their leader one last desperate time. Deen-dih carried her own newborn baby on her back, two hundred miles, all the way from San Carlos Agency.

Deen-dih and Cray-gee, both widows with infants, agreed to run toward the Sierra Madre with Geronimo and his small band of hostiles. Four other women were with them too; the rest were men. All knew escape from the reservation could lead to imprisonment or death. "If we make it—we make it. If not, well, all is lost anyway," Cray-gee reasoned.

"Anything is better than life on a reservation," Deen-dih agreed. Just like the men, the women felt a storm in their hearts. They were only women, but they decided to take their chances with the men.

Three days later, Deen-dih's baby still hung from a leather sling on Deen-dih's back. Scrambling along behind the men, she felt her feet slide on the hot shale. Suffocating wind blew through the hills drying her tongue till it felt like leather. Her eyes rolled grudgingly in their sockets. Her parched throat begged for water. The earth was so hot, walking on rocks was like treading stovepipe. The summer mountains were baked colorless in a silent, heat-ridden vacuum. Arizona Territory was an endless furnace that late August of 1886.

Far below, winding like slow blue ants, came the column of soldiers...relentless...coming...coming. Hundreds of them. On horseback, leading pack mules, they had plenty of food and water...and guns.

"White Mountain Apache scouts do the tracking," Geronimo said, spitting. He ordered his followers to find what shade they could against the rocks and bushes on a hillside. "It takes an Apache to trail an Apache."

"General Miles has orders to find us this time, no matter what," answered Naiche, a warrior of importance. He sat on a rock beside Geronimo. His dark eyes had not left the cavalry column snaking along the Apache trail. Horseshoes clicking against rocks caused metallic echoes to reach Apache ears. "Many soldiers follow us. They have learned we are not easy to catch."

Gasping for breath, panting shallowly to conserve energy, Deen-dih leaned on a boulder beside her sister. Looking high on a hilltop, she saw light flashes sending mirror talk across the vast miles from heliograph stations. Back and forth...back and forth...messages in the air much quicker than worn moccasined feet.

Geronimo saw it too. "White eyes lightning talk," he said, frowning, pointing back and forth at the pinpoints of light making signals. His leathery face was rugged as the hills; mouth dry as chalk. He ordered everybody to move on.

Throughout the long hot afternoon, they trailed higher into the peaks. The fleeing Apaches could not understand what was being said with the mirrors, but they knew the signals could only be a bad omen for them.

The next day, Deen-dih's baby was ill, fussing like a restless bird, struggling for breath. Deen-dih offered her milk, but the infant had too many miles of desolation behind her. Geronimo himself stood over the woman and child. Geronimo with long, downward-slashed mouth, arms crossed, feet slightly apart, his skin the color of earth. Without saying anything more than her name, "Deen-dih" and pointing with a bronzed finger, Geronimo's eyes told her what she must to. Deen-dih gathered her courage. The child must be killed. Its cries, carried on the wind, might alert the soldiers to the Apache whereabouts. Sacrificing one to save the others while on the march had always been the Apache way.

"Do it now," Geronimo said. He turned swiftly and was gone. There was nothing else to talk about.

Deen-dih stiffened, understanding her duty. She had hoped it would not come to this, but it did. The high wind currents blew in sand-ridden stings across her face. The vastness of a dangerous desert night caused her to tremble once. She slid quietly away to a small arroyo in a bleak brown canyon. Deen-dih bit her own lip to keep from crying out. After strangling her own child before she could have second thoughts, she quickly slid the small limp form rolled in buckskin thongs deep inside a crevice between some rocks. Deen-dih covered everything by scooping sand with her hands until her palms bled. Her fingers bloody and burning, it felt good to punish herself.

Deen-dih staggered back to camp, and joined Cray-gee. She slid, breasts aching, under the threadbare blanket shared with her sister. Cray-gee was awake, but she said nothing. Sisters of the wilderness, their sorrowing unspoken feelings were passed back and forth like silent flame.

Up at first dawn, the Apaches climbed the narrow sliver of high trail. Farther into the mountains, the renegades glanced like furtive coyotes over their shoulders at the endless blue column still advancing.

Long hair tied back with a headband made of some white woman's dress, Geronimo's face was creased with gray alkali dust. He hesitated briefly, then led his band forward again.

Parched throats, painfully empty bellies, hearts throbbing, legs moving on little more than well-practiced determination, the Apaches struggled on. Sometimes bullets bounced around the rocks—random shots from soldiers intended to keep their quarry on the move.

Late that afternoon, Cray-gee weakened and fell back. After missing her, Deen-dih retraced their steps. Deen-dih found her sister sprawled in the dust below a big tan rock where she panted like a sick dog.

"What is it?" Deen-dih asked.

"I am dying." Cray-gee's words came in a rough rope of breath. "I am too weak to go on. Here, take my baby." When Cray-gee slid over onto her side, Deen-dih saw the bloody hole in her left flank. Pressing her fingers against the oozing blood, Deen-dih understood a soldier's bullet had found its mark. Cray-gee had not complained.

Geronimo, bronze and sinewy, appeared suddenly. "What is wrong! Hurry up! We go!"

"My sister is dead—a soldier's bullet," Deen-dih whispered.

"Ih! Cover her quickly and follow us. Now!"

After dragging the corpse to a crevice between two large rocks, Deen-dih scooped frantically, no time for rituals. Only a woman. Hurry. The others must not be jeopardized. She finished the burial, then held Cray-gee's baby girl in her arms, and ran along the trail. Head low, she was disoriented now and worried the others scurrying like fallen leaves had left her behind. Her brain whirled with thoughts of her own dead baby, and now her dead sister.

Gasping, Deen-dih found a high spot and let her eyes travel the way the others might have gone. At first she could see only the dry and wrinkled land, the rocks the lofty pinnacles...a harsh blue sky...Apache land. Suddenly, there in the high cliffs she saw two warriors watching from their stone perch. Long hair swaying, solemn dark-skinned faces surrounding darting black eyes, Fun and Chapo signalled Deen-dih to hurry. They turned their backs and disappeared with a silent swish of their breechclouts.

In the blue haze of late evening, the men found a narrow cave entrance in the canyon wall. One by one, everybody slid inside. Scraping backbone against rock, they stepped off a short drop into a chamber just large enough to protect them during the night. Exhausted from the long day's hard traveling and lack of food, the fugitives rested on their haunches, breathing deeply, waiting for Geronimo's command. The water flask was passed around until it was empty. A fire was started with sticks the women had picked up on the trail. In the firelight everybody feasted on wood rats caught during the day, and a few strips of horse jerky left over from the reservation. The crackling fire only seemed to remind them of better days.

Deen-dih sat with the women at the back of the room while the men kept their own spirits up with long-winded talk. They boasted about leaving their mark, and fighting on to the last man. They sat smoking rolled oak leaves, their white man's tobacco long gone.

"We are not easy to kill..." Fun said, "the white eyes will remember." Geronimo nodded, rattling his long gun that had few bullets. His long black hair hung in ragged points to his shoulders. "Besh-e-gar! With more rifles we can still win."

"Sh-yeh!" Fun added, "We keep going!"

"Llini!" another said. "In Mexico we will find ponies."

"Enju," Geronimo said, "It is well to be remembered how the Chiricahua did not give up."

The men droned on, reliving their old victories while there was still time. One by one they drifted off to sleep leaning back on the stone floor, snoring, filling the cave with their sweaty smell. And finally not even Geronimo had anybody left to listen to him.

Deen-dih waited until the men fell asleep. Then she drifted quietly across the room, and stepped out between the slitted rocks where cool night air met her body. A blanket of stars spread across the black sky caused her to stare in fascination—there were so many things in the world she did not understand. Like stars—where did they come from, and why? How did they light up at night? And could her sister Cray-gee be up there someplace? And Deen-dih's baby? Deen-dih knew a spirit went on after death. But where? And how?

Chapo, standing guard with his rifle in his hands, turned to Deen-dih as she walked to the cliff-edge. "You should not come out here," he said. "Stay inside with the others."

Deen-dih stood against the sky. Swaying gently, she held Cray-gee's restless baby in her arms. "Soldier fires light up the night." She watched the yellow-gold flickers dotting the mountainside. "They have no fear that we see their camp."

"Why should they? There are few of us compared to them." Chapo joined her, staring sullenly into the canyon. He was Geronimo's oldest son. Geronimo's children from his first wife, older than, had been killed many years ago by Mexican soldiers in Sonora.

"Anh. It has come to the end of our people," Deen-dih said.

"But we end bravely. We will show them we know how to die," Chapo answered.

"The end is still the end," she said. "Why would they remember how we die? Who will care?"

Chapo stiffened. "We fight!" His eyes caught a glow from the sky and valley, showing the same dull glare.

Deen-dih shivered against the new breeze touching her skin like Ghost Face; winter. The baby squirmed harder in her arms. "Anh. But our memories will fly away like dust in a storm. Perhaps we will end up in the sky to make our own stars?"

"I have no time for women's talk. Ugashé. Go inside!"

Deen-dih's belly growled. Dizzy with hunger and fatigue, she thought of finding her way down the mountainside to demand food from the soldiers for the child and herself. She knew they would take her and the baby in. Feed them. Then send them back to San Carlos. But that was only a fleeting thought, a moment of weakness on her part.

As if reading her thoughts, Chapo took a quick step toward her, motioning with his gun. She bowed her head, wending slowly back into the cave where the last of the Apache fire threw wavery light around the room. Looking up, she noticed strange patterns on the walls. It occurred to her some mysterious ancients had left drawings here. Someone had been inside this place even before the Apaches. Deen-dih flinched, nerves tingling like telegraph wire. There were animal and human figures etched in story-form on the walls. She walked quietly around the cave, studying the figures depicting somebody's life history. She saw horses, and deer, and women grinding corn. There were snakes, and strange horned animal figures with humps on their backs she did not recognize. She looked and looked, fascinated, tracing her fingers across the dark pictures drawn on the rough stone.

Later, during the night, Cray-gee's child became restless. A pallor came into the small one's little red face, making the mouth pinched and eyes glazed—the same way Deen-dih's baby had looked two days ago when it first got sick. The infant's whines did not go unnoticed by the men.

At dawn Geronimo watched Deen-dih from his position near the dead fire. "The child makes noise." Those cougar eyes of his followed her movements while outside the black night lifted into slate-gray dawn. Morning broke in white slashes across the eastern sky; the Apaches awoke for their orders.

Geronimo stood before them, arms crossed, staring around at the sunken faces full of suffering but still dangerous, like so many panthers, ready to turn one last time to make their stand. Finally his eyes fell on Deen-dih for the second time that morning. He gave the same simple order he had given her two days ago. "You know what to do."

"Anh, Yes. I know what to do. Leave me here to do it. I will follow you." But her eyes did not meet his this time. Facing Geronimo while harboring her own secret thoughts was like licking honey from a knife edge.

Geronimo swept his arm in a quick circle and the silent Apaches rose, slipping one by one from the slit in the cave entrance. Deen-dih stood alone with the sick baby in her arms.

She made a choice. The men would go on. Let them fight and be remembered in their own way. She would remember Cray-gee in hers. Deen-dih pressed Cray-gee's child to her own breast to stop its fitful cries. Then, she stooped to pick up a handful of cold charcoal from the banked fire. Mixing this with bits of brownish powdered sandstone she scooped from the floor, Deen-dih pinched the mixture between her thumb and forefinger. Finally, she pressed this between her lips, and, sucking hard, brought saliva to her mouth. She chewed the bitter compound into a cud. She spat it back to her fingertips and slowly pressed the dampened color into the wall with her thumb.

Deen-dih began her sister Cray-gee's story simply, as a woman's story. It started with a cradle.

JULIA BULETTE

Julia Bulette was an elegant Creole beauty who, in 1859, began her legendary career in Virginia City, Nevada. Men of this booming mining town appreciated her flamboyant style. She built Julia's Palace—a center of "social activity" that boasted of the finest food, liquor, and female companionship. By 1863, Virginia City swelled to a population of 30,000 inhabitants, becoming the second largest city west of Chicago. Julia's Palace was the most elegant structure in the city's Red Light District, and Julia Bulette herself commanded $1,000 per night from any gentleman able to afford her company. Julia's shocking murder in 1864 threw the entire city into excitement. The day of her funeral was declared an official day of mourning. Eventually, John Millain was convicted of the murderer. But he went to the gallows professing his innocence.

Julia Bulette's biggest opportunity presented itself in Virginia City, Nevada, where the fabulous Comstock Lode made hundreds of men wealthy overnight. The scarcity of women allowed a beauty like Julia Bulette to cash in on a large part of their fortunes.

Julia's personal maid, Colette, huffed and puffed, lugging Julia's hat boxes and baggage across the West from one boomtown to the next. For even though Julia barely scratched out a living, she always acted like a highfalutin' lady—it was all part of her act. Julia and Colette met in New Orleans, just as Julia's "career" was blossoming, and Colette's was fading. At twenty-five, Julia Bulette was in her prime. But at fifty, Colette worked grudgingly as Julia's personal "French maid."

They arrived in Virginia City on a summer afternoon in 1859. The stagecoach was full of passengers, including a six-foot-tall blonde with a Roman nose and a cracked voice calling herself Antoinette Adams. Antoinette billed herself as a great actress who had come to Virginia City to entertain

71

the miners. She droned on and on in a most boring fashion, and both Colette and Julia were glad when the stagecoach finally came to a rocking halt at the Virginia City stage office.

The town was made up of hastily thrown together buildings bordering the dusty street. Horses, wagons, dogs, burros, and men moved in hurried swarms as Julia and Colette checked into the hotel. They decided to see Antoinette's act after dinner, since there was little evening diversion except for the rowdy saloons. Besides, Julia was anxious to look around.

The theater consisted of rough planks nailed across two rows of felled trees inside a tent. The miners crowded inside; some brought buckets to sit on while the rest either stood or sat on the floor. Julia and Colette were given places near the stage, since the men were astounded to find a female of Julia's beauty in camp. As yet, few other women had arrived in Virginia City, so Julia's timing was right.

Antoinette performed a batch of bawdy songs and awkward dance skits. The miners got restless because Antoinette looked nothing like the curvaceous sprite pictured on her publicity posters. Besides that, her voice was a pretty good imitation of a braying mule. Right away the witty miners shortened Antoinette's name to "Aunty," and they laughed and howled, which did not do anything for her confidence. Every time she tried to start a new song the miners cheered, "Huzza, Aunty!" drowning her out while they laughed and stomped their boots.

When they figured they had teased her enough, they started tossing silver coins up onto the stage. In a few minutes the planks were covered with money. By the time

Antoinette finally left the platform, she grunted under all that weight since the coins filled two cloth sacks.

"Aunty" took the hint, and left on the morning stage. But Julia was inspired after seeing what happened. She realized these miners were lonely, generous and good-natured. She rented a house at the end of the street. She began entertaining discriminating gentlemen who knew how to behave, and who were willing to pay dearly for an evening with a real lady.

Julia liked to tell everybody she was French, having perfected an oily-voiced accent mixed with a lilt to match her coquettish smile. She had a wide mouth, good teeth, and short, curly black hair. Her creamy smooth caramel-colored skin bespoke of her Creole ancestry.

Within the year, she demanded $1,000 per night, and was soon able to build "Julia's Palace" on D Street. The building's rococo lavishness was in keeping with Julia's elegant taste. Each day, Wells Fargo delivered fresh-cut flowers from California. Julia's personal possessions swelled drawers and closets with jewelry, money and furs.

Colette lived in a dark little room off the kitchen, seemingly content to oversee the cooking and cleaning. Julia hired young women who displayed charm and beauty to occupy other rooms in the house. The place with its aged wines and French cooking was all very posh—but the only thing Colette was allowed to sip was cheap "tarantula juice."

By 1863, Virginia City was booming. With a population of 30,000 inhabitants, it was the second largest city west of Chicago. It now had a Red Light District, but nothing could compare with Julia and her Palace.

"I want a raise in my salary," Colette told Julia one day. Colette had been fetching and carrying for nearly six years.

73

Meanwhile, the past four years in Virginia City had brought Julia such wealth that Colette thought it was time Julia showed Colette her appreciation.

"What do you need money for?" Julia asked, dabbing charcoal on her eyebrows with a fine, silver-handled brush. She sat in front of her dressing mirror. The room smelled like lavender water, roses, and stale cigar smoke.

Colette gathered up Julia's green silk dressing gown from the floor after opening a window for fresh air. "What difference does it make how I will spend it? I deserve it. That's all."

Julia pouted in that indifferent way of hers that Colette had come to despise—it was the same look Julia wore when smashing a fly. "Twelve dollars a week, including room and board is already more than any other servant in this town makes."

"I am not any other servant!" Colette cried. "I oversee everything in this house—cooking, cleaning, laundry. Besides being your personal maid, I am expected to pick up after the other girls, too. You make more than one thousand dollars a night. I think it is only fair that you appreciate my worth."

Julia opened a new box of pink rouge, finally dabbing fiercely at the hollows of her silky tan cheekbones. "Colette! Do not bore me with your prattle." She got up from the dressing table and wiggle-hipped away to change her clothing behind the hand-painted black and yellow Japanese dressing screen.

Seething, Colette stood in front of Julia's mirror, looking at her own large hands that were calloused from work. Graying hair, thick waistline and sagging chins reminded Colette of her age. Had she been thirty years younger she

74

could have given Miss Uppity a run for her money in Virginia City. Some real competition! Colette had been in this business before Julia was born, but Colette could only be a madam now. Starting new meant an investment—a large house—hiring girls—offering the ambience that men were willing to pay a high price for. It infuriated Colette, remembering she had given Julia all of those ideas in the first place.

While Julia rustled about behind the screen, Colette's eyes fell on an opened dresser drawer overflowing with strings of pearls, jet beaded collars, gold chains, and diamonds and rubies set in elaborate rings. It was not fair that Julia treated Colette this way! She stalked out of the room.

During the following weeks Colette did not mention a salary raise again. She kept busy, paid attention to the details of her job, and even drew a few compliments from Julia, who noticed how sweet-tempered Colette had become. But late at night, in the privacy of her room, Colette pried up a floor board and took out her cache, hoarded in a green leather box. For a few wonderful moments she'd fondle the coins, rings, bracelets, watches...if Julia would not pay Colette her worth, then she felt it only right to take steps in feathering her own nest. After all, Colette was not getting any younger.

It was July. The heat was oppressive. A late breakfast brought the six girls who worked for Julia together around the kitchen table for a bit of mutual gossip and toast. Suddenly Penny said, brushing her dark curls away from her damp forehead, "My gold ring is missing. And my amethyst!"

"Really?" Julia asked, frowning. "I too have lost a strand of pearls.

75

Rosie sipped her coffee. "My emerald bracelet is missing. I bet a customer took it, but I have not yet figured out who."

Lulu piped, "I miss no jewelry, but some cash is gone from the shoe box in my closet where I keep private papers."

Birdie stormed, "I didn't want to say anything, but my ruby necklace has disappeared."

Julia looked sharply at Colette. "Colette! Do you know anything about this?"

The stack of china rattled in Colette's hand. "No! Nothing!" She tried keeping her voice calm, but felt her face redden under Julia's harsh stare.

The girls continued with breakfast, but a pall hung over the table. Colette could see them casting suspicious glances at each other. Julia was especially slit-eyed, for while she had only admitted to missing the pearls, Colette had relieved her of many more things that Julia was either not aware of, or was unwilling to disclose for now.

Julia said, "We have many customers who come and go from here. It could be any one of them. Be careful from now on. Do not leave your valuables exposed."

The girls burst out laughing then, having taken her comment in an off-color way. Colette too laughed, glad the subject was changed.

Suddenly from far down the street was heard the frantic clang of the fire bell.

"Fire!" Julia screeched. It was her great delight to rush from the house when the fire engine raced by. If she had it timed just right, the driver would slow down to pick her up. She especially enjoyed working the water pump, and on July 4, 1861, the Virginia City Fire Company made her an honorary member and allowed her to be the Queen of the Independence Day parade. Ever since that time, she entertained people with stories of how she wore a fireman's hat and carried a brass fire trumpet filled with fresh roses when she rode Engine Company Number One's best vehicle through town.

Julia leapt up from the table and raced away to her room. Colette knew Julia would dress quickly so that she could join the firemen. The other girls got up from the table too, rushing to the porch, hoping for a glimpse of the clattering fire engine, excited horses, and shouting men.

Colette followed Julia to her room to see if she could be of some help, but Julia was already running back down the hall. In her flight, Julia struggled to hook the front of her dress. An outrageous hat covered with red ostrich feathers and gold silk flowers bobbed on her head.

"Prepare coffee for the firemen, Colette! I will invite everybody here after we have extinguished the fire!" she cried.

"Extinguishing a man's fire is your forte," Colette muttered. But Julia did not hear the remark, which was just as well, because Julia did not have a sense of humor.

Entering Julia's room, Colette began picking up the clothing Julia had tossed here and there. Shoes were flung into the corners, the sheets were rumpled on the big brass bed. Colette dusted around the dresser, and then she spied the emerald ring Julia liked to flash. Julia had just tossed it into the soap dish near the ceramic bowl and pitcher. Colette was filled with disgust for Julia's apparent insensitivity to the riches she had accumulated. Colette knew she could not dare touch that ring now, especially after that morning's breakfast table discussion concerning theft. But in a fit of rage, she stomped to Julia's dressing table and slid a gold chain from the bottom of the jewel box. Julia hardly ever wore it—the chain was much too plain for her taste—just another gift to her from an admirer. She would not miss it. Then Colette noticed a huge opal in an elaborate silver setting. She could not resist!

Suddenly a hot hand clamped onto Colette's wrist while the other hand slapped her full across her face. "You!" Julia hissed. "Thief! I have suspected you for many weeks. Now you are caught in the act!"

"I was only dusting the jewelry...." Colette tried to lie. But of course Julia knew Colette well enough to perceive her guilt.

"Liar!" Julia screamed. "I want the rest of my jewelry returned! And what belongs to the other girls, too. And then I want you out of this house by tomorrow morning!"

"You can't put me out," Colette whimpered.

"Oh, no? Only our long relationship keeps me from reporting this to the police."

Colette knew Julia would not dare make an official spectacle out of the missing jewelry. Much of it had come from certain men who ran the community—men whose wives would be infuriated if there was a police investigation to find out where their valuables had ended up.

Colette was much taller and stronger than Julia, but for the moment Colette was weak with embarrassment. Julia's wrath seemed to burn a hole in Colette's wrist where Julia held her. "What will I do if you send me away?" Colette whined. "How will I live?"

"You can do laundry for the miners at fifty cents a tub! That will keep your big paws too busy to get into trouble!" With that, Julia shoved Colette aside before grabbing a pair of shoes that she had forgotten during her earlier frenzy. She ran down the hall and out of the house in time to flag down the fire engine.

Beside herself with nervous energy, Colette finished cleaning Julia's room. The other girls got bored after the fire engines raced away, so they returned to their boudoirs. Later, after the fire was extinguished, Julia invited the entire crew of nearly fifty men to the house. They guzzled coffee and relived the exciting and dangerous details of that day's fire fight.

Colette busied herself dashing hither and fro with coffee cups and pastries. Julia was in her element, chattering and laughing brazenly while the men complimented her as if she had single-handedly put out the fire.

Colette was glad for this distraction, because it gave her time to figure out a plan. While the firemen were busy talking and laughing, Colette slid the gold chain and opal ring out of her bodice and into the pocket of a coat one of the men had carelessly tossed over the back of a chair. The coat belonged to a man named John Millain.

Early the next morning, shrieking wildly, Colette dashed back and forth down the long upstairs hall. She aroused the entire house with her hysteria. She'd found Julia's dead body stretched nude across her bed. When the police arrived, Colette explained that she had seen some strange men leaving the house during the night. She did not recognize any of them, because their coat collars had been turned up.

Later, after the doctor gave Colette laudanum to calm her nerves, he announced that Julia Bulette had been strangled sometime during the night. Enormous blue welts on Julia's delicate throat could only have been made by large hands.

Virginia City went into official mourning as the saloons hung black wreaths across their doors. The fire company covered the engines Julia loved with long black streamers. The funeral procession consisted of thousands of miners trudging sadly behind the black-plumed, glass-walled hearse as the militia band played "The Girl I Left Behind Me."

The men in town were enraged when no murderer could be immediately found, which caused rumblings and threats that a vigilante committee should be formed. But in time one of the miners was accused of the murder. His name was John Millain. His partner discovered Julia's gold chain and opal ring hidden in John's cabin. At his trial, Millain begged the jury to believe he'd found the jewelry in his coat pocket, he had no idea how it got there. The jurors of course laughed at such a silly excuse.

For weeks preceding the execution, the housewives of Virginia City gathered together. Campaigning to save the life of John Millain, they insisted the murderer had actually done Virginia City a favor by ridding the community of the wicked Julia. But in the end, the ladies were shouted down. The execution took place as scheduled.

Colette took the stagecoach to San Francisco on the morning of the hanging. The coach rumbled past the Virginia City gallows shortly before noon, just as John Millain, still professing innocence, was ushered up the wooden steps. Colette, peering from the coach window, saw Millain kneel for the blessing of a priest. She was glad the stagecoach did not stop, because the huge crowd was stifling. All of the mines, schools, and businesses had shut down so that the entire populace could attend the hanging. It turned into a holiday, so anxious were the grieving miners to see Julia Bulette's murderer brought to justice.

Colette turned her face away from the window. The gallows trap door snapped open. The crowd let out a cheer. Colette concentrated on holding her precious green leather box on her lap. She had not trusted the conductor to toss it recklessly into the boot with the rest of the trunks and baggage.

NA-SHA-SHAY

Born in Arizona around 1860, the Apache Kid was a member of Capitain Chiquito's band of Aravaipa Apaches. The tall and handsome boy learned white man's ways, and spoke passable English. While in his early twenties he joined the U.S. Army and became a First Sergeant of Scouts. After a series of tragic misunderstandings, Kid was arrested and sentenced to Yuma Territorial prison. An attractive Apache girl named Na-sha-shay spoke on his behalf at his trial at Globe, Arizona. She attested to his good character. On the way to prison, Kid escaped, and became the most wanted man in Arizona Territorial history. With a $15,000 reward on his head, he outfoxed everybody who set a trap for him. It was known that Kid took Apache girls with him into the Sierra Madre. Apache Kid's ultimate fate remains a mystery.

"That pesky owl hoot fools nobody," Grandmother sighed, turning under her blanket. "About time he's come back," she added with a sly chuckle.

The desert night settled upon us. Strips of moonlight coming through our wickiup glimmered like snow against Grandmother's white braids. The evening fire had nearly smoldered itself out while we huddled under our thin blankets. My older sister, Na-sha-shay, who was seventeen summers, always curled against me during these chilly nights. But I realized suddenly her space was cold. She was gone!

I strained to listen. The mournful owl hoot came again, strong and clear. Heart thumping, I suddenly understood what Grandmother meant. Scrambling from under my blanket, I tried to be quiet. I slipped into my moccasins, making only soft padding sounds on the cold earthen floor.

Grandmother muttered, "Ih! He has come for her at last. Ah, well, it is better this way. Her heart is withering since he took up the bronco trail. She might as well join him and be done with it." Grandmother continued mumbling under her breath, but I heard no more because I was already running out of our wickiup to spy on Na-sha-shay.

At thirteen summers, I was short and fat, not willowy like my sister who enchanted everyone with her large eyes and soft mouth. My own face was plain, with a nose too wide and flat to allow anybody to think I was beautiful. "Chipmunk" was the cursed name I inherited. But my poor looks had nothing to do with what I felt inside my heart for Haskay-bay-nay-ntayl. He was known by the white soldiers as Apache Kid.

Kid would have already been my brother-in-law had he not gotten into trouble with the white people. After serving as a faithful scout for nearly six years, he was suddenly the most hunted Apache in Arizona Territory with a fifteen-thousand-dollar reward offered for him. Dead or alive.

My sister pined when he disappeared into the Mexican Sierra Madre to avoid capture. But tonight the owl hoot signal meant he was back, and in my sorrowing Apache heart I knew this might be my last chance to catch a glimpse of him. I, too, loved him, but I was determined that no one must ever know.

In the dappled darkness near the horse corral, I saw the legendary chevrons and ragged blue cavalry coat as Kid embraced my sister. Tall for an Apache, his wide shoulders bent over her. The lovers hugged, faces close together, arms entwined as if two slender trees had grown together.

My own breath made nervous gasps while my heart pounded. I was fearful of discovery, yet mesmerized by the sight of the bravest, most notorious Apache. The year was 1891, five years after Geronimo surrendered and the Apache wars in Arizona had ended. But bronco Apaches

83

and renegades still roamed from San Carlos to Old Mexico, and Kid was the wildest of all.

Two years ago, Kid was mixed up in the escape of eight Apaches being taken by stagecoach to Yuma prison; the incident was known as the "Kelvin Grade Massacre." In the fight, Sheriff Reynolds and his deputy were both killed. Since then, Kid was blamed for every murder and robbery in Arizona Territory. It seemed like everybody was after him.

Na-sha-shay swooned. I strained to hear what Kid was telling her. While leaning forward, a cursed twig snapped under my moccasin; Kid disappeared in the blink of an eye. Suddenly a hard hand grabbed me from behind, spinning me around while rope-like fingers clamped across my mouth.

"Chipmunk!" Kid hissed, "You are lucky I did not slit your throat!"

I knew he was only trying to scare me. He had not even pulled his knife. Just when I was enjoying the sensation of his hand on my face, Na-sha-shay dashed toward us, scolding.

"Chipmunk! Why have you followed me?"

Kid glared, dropping his hand from my mouth. "What should we do with her? If she goes back to camp, she will talk like the little squirrel she is named after." He was not pleased to see me, and I was sorry because he was the only thing I had been thinking and dreaming of. Even though he belonged to my sister, and she to him, it did not change the feelings I had for him.

Na-sha-shay patted my shoulder. "Poor little Chipmunk, always concerned about me. Do not be angry with her," she said to Kid, who kept scowling, which I thought made him look handsome.

Since the first time I saw him, I dreamed of that straight mouth, dark brooding eyes, tall, lean way of moving, and his smooth voice. He swaggered around in that blue coat, proud to be a scout, that is, before he got into all the trouble. Meanwhile, my sister's talking about him hour after hour, year after year, only added to my own warm feelings for this man I could never belong to.

"Chipmunk," Na-sha-shay said softly, "promise to go back to our wickiup. Do not tell anybody what you have seen here tonight."

"Grandmother already knows," I said. "She heard the owl hoot signal, and she is glad Kid came for you at last. She said she is tired of looking at your sad face and listening to your carping about life without him."

"Anh, yes," Na-sha-shay said. Her face turned red. "That is just what Grandmother would say."

Kid's eyes bored through me, black as death. "I cannot risk that she goes back to tattle," he said to Na-sha-shay about me.

"Then take me with you!" I said hopefully. "I am strong, and willing to help in camp. I ride, and cook, and gather wood. That way you will know exactly where I am all of the time."

"Better yet, I can knock you in the head," Kid warned. "That way I won't have to worry about you at all."

"The famous Apache Kid is not a woman-killer," I giggled.

He clamped his jaw so tightly the muscles of his face rippled like twisted rope under his bronze skin.

"Let's take her," Na-sha-shay said. "It will be lonely in the Sierra Madre without members of my family...and she is old enough to leave our camp soon." Her smile implied I was nearly ready to take a husband of my own. Little did she know I was interested in only one man—hers—a man I could never have. Nevertheless, I was willing to be nothing to him if only I could be near him.

"You know I cannot be trusted with secrets," I said to Kid. "When The People here begin to question Na-sha-shay's disappearance, I might say all the wrong things. So for your own safety, you better take me with you."

Groaning, Apache Kid grabbed my elbow and pushed me in front of himself, across the clearing toward the horses tethered in the brush beneath a sycamore tree. "Hurry, Chipmunk pest. Ride the old pack mare," he growled.

Without further talk, the three of us mounted, then guided our horses down the steep descent angling toward the valley floor. We rode for a long time, crossing through humped prickly pear cactus surrounded by small scattered flowers glowing silvery in the moonlight.

Kid, ever watchful, had the wolfish expression of one who lives by his wits. He kept his eyes on the trail while at the same time paying attention to the movements of the horses' ears, which could spell trouble. But we rode all night, traveling many miles from the boundaries of the San Carlos reservation. At dawn we entered the mountain range north of the white settlement called Tucson. From here, Kid planned to follow the San Pedro River south until we crossed the Mexican border.

Kid led us into a high canyon where he hid the horses while Na-sha-shay and I made camp. We could not travel during daylight hours. Our hiding place was a cave whose ceiling was black with fire stains from centuries of Indian camps. The dusty floor held moccasin prints I recognized, since they toed-in, made by one who was slightly bowlegged: Kid. He had camped here before.

We ate cold ashcakes made of ground mesquite flour, and drank water from the battered army canteen Kid carried. Later, while Na-sha-shay and I rested on saddle blankets at the back of the stuffy cave, Kid crouched at the entrance holding field glasses against his eyes.

When Na-sha-shay fell asleep, I crept forward to join Kid at his watch. "I will stand guard," I said, scanning the barren valley surrounded by craggy pinnacles. "You need sleep more than I."

He took the field glasses away from his face and squinted at me through reddened eyes. "All right. But you must watch carefully, especially along the river. The deep dry sand makes an easy trail for trackers to follow. Further, be careful you do not direct the glasses toward the sun. The rays flashing against the glass can be seen many miles away."

I nodded. I knew this. Even though I did not understand how that could be, except that the sun was bright and glass was shiny. "Perhaps when the two meet there is a spark between them," I said. "Like a man and a woman?"

"Do not question everything," he said, tensing his shoulders. "I learned when I was First Sergeant Kid, Company F, Indian Scouts, Third U.S. Cavalry, that windy talk means nothing."

"You still speak proudly of being a scout," I said, "even after what the white men did to you. Even though they hunt you and want your dead body for the reward."

He flinched. "Some things have already been decided for us by men of power. We must accept those decisions and go on to other things in life. I am what I am. All I want now is to make a good home with Na-sha-shay." He walked away, leaving me to hunker at the entrance of the cursed cave pondering his words.

Later, when my arms were tired of holding the heavy field glasses, and my eyes grew sore from squinting, I darted a glance where Kid rested close to my sister. The lovers slept side-by-side, fingers touching. I knew there was nothing else they would do together until this journey ended, and they could finally be alone at Kid's camp deep in the Sierra Madre. According to the Old Law, a dedicated Apache does not consort with his woman during a long march on the trail. I already knew he and my sister had never done any more than hold hands and do a little hugging. I only wished I was there...close to him...on the blanket.

Sighing, I put those thoughts away because kindly Na-sha-shay was my sister. Not only did she love Kid with all her heart, but he was in love with her, too.

That night we sipped the last of the water from Kid's canteen before finishing the ashcakes. Kid told us he did not want to use his gun to hunt game until we were farther south because of sounds the shooting would make. That was all right because we knew how to gather herbs and roots; Apaches are never far from nourishment.

On our horses again, we rode along the sandy cliff edges skirting the San Pedro, staying off the main trail as much as possible. We stopped briefly while Kid gouged juice for us with his knife from ripe prickly pear fruit. We laughed softly as the sweet red pulp dribbled juicily down our chins. Kid caught some drops with his fingertips from the parted lips of Na-sha-shay, who quit laughing as the two people gazed like sheep into each other's eyes.

Embarrassed, I busied myself by loudly spitting tiny black seeds of the prickly pear fruit, hard as buckshot, to the ground. I waited for the lovers to quit gawking at each other. Sighing, I crossed my leg over the withers of the thin pack mare. I had not ridden horseback such a long ways at one time before, so I stretched myself stiffly, remembering that we still had four long nights traveling to Sonora.

Our horses kicked little pebbles under their hooves as we continued on our journey. We crossed through brush and timber and slashed-up hills. The path angled into a single black scar. Mesquite clawed our legs, and yellow-bloomed desert holly bent twisted branches across our trail.

Ahead of me, Na-sha-shay rode quietly, slim-bodied, high-chinned and proud to be with this man she had waited for. My gentle sister had spoken little since we left home, but I could tell by her glowing expression she was happy at last.

Kid signalled us to stop. We pulled the horses together on the narrow trail while he slipped from his roan gelding. He handed the reins to Na-sha-shay before he disappeared in a clump of willow trees.

We were near a spring in the lower end of the mountains, and we badly needed to fill the canteen before riding on. The horses snorted, smelling water, restlessly pawing for a chance to drink.

I dismounted, putting my hand over the fluttering nostrils of Kid's roan, for he was a strong horse and more aggressive than the mares.

Kid returned, limbering his Winchester. "Something is wrong at the spring. Na-sha-shay, you must go alone."

Na-sha-shay nodded. She understood what was expected of her. It was the Apache way for the woman to appear first when there was danger on the trail. Orders had gone out from the United States government that women should not be shot by soldiers. Learning of this, warriors sent the women ahead as decoys when suspecting ambush. She hopped like a nervous bird from her mare, looking at Kid for instruction.

"Go to the spring. Stay close to the willows," he whispered. "In case of trouble, run to the opposite cliffs where you will find your way to a wide ledge. Wait for us there."

"Anh, do not worry. I will go carefully," she said.

The two looked at each other like heartsick doves. I wondered if their lives would forever be filled with the fear of what lurked at every spring.

"Let me go!" I said. "Give me the canteen. If anybody stops me, I will say I am just a little Apache girl, alone, looking for water."

"My canteen says U.S. Army on it," Kid reminded me.

"So? I will say I found it in the desert." Before he could argue, I ran down the narrow trail toward the water. Hands shaking, I uncapped the canteen and lowered it into the pool. I heard lapping gurgles as the container filled. My cursed heart pounded like drums. I strained to listen, while at the same time watching the edges of the pool. Perhaps at any moment a crackling bough or click of a rifle being cocked would tear the stillness, but no sounds came. Quickly, I re-capped the canteen before dropping my mouth to the surface of the water for a long drink.

Still...nothing stirred. Near the spring the air smelled salty, like the desert after a rain. Wiping water from my chin, I hurried through the trees toward Kid and Na-sha-shay and the horses hidden in the bluffs.

"Nothing!" I said, proudly handing the heavy canteen to Kid. I was anxious to show him how brave I was. He paid little attention to me while he and my sister took turns gulping long swallows of water. The horses kept pawing, sniffing in the direction of the spring.

Finished drinking, Kid said, "Perhaps nobody...or perhaps somebody waits who knows the women go in first. In that case it could be my old enemy, Wallapai Clark. He lives close by in a cabin at upper Fish Creek." Kid nodded to the west.

I shivered. I knew Kid was accused of murdering Wallapai Clark's partner, Bill Diehl. Wallapai Clark had vowed to avenge his partner's death. Wallapai Clark was an ex-army scout, very wise in the ways of trailing and killing Apaches.

I panted with fear and excitement. "Let me take the horses to the spring. You keep the water and guns. If there is trouble for me, you two can still get away."

"You giving orders now?" Kid grumbled.

I whispered, "I do this for you...and Na-sha-shay, of course." I looked steadily into his eyes and in that moment I think he finally understood what was really in my guts.

His shoulders stiffened when he said, "Enjuh, little Chipmunk. Good luck."

Nodding, I took the bridle reins and led the horses back through the trees toward the spring. I felt better this time. I thought if anybody was around here he would have grabbed me when I first came to fill the canteen. But as the horses greedily dipped their noses into the water, I was taken by surprise. The blue-gold reflection from a gun barrel flashed in the moonlight from the west side of the spring.

I jerked at the bridle reins just as a bullet whopped into the pack mare, dropping her into the stream like a floundering sack. Blood swirled from her belly as she slid under the surface of the water, legs kicking. Kid's gelding and the other mare scrambled away, bucking, plunging through the water and running south away from the whanging gunfire.

Clinging between the horses by gripping the stirrup leathers, I let them drag me up the hill into a thick cover of mesquite and black oak. I fought to hang on.

"That damned little squaw!" I heard shouted in white man's words. After that more excited yelling came to my ears, but I did not understand the words.

Another volley of shots brought the mare to her knees. I let Kid's gelding go and the horse disappeared in the brush as the mare fell on top of me, pinning me to the ground. Crushed under the weight of the dying mare, I sank my teeth into my lip to keep from crying out. My left leg was bent painfully backwards, and I knew the cursed thing was broken. Two white men, gasping for breath, approached with their guns pointed at my head. The tallest, with a thick gray beard, spoke in Apache.

"Where is Niño? Apache Kid?"

I knew Niño meant "kid" in Spanish, and some people who had known him in the army called him that. But I said nothing.

The big man leaned over me, smelling of sweat and tobacco. "You are the little sister of Na-sha-shay. I saw you at San Carlos. Everybody knows about Kid and your sister. What are you doing off the reservation?"

I muttered some words. The warm sulphur-smelling gun barrel was pressed against my head, and I thought I better say something. "I stole these horses. I live with my sister and grandmother. We are poor now. The men in our family are dead, or in prison in Florida."

He laughed. "You little liar. I recognized that roan gelding. Apache Kid's horse. Since when do fat little girls steal horses from the great Kid? Eh?" The warm, sharp steel pressed harder.

The other man, smaller and older wearing leather boots and baggy miner's clothing, said something in the white tongue I did not understand, except that he called the big man "Wallapai."

Wallapai Clark said to me in Apache, "This man thinks you are suffering bad, and I should kill you. I will if you don't tell us what you are doing here. Where is Apache Kid?"

"I know nothing about him," I said. "I am stealing horses." I gritted my teeth as he pushed the cursed gun against my face so hard my left ear was forced to the ground. And that is how I heard the soft striking of unshod hoofs against stone. A horse trotted south, led down the trail by two pairs of moccasined feet moving lightly as butterflies' wings.

93

ELIZABETH CUSTER

Elizabeth Bacon, the only daughter of a judge, was born in Monroe, Michigan, in 1842. In February, 1864, she married the love of her life, Civil War hero George Armstrong Custer. A lady of high breeding, Libbie nevertheless followed her man through the Civil War, and later into the Indian Territories. After Custer's tragic death at the Little Big Horn in 1876, Libbie returned to the East where she defended her husband's reputation. Too, she did everything in her power to help the widows of the officers killed in her husband's command. Libbie Custer liked to say, "Where there's a widow, there's a way." She spent the rest of her life alone; there would never be another man for her. At the age of 91, Libbie died in New York City in 1933. She was buried beside her husband at West Point.

Early February of 1864, Civil War raged all around. Soldiers were running and shooting through the second-growth timber along both sides of the road. Shells dropped close to a group of Negro refugees in a foggy rain. A teenage girl, Eliza, screamed and covered her face, wishing she was still back on the plantation.

The girl traveled with a group of newly-freed slaves. They were anxious to go North, away from a little town called Stevensburg, about five miles south of Brandy Station, Virginia.

"Come on, girl! Run!" One of the Negro men shouted at Eliza, while he carried a crying baby in his arms. Eliza was a nearly-grown woman, expected to fend for herself. She struggled along carrying a raggedy bundle of clothing on her back—every worldly thing she owned.

Crackling gunfire and blasts of artillery mingled with screams in the woods. The refugees had been caught on the road between Federals and Confederates. Eliza did not know which way to run. A group of horsemen galloped down the road toward her followed by lathered teams pulling caissons laden with ammunition. She saw blue uniforms, and was glad to know at least she was not being run down by Confederates.

Eliza scurried to the side of the road when one of the officers pulled his brown horse to a plunging halt. He looked the girl up and down. The man had long brown curls, steady blue eyes, and a yellow mustache. His face jutted from under a flat-brimmed hat. "You want to come work for me? One dollar a week, room and board. I need a cook and a housekeeper. My bride is joining me in a few days."

The invitation was kind of fast, but then Eliza reckoned the war did not leave folks much time for manners. They were in Rappahannock County, Virginia, a long way from Washington where she hoped to go. But, willing to do her part in the war effort, helping this Yankee officer sounded like a good thing to do. He was abrupt, but there was something about him she trusted. Besides, she had never been offered money of her own before. So she answered, "I reckon I would."

"Good! If you can get to that farm house beyond the woods," he pointed, "you will find Army headquarters. My rooms are upstairs. What is your name?"

"Eliza," she answered.

"I am General Custer." He tapped the edge of his hat before galloping madly down the road, spurs pressed deeply into the flanks of his steaming horse.

The folks Eliza was travelling with had already disappeared around the bend in the road. She climbed through the split rail fence. Eliza found her way through the brush, heart pounding, scared to look at all the wounded men writhing around in the mud calling for help. There were so many—but she knew nothing about doctoring.

The white wooden farmhouse had green shutters and a high pointed roof with a sooty brick chimney that had been mostly shot off. A Virginia family lived downstairs. General Custer's living quarters were upstairs like he said. Military staff lived in tents all around the yard. Horses and men trampled the garden and flower beds into a boot-sucking quagmire.

The family downstairs used the wood stove. Since Eliza had been taught by her mother that two women don't get along in the same kitchen, she set up a cook camp out in the yard. The Federal soldiers paid little attention to her once she told them she worked for General Custer. At first she was lonesome, and afraid of everything that had to do with war. But in a few days, like the general promised, she got to meet his bride, Libbie.

The morning the new Mrs. Custer arrived, she drove a little black buggy loaded with trunks and bundles while her husband rode his horse alongside. It was easy to see how happy the newlyweds were by the smiles and glances they exchanged. Mrs. Custer was barely five feet tall, with blue-gray eyes and chestnut hair.

"Eliza," General Custer said, "this is my wife, Mrs. Elizabeth Custer. Please help her with this luggage—enough to clothe the whole army!"

So up the narrow wooden steps they dragged Libbie's possessions. All the while General Custer, whom Libbie affectionately called "Autie" on account of his middle name being Armstrong, hummed and fussed and tried to direct the women. But they soon drowned him out with their chatter. They laughed and talked, getting all excited about decorating those cold little rooms. Miss Libbie reminded Eliza of a bird trying to feather her new nest.

"Dogs off the bed!" Miss Libby scolded, clapping her hands. Her husband had a bulldog and a greyhound that enjoyed the run of the house. General Custer soon got tired of the fussing, so he went outside to visit his horse. The dogs scrambled after him.

While unpacking Libbie's dresses, Eliza said, "Miss Libbie! You have the tiniest waist, and the most beautiful feminine ways. You do not belong in the middle of this war."

"You talk just like Autie," she said, while hanging up a fine silk dress. "He does not approve of my joining him so close to the front lines. He wants me to stay in Washington. But I want so much to be with him. My mother died when I was young. My father, Judge Bacon, taught me to be my own person."

Eliza nodded, thinking that meant Mrs. Custer was a mite headstrong and spoiled, but Eliza could not help but admire Libbie's spunk.

Libbie said passionately, clutching a fur muff to her breast, "General George Armstrong Custer is my Boy General! Wherever he goes, I will go with him!"

Eliza raised an eyebrow, thinking Mrs. Custer did not yet know what war was all about. It saddened Eliza to think that they would not be in this house very long. She'd heard the soldiers say the Michigan Cavalry Brigade led by General Custer could move out at any moment, so it was only a matter of time before Miss Libbie would have to pack up again.

Those two little rooms at the top of a shot-up farm house, surrounded by the uncertainty of war was the place the Custers spent their honeymoon. Every chance they had to be alone, the general gathered his little bride into his arms and they'd kiss and giggle and seem not to care that Eliza hung around, grinning.

Miss Libbie was cheery, always fussing about her Autie... he was her life. And Eliza could see that no matter how tired or worried he was, he'd turn dashing and happy in Libbie's presence, sort of like a bragging rooster strutting around his little hen.

Eliza did all the cooking and washing. The general did not want Miss Libbie to fret and stew over common chores. One day he took Eliza aside, saying, "Eliza, I want my wife to be as carefree as possible. She must save her strength for the privation and dangers she must face following troops in the field."

"Yes, sir," Eliza said, thinking that was mighty thoughtful of him. She wondered how a man so young (he was in his early twenties at the time) could make such a good husband.

"Miss Libbie," Eliza said one day while admiring one of Mrs. Custer's dresses—a white silk with hoop skirts and lace. "My! Ain't you a queen in that fine dress? I ain't never had a dress like that, and most likely never will."

Libbie turned to Eliza, skirts swishing, smiling that pretty little smile. "Oh, Eliza! You have been such a wonderful help to Autie and me. How good of you to stay here with us when you could have been in Washington by now. This white dress is Autie's favorite—I wore it the night he proposed to me. I will never part with it. But I'll give you my blue silk dress—it's the least I can do to thank you for all your kindness."

Eliza's jaw dropped. "But, Miss Libbie, it will take a heap of fixing to get that dress to fit me." Eliza eyed Libbie's waist, so small she'd seen the general nearly circle it with his two hands.

"Oh nonsense, Eliza! You are so good with a needle. I've seen you mend uniforms for soldiers. You are quite expert. You can make alterations in no time. I'll help you."

That is how Eliza became the owner of a fancy dress. She worried General Custer would not approve of his wife's generosity, but he just smiled and said that whatever made Miss Libbie happy, was fine with him.

One cold morning Libbie told Eliza to prepare her sidesaddle dress. Her husband had invited her to ride with him that day, so out came her riding clothes. Eliza had to laugh because Libbie looked like a little girl, pout and all.

"Miss Libbie, you look mighty elegant in that purple velvet sidesaddle suit. Look at the way the gold braid shines on your sleeves. Be careful you don't lose that red feather drooping from your cap—there ain't a chicken left in Virginia to replace it."

"Oh, Eliza, never mind the hat. It's the heavy skirt that worries me. Autie loaded the hem with shot." Libbie staggered across the room barely holding the skirt up in front of herself like she was lugging a sack of potatoes.

Eliza laughed at Libbie's struggles under all that weight. "The general has invented a clever way to keep a lady's skirt from flying up by stuffing the hem with buckshot.

Now the soldiers can't see your ankles when your horse goes flying at a gallop."

"Oh pooh! That dreadful little pony Autie's given me can't get out of his own dust!"

"Now, now, Miss Libbie," Eliza chided, "big fast horses are scarce in this war. Besides, General Custer paid dearly for that little horse who is so smart with all them tricks."

Libbie clumped down the stairs, riding whip tucked under her elbow. "I could do with fewer tricks and more speed." Her nose was stuck in the air.

Everybody knew General Custer bought his wife a small, gentle horse that had been a child's pet. It was trained to kneel down when the rider wished to mount, but it had a bone-jarring gait. When the little animal trotted beside the general's snorting charger, poor Miss Libbie looked like a monkey bobbing on a stick.

One of the officers teased Miss Libbie by telling her she "rode just like the infantry" which brought embarrassed blushes to her face. But it was all in good fun. Miss Libbie, being the gentle lady that she was, went along with all their jokes. She whispered once to Eliza that teasing from the men was worth it, as long as she could be close to Autie.

In late February, Eliza knew something big was about to happen because the men stirred and mumbled among themselves. Some of them asked Eliza to take care of personal property they wanted her to send to their kin folks in case they did not return from the upcoming fight. Eliza's skirt and apron pockets swelled. Sometimes when Eliza dug around for her handkerchief, money and watches tumbled to the ground. All that stuff weighed her down. While working around the outdoor cooking fire, it made her clumsy when she tried to run away from a shell dropping too close. But Eliza figured some of these poor men would not be coming back, so she did not complain.

Miss Libbie noticed the changes too. While she eyed Eliza's bulging pockets, Libbie did not ask questions. It was as if she did not want to deal with answers.

Late in February the cavalry moved out. General Custer told his wife only that he was assigned to a special mission. He rode away at the head of 3,500 men with orders to free 15,000 Federal prisoners held in a Confederate prison in Richmond, Virginia.

Miss Libbie did not know it until years later, but General Custer did not expect to return alive. He kept the dangers of the mission secret from his Libbie so that she would not be worried.

When the lovers parted that cold wintry morning, they embraced with a fierceness that can only come from an underlying fear that they would not see each other again. Miss Libbie knew in her heart that at any moment disaster could strike her man.

Meanwhile, the general was filled with anxious bravado; worrying about his wife, while at the same time happy and anxious to be off at the head of his troops.

Eliza thought to herself, *Men!*

Camp empty, dangers all around from renegades and deserters, Miss Libbie and Eliza packed up the buggy and skedaddled for Washington. So, nineteen days after their wedding, the Custers were separated by war.

Miss Libbie became a great social favorite in Washington. Folks were intrigued with her beauty and charm. It helped that her husband was one of the most famous military heroes of the time. Not a day went by his name did not appear in some newspaper, giving details of his derring-do. Thirteen horses were shot out from under him during his Civil War career, but still he got through it.

Miss Libbie worried about her Boy General. Letters flew back and forth between the two. In a short time her sweet little face became lined with strain. There was an anxious look in her eyes. She and Eliza sometimes passed hospitals overflowing to the point of men groaning in stretchers on sidewalks and steps, waiting their turn for attention. Ambulances clattered up and down the streets, making way only for black hearses.

Eliza got a job helping in one of the hospitals. She did not see Miss Libbie again until after the surrender came in April of 1865. A great victory parade was scheduled to take place in May. Endless columns of soldiers marched down Pennsylvania Avenue. Flags hung from every window. The atmosphere was clogged with masses of bunting, military bands, and throngs of people. In the great and stirring parade, artillery, infantry, and cavalry passed in review.

While joining the crowd, Eliza found herself shoved in close to the reviewing stand that day. Every Washington bigwig watched as the Army of the Potomac marched by. Girls from an academy sang "Hail To The Chief" while flinging bouquets to the cavalry. General Custer, riding at the head of his troops, grabbed for a handful of flowers only to lose his reins. His already fractious horse took flight, bucking and plunging out of control.

A voice near Eliza cried, "Oh, Autie! Hang on!"

Shocked, Eliza realized Miss Libbie was standing right next to her. Libbie gasped when General Custer lost his hat and even his saber! His runaway horse bolted down the street. Somehow General Custer stayed in the saddle, grabbing reins, hauling the berserk animal in a circle to avoid trampling bystanders.

Some fat old general sitting above Eliza and Libbie in the reviewing stand turned to President Johnson and said, "Oh! It's only Custer showing off again."

Eliza tugged on Miss Libbie's sleeve until she got Mrs. Custer's attention. They both started laughing and hugging, seeing humor in the situation.

"Miss Libbie," Eliza gasped, "don't worry about the general! He won't dare fall off his horse in front of a million spectators."

"I told him not to ride his new horse today," Libbie finally said when she quit choking. "It's a Thoroughbred stallion named Don Juan who has not seen military service. I just knew this crowd would scare that poor nervous creature to death. Luckily there is no cannonade today!"

"Miss Libbie, you know your husband likes nothing better than mastering a spirited horse."

Libbie laughed, nodding in agreement. "Eliza, how have you been?"

"I'm fine. And yourself?"

"Autie has a new commission now the war has ended. We need a housekeeper. Would you like to join us?"

"Thank you, Miss Libbie. But I am to be married soon to a man who is studying law. I'm learning to read!" That last part Eliza gushed over because reading and writing were so important to her.

"Eliza, I am happy for you. It seems everything has turned out wonderfully for all of us. I'm so excited—Autie and I leave in three days for the western frontier."

The next time Eliza saw Miss Libbie was quite by accident. It was November of 1886, ten years after the Battle of the Little Bighorn. Eliza heard that Miss Libbie was living in New York City, struggling to get by on a $20 a month government widow's pension. Mrs. Custer tried to earn additional income from writing, and giving historical lectures about life on the plains.

Eliza was in New York for a few days with her husband. While he had some business to attend to, Eliza took a swaying, noisy horsecar to Madison Square Garden to see a grand spectacular called the "Buffalo Bill Cody Wild West Show" that everybody talked about.

While sitting in the audience, Eliza gawked at the Grand Review when all of the characters in the show rode out on horseback. Flags flew; a band blared music—everybody in the crowd cheered till they nearly lost their voices.

The acts were fast and furious. Cowboys did a roping exhibition. Indian boys raced their spotted horses in a cloud of dust; bodies smeared with paint, feathers flying. A cavalry drill brought back sentimental memories when Eliza saw those yellow-striped blue uniforms and glittering sabers. Before she got too weepy, a band of outlaws bristling with guns plunged across the arena to rob the Deadwood stage.

Finally, Buffalo Bill himself accompanied by a pretty little sharpshooter named Annie Oakley did trick riding and fancy shooting the likes of which impressed the whole crowd. That tiny lady with flowing brown hair, wearing a fringed skirt and vest, stood on top of her galloping horse. If that was not spectacular enough, she shot flames off candles spinning around on a wheel.

While the final act was announced, Eliza studied the people sitting in boxes above the arena, where dignitaries were seated. It was easy to pick out the Generals Tecumseh Sherman, and Phil Sheridan. Not that she had ever met them, but their pictures were familiar to everybody on account of their being Civil War heroes. Suddenly Eliza jumped right out of her seat. She recognized Miss Libbie! Dressed in widow's weeds, Libbie Custer sat fanning herself beside General Sheridan.

When the final act unfolded, Eliza spent as much time watching Miss Libbie as she did the show. Sadly, it was a reenactment of the Battle of the Little Bighorn. The cavalry rode into the arena to the tune of "Garry Owen," General Custer's favorite, to which his regiment had gone out to battle. Moments later there was shooting and shouting, dust flying, sabers ringing, horses falling. Finally, war whooping Indians surrounded the valiant soldiers of the Seventh Cavalry, who fought to the last man.

The tall, blond, curly-haired Buffalo Bill Cody portrayed General Custer. Eliza's heart fluttered when she noticed the stunning resemblance. Buffalo Bill was tall and broad-shouldered, with a reddish complexion and well-defined mustache. He had that slim waist and swaggering way of moving, like a man who rides horses and takes charge of things.

Miss Libbie's face retained that calm look, although her eyes darted at all that was happening in the arena. When the show was over, "General Custer" mounted his horse and rode to within a few feet of Miss Libbie. There, he gave her a salute that brought the crowd to its feet.

Later, Eliza struggled through the throngs of people to the backstage where she hoped she would see Miss Libbie. Eliza could not imagine Mrs. Custer leaving without visiting Buffalo Bill. Eliza knew Buffalo Bill worked as a scout for General Custer when they were on the frontier. Eliza wanted to at least shake Libbie's hand and let her know how sorry she was about what happened to Autie.

Sure enough, Eliza saw Miss Libbie and Buffalo Bill talking quietly to each other. Suddenly Annie Oakley joined the couple. The three people laughed and chatted amiably, and Eliza was too shy to interrupt. She watched them stroll away through the horses and riders and choked dust—images from the past.

Forty-four years went by before Eliza saw Miss Libbie one more time. Mrs. Custer lived in an apartment at 71 Park Avenue in New York. Eliza was advised to send her card before being admitted, even though she had made an appointment with Libbie some weeks in advance. Eliza's husband was dead. She herself had come to New York to visit a sick relative. If possible, she wanted to see Miss Libbie one more time. Eliza planned to return to her daughter's home in southern Ohio, and knew she was too old ever to make this trip again.

A housekeeper named Miss Merington let Eliza in. Finally, Eliza was greeted by Miss Libbie. Frail, white-haired, Miss Libbie was dressed in a straight black dress, fashionable of the 1930s. Of course it was nothing like the hoop-skirted elegance Eliza had remembered from the past.

Eliza felt tears come to her own eyes when she and Miss Libbie embraced. They had shared memories from a special time in their lives when Libbie's Boy General was at the height of his career. Libbie's blue eyes seemed paler now, but that knowing sparkle full of joy and remembrance radiated when she looked at Eliza, and Eliza felt weak in the knees.

Libbie offered Eliza a chair. They sipped tea for a long while, unable to speak. Eliza was overwhelmed by old memories. Without saying a word, she knew they both felt the presence in that room of General Custer.

"Dear Eliza," Libbie said finally. "Has life been good to you?"

Eliza nodded. "Better than for most, I expect. A good husband, a family... I have come a long way from that camp on the Rappahannock."

"I have too," Libbie said. "But you know what? I'd give anything to go back, and relive one more day." Her silver hair glowed in the afternoon sunlight peeping through the heavily-curtained window. Being it was a summer day, Miss Libbie fanned herself and seemed almost dim-witted compared to the bundle of bubbling energy Eliza remembered.

"You are wearing the velvet collar the general gave you," Eliza said. She recognized the hand-painted figures on glass attached to a black velvet ribbon. It rested at the center of Libbie's creased throat.

Libbie smiled, while fondling the metal filigree edges with her unsteady fingertips. "It has kept me in good stead all these years. Knowing he once touched this, it helps me to be brave."

Eliza nodded, having heard of Libbie's relentless battle to keep the memory of her husband untarnished.

"Travel, readings, work on special collections for museums," Libbie began, "it seems there is no end to my effort.

But I have had some successes. Many misconceptions about Autie have arisen over the years. People do not think of him in much else than his part in the Battle of the Little Bighorn."

Eliza flinched, and Miss Libbie must have noticed the sadness in Eliza's face. Eliza did not come here to question the circumstances surrounding General Custer's death. She remembered him in life, and for Eliza he was a brave and honest man, always full of energy and fairness that she appreciated. Poor Miss Libbie had grown old defending his memory. He would always be her Boy General. She, his lifelong crusader.

"Eliza," she said in that soft voice, for she smiled a lot, but Eliza noticed Libbie never laughed now. Her hands were clasped gently in her lap. She did not use them when she spoke. "My life ended with Autie's. I wanted to die. I am not afraid of dying, but I am afraid of being dead. You see, my husband's reputation is being assailed by those who make profit by defaming the famous. And only I, from my arsenal of facts, can refute the many lies written about him."

Eliza could see Libbie was consumed by it, and there was no drawing her attention away. The afternoon wore on. They drank more tea. Eliza encouraged Libbie to talk about her adventures after the Civil War. Libbie spoke of her life with Autie in Texas, traveling by wagon across the frontier where she faced every privation from illness and loneliness to drinking water that tasted like tree roots. She spoke of famous men such as Wild Bill Hickok, and Buffalo Bill. She mentioned the names of Autie's horses, Vic and Dandy. She laughed remembering how he bought a horse for her known as Custis Lee, named after General Lee's son.

Eventually Libbie spoke of the museum being planned for the Custer Battlefield in the Dakotas. She told Eliza about the Custer Institute, and the statues that had been erected in her husband's honor, including the one at West Point.

While Mrs. Custer talked on and on, Eliza understood how totally involved she was in her husband's lifetime memories. Her devotion was miraculous. Libbie's only sorrow, apart from having lost her precious Autie, was that they had not had children. She blamed herself of course, but everybody knew cavalrymen were often sterile.

They parted late that afternoon. When Libbie smiled, Eliza could see that Mrs. Custer's expression was somewhat hollow, as if she had talked herself into exhaustion.

Eliza did not see Miss Libbie again. But she read in the newspaper in April of 1933 that Elizabeth Bacon Custer, two days short of her 92nd birthday, died of a heart attack at her home in New York. She was buried beside her husband at West Point, joining him at long last. Elizabeth Custer requested that she be buried in her best white dress from the 1860s because it had been Autie's favorite.

MADAME MUSTACHE

Eleanore Dumont was well educated, had a French accent, and claimed to have come originally from New Orleans. Her career began around 1854 in Nevada City, Nevada where she opened a gambling house, specializing in blackjack. She accumulated considerable wealth working at her profession in a succession of gambling saloons from Nevada to Arizona. Unfortunately, she fell in love with a handsome gambler named Jack McKnight who took her money, and deserted her. She then found herself middle-aged, broken-hearted, and down on her luck. To make matters worse, she began growing unwanted facial hair which earned her the hated nickname, "Madame Mustache." Eleanore turned to prostitution in the mining camps throughout Nevada, and finally became a track follower along the route of the Union Pacific Railroad. In 1879 her brief obituary appeared in a Sacramento newspaper: "Eleanore Dumont was found dead today about one mile out of town, having committed suicide."

Gasping and terrified, Eleanore Dumont staggered to the wagon where she burst into one long howl, causing everybody to jump. A tan and gray prairie rattlesnake hung from the front of Eleanore's long dress. Mad as hell, its fangs were hooked through the cloth. The snake's quivering rattles sounded like dry beans clicking inside a tin can.

Muley, a big rough woman nearly twice Eleanore's size, grabbed the longest knife in camp, and told Eleanore to hold still. Meanwhile, Cuddles, Beeb and Kerosene Kate were no help. They ran around yelling like they had never seen a snake before.

Muley caught the big rattler behind its head and lifted it off Eleanore's dress. "You're lucky you're wearing all them petticoats," Muley told Eleanore.

"Oh, God!" Eleanore gasped, leaping away. "It surprised me back there in the gulch." She pointed to a sandy arroyo where she'd been walking.

"I told you girls to watch for snakes around here," Muley said. The rattler whipped its tail-end around Muley's calico skirt. The girls would not come any closer. "It's August. Wyoming rattlers are mean this time of year," Muley reminded everybody.

"They're hard to see in the morning," Kerosene Kate said. "Never know when one of the devils will jump out at you."

"They're always hard to see," Cuddles added. "It's those crossed eyes of yours that don't see things quick."

Kate made a face at her.

Eleanore got her composure back. She put her hand over her eyes to protect her face from the sun while looking east of their camp. The Union Pacific Railroad crews were laying track. Hundreds of men, a quarter of a mile away, milled like ants around the railroad bed. They leveled and graded with horse-drawn fresno scrapers. "God, will the noise never end?" Eleanore muttered, more to herself than to the other women.

"Be glad they are working," Muley told her. "The anvil chorus means there will be another payday for them and for us, too."

Eleanore's dark eyes continued scanning the crews. Muley knew that Eleanore watched for one special person, the one Eleanore could never forget—the man who jilted her, broke her heart, took her money, and disappeared a long time ago. But Eleanore still loved him and made a sorry figure out of herself, always looking for Jack McKnight.

Cuddles and Beebe slumped back over their washtubs. The men paid Eleanore's girls good wages—fifty cents a tub, plus providing water. That was daytime business. At

111

night they had other business to attend to, that is, all but Muley. Muley was too old to be anything but camp cook and mule skinner, which earned her the name Muley. That name was fine with her, since none of the women wanted anybody to know their real names anyhow. Being a track follower was not something to be especially proud of.

This enterprise belonged to Eleanore. She once ran some of the fanciest gambling saloons in the West. But time and misfortune had taken a toll on her. Track following is what she did now.

Kerosene Kate said to Eleanore, "Are you going to be all right?" Kate's dust-reddened eyes rolled toward the writhing snake Muley still held in her big calloused hand.

"Yes, thank you," Eleanore said in that French accent of hers. She had been educated in New Orleans when she was a girl. Plump now, and way past her prime, Eleanore still carried an air of modesty. She tried not to show that she was annoyed when people gawked at the dark fuzz growing on her upper lip. It had earned her the name "Madame Mustache."

Muley turned back to her cooking. That morning she'd found wild onions and a patch of purslane growing near a spring above camp. The railroad made two miles a day, so the women had to work in a hurry to get ready to move on with the crews. They seldom camped in the same spot two days in a row. Looking at Eleanore, Muley said, "You better take that dress off, so I can wash it. Might have venom stuck in the cloth."

Eleanore began unbuttoning the dress. "We're nearing a settlement called Cheyenne." She stepped out of the dress, suspiciously examining the front of the billowing cotton skirt. "I don't think I want to go farther with the crews.

I am tired of all the wagon travel. Perhaps we will go south from here, back to Nevada."

"Suit yourself," Muley said. It didn't make no never mind to Muley which way they went. As long as there was activity around like men working on railroad tracks, or a handy saloon, Eleanore's girls made out all right. "The girls are looking kind of peaked, anyhow," Muley told her. "Scrubbing all day and not getting much sleep at night has taken its toll."

Eleanore gave Muley that hazy, faraway look of hers.... It was hard for Eleanore to take anybody else into consideration. She was a good person, but her brain had gotten addled long ago over Jack McKnight.

After dropping her dress on the ground, Eleanore walked away wearing only her chemise and pantaloons. She headed toward a stand of trees. Muley got busy cutting up the snake. Fried rattler was as good as chicken any day.

Cuddles dropped the shirt she was pounding against the scrub board and asked Eleanore. "Are we really going to quit following track?"

"I'm thinking about it," Eleanore admitted.

Cuddles joined Eleanore, facing her. She looked desperate. "I want a room, a real bedroom! With a bowl and pitcher and clean water. And a mirror! I will work for you, Eleanore. You know I am a hard worker. But this dirt and dust and living out of a wagon has damaged my hair and my skin until I look like a fried lizard!"

"Quit complaining," Eleanore answered. "You know I am trying to save money to establish us in a house. You think I've enjoyed following a railroad crew across the whole Wyoming Territory?"

"Why not?" Cuddles threw at her. "You're always dreaming of that scalawag, Jack McKnight. Thinking he will step out of the crowd to fall at your feet!"

Eleanore whirled at Cuddles. "And what if he does? It is no concern of yours!"

"It is a concern of mine! I think you would go away with him! Give him all of your money again—do whatever he wanted. And where would that leave the rest of us?"

"I don't care about the rest of you!" Eleanore cried.

"Ah! Then you admit it!" Cuddles turned to face the other women. She brushed her long red hair away from her narrowing eyes. "Did you hear that? At the first chance she'll abandon us. We're only good enough to work until she finds her precious Jack McKnight. That good-for-nothing thief!"

Eleanore slapped Cuddles, who slumped to the ground. "I run things around here," Eleanore said, hand poised to strike again.

"You hit me!" Cuddles whined.

Nose in the air, Eleanore walked away. Muley, watching the scene, had to admit Eleanore looked funny acting huffy, dressed only in her underclothes.

"She has nerve slapping you just for mentioning Jack McKnight!" Kerosene Kate chimed in, leaning over Cuddles.

"We should ask for more money," Beebe yelled. "We're not paid enough for the work we do. We should have something saved in case Eleanore deserts us."

"We're no good out here unless we stick together," Muley said, gutting the snake. She spit tobacco juice into a nearby clump of bushes.

Cuddles shot a cool glance at Muley. "Of course you would take Eleanore's side in any matter. Look at you! What else can you do but drive mules, and...and...kill snakes!"

Muley rolled up the hide. It was a big one. She'd be able to get a good price for it after tanning. With those nice big rattles attached to it, some man would be anxious to make a hatband out of it and brag to everybody he'd done the killing.

"Well?" Cuddles said, still sneering at Muley, waiting for an answer.

Muley ignored her. Cuddles was always looking for trouble. Muley knew that her own loyalty had to be to Eleanore. After all, Eleanore owned this outfit. Besides, Cuddles was right... at sixty years old, Muley was withered, crotchety, and too set in her ways to be anything but a mule skinner.

Thunder rattled the sky like sheets of tin that night. Everybody huddled inside the wagon, listening while water ran in rivers down the slopes. The women hugged themselves inside old coats and blankets—the temperature dropped nearly thirty degrees in a few minutes.

Cuddles and Beebe and Kerosene Kate nested against one another to keep warm. From the sounds of the snoring, Muley knew the three of them had conked out. There was too much storming tonight for any of the men to venture over to the women's wagon—which was just as well. The outfit was in a fractious mood after the fight between Eleanore and Cuddles.

Eleanore sat close to Muley at the opposite end of the wagon from the others. Together, they were bundled in blankets, while resting their heads against flour sacks and lard cans. Eleanore worked on a bottle of sippin' whiskey. Muley took a taste now and again—it warmed both women up.

"What's this?" Eleanore asked, squinting at the coffee cans and preserve jars in the dark. Of course she knew what it was, but she had little else to talk about.

"Our food stuff," Muley humored her. "Everything we brought from our last stop. Pocatello. Remember?"

"Oh. And what is this?" She found Muley's old rusty tobacco can where Muley kept the dried mushroom powder. It was poisonous. It came in handy when they got into areas where vermin or coyotes raided their camp.

"Don't ever touch that," Muley told her. "It's my poison concoction. Learnt it from the Sioux."

"Yes! I remember. You got rid of that coyote last spring when it killed our chickens."

Muley nodded. "Hauled them hens in crates two hundred miles, only to have a sneaky coyote eat 'em!"

Eleanore shivered, turning her attention to Kate and Cuddles and Beebe. "Look at them. Sleeping like they have not a care in the world. They think it is easy for me to worry about business. I must fuss over every detail while we struggle along with the crews each day. Listening to the...what did you call it? Anvil chorus!"

"They're good women," Muley said. "Don't be too hard on them. You know that Beebe was orphaned when her pa abandoned his family, and Cuddles' husband was killed

116

in a mine cave-in. Kerosene Kate's man was hanged by vigilantes for robbing a bank."

"Every woman has a sad story connected to some man!" Eleanore said. "But I was born in New Orleans, educated, from a good family. I came West for adventure. There was no man in my life until...Jack McKnight. And now I am as ruined as these poor fools are. All because of a man!"

Muley pondered that remark. She had not thought much about it. But Eleanore had a point. Muley herself had been happy on a homestead with a husband and two good sons until they were killed by a Sioux war party. For all practical purposes, her life ended then, too.

"It's the men!" Eleanore cried passionately. "Men! Why do we allow our hearts to lead us by our noses?"

Muley took another sip of whiskey.

Eleanore fiddled with the poison can, then put it down. "Do you think I was wrong striking Cuddles today?"

"She didn't need to remind you of Jack McKnight," Muley said. "She knows that is a sore spot with you. But maybe you were too quick with your fists. Now she has Beebe and Kate siding in with her. It has caused tension among us. You should be more patient with people in camp."

Eleanore's dark eyes glowed. Lightning flashes zig-zagged outside the wagon. Eleanore's mustache twitched. "You, Muley, have learned to have patience in camp."

Muley nodded. She did not like to talk about her past, but Eleanore and she had spent a lot of time together. And since they both brooded about things that happened to them,

117

they learned about each other—especially during nights like this when they had whiskey to work on.

"Five years in a Sioux camp would have taught anybody patience," Eleanore said, pursing her lips as if she really understood.

There was no way anybody could understand a thing like that unless she lived it. But Eleanore was really a sensitive person, so Muley humored her by repeating the story she knew Eleanore liked to hear. "A war party raided our homestead, killed my husband and sons, and took me captive."

"The Indians do not usually take grownups captive, do they?" Eleanore's voice was breathless with horror even though she'd heard the story a hundred times.

"No," Muley said. "It was only the whim of one warrior that kept me alive. I was already well into middle age, but he needed a woman to work in his camp because some of his female relatives died of the pox, which he knew was a white man's disease. So, he figured I owed him."

"Think of it!" Eleanore cried, guzzling from the bottle. "Five years in a Sioux camp. Tell me, Muley, did the Indians possibly take a white man named Jack McKnight captive while you were with them?" Her eyes glazed with the thought of it.

Eleanore's sympathy for anybody else was very limited. No matter what, her thoughts quickly turned to herself and Jack McKnight. That was good, because Muley did not want to remind herself of life as a slave in a Sioux camp. She was still kickin' only because soldiers raided the camp by surprise one day, when Muley's captor was out hunting. She was rescued before any of the other Indians thought to knock her in the head.

Licking her lips, Eleanore said, "Jack McKnight is the most handsome man in the world. You would know him! Strong. Black wavy hair. White skin. Good teeth. Beautiful clothing. Long slim fingers that tickle the cards into happy submission!" She swooned.

"A gambling man. I can see how you lost your heart." Muley agreed with her just to keep peace. Muley did not think much of gamblers. No matter how good-looking Jack McKnight might have been, he treated Eleanore like dirt—stole all her money. So he did not have Muley's admiration, but she didn't let on to Eleanore.

"He took my money!" Eleanore said suddenly. "He stayed with me until my property was sold, and the money spent. And then I began to lose my beauty. Thank God he left before I became middle-aged and grew this hideous mustache."

Only because Muley was drunk she blurted, "You mean he never saw you with your mustache? If he left you twenty years ago, before you grew a mustache, he sure as hell won't come back to you now!"

"Oh, Muley!" Eleanore cried, clamping her hand across her mouth. "I had not thought of that!"

"There! You see? All this time you had good reason to be glad he's gone. You don't really want him to see you with a mustache, do you?"

Eleanore gave Muley a sad smile. She was silenced in thought, for once.

"No more Jack McKnight," Eleanore cried. "NO MORE JACK McKNIGHT! You are right, Muley. I would rather die than have him see me this way."

Muley felt good knowing she had helped Eleanore out of her trouble. Muley fell asleep listening to rain running off the wagon sheet.

The girls dragged around camp in the morning, stretching and yawning, waiting for coffee to boil. Muley had taken the mules up to a grassy spot to graze. She had not seen Eleanore around camp yet, but that was not unusual. Eleanore sometimes lit out early to conduct her morning ablution before the rest of the women got up.

Muley mixed leftover fried rattler and boiled purslane, sniffing the aroma as it lifted from the iron frying pan. Suddenly a bandy-legged Chinese fellow ran up the slope toward the women's wagon. He waved his arms, chattering something Muley hardly understood.

"Madame Mustache! Madame Mustache!" He pointed wildly back toward the crews bunched at the side of yesterday's newly laid track.

By the time Muley got down there Beebe was already carrying on, and Cuddles was crying as if she'd lost her best friend. Kerosene Kate stood staring like a poleaxed calf.

Eleanore Dumont's body was stretched along the side of the track. Bluish bubbles were dried around her mouth. Muley's old poison can was held in Eleanore's stiff hand.

"She's poisoned," the crew foreman said, while carefully rolling the can with the heel of his boot.

A doctor who travelled with the railroaders stood up, adjusting his glasses. "Yes, poisoned. Looks like suicide. See? This blue powder is all over her fingers, as well as her mouth. And there are no other tracks here in the mud but her own." He looked at Muley. "You know anything about this?"

"Only that she said, 'No more Jack McKnight.'"

The girls helped Muley pick up Eleanore's body while the men walked away.

KITTY LE ROY

Kitty Le Roy was a rare beauty who ran a Deadwood gambling den in the Dakotas known as "The Mint." She was handy with revolvers, bowie-knives, horses, and men. Kitty grew up in Dallas, Texas, and learned to deal faro at an early age. By the time she headed for the Black Hills, she was already a woman with a reputation for taking care of herself. Hot-tempered, quick on the draw, Kitty dressed like a Gypsy, and attracted attention wherever she went.

The big German begged Kitty for just one more night. What a pathetic man he was! She turned away from him with a quick shrug, causing her red dress to swirl from her curvy hips. A bowie knife was stuck in her waistband. A red scarf tied around her head suggested a gypsy. Everybody knew she carried an arsenal of derringers hidden about her anatomy.

"Get out, Hans!" she ordered. "I have other customers to tend!" Kitty's business, known as The Mint, lived up to its name—the busiest gambling saloon in Deadwood.

Gertie, who worked for Kitty, watched the spectacle. Gertie was not her real name, but none of Kitty's girls used their real names. Three girls worked for Kitty. They made good money, too, selling drinks and entertaining lonely men. Gertie liked the excitement of The Mint—always plenty of cash, whiskey and music.

Kitty Le Roy owned everything, and she worked hard. She dealt faro and had the say about all that went on around the place. At twenty-five, she'd already had four husbands. People laughed and made jokes about who would be fifth. But the jokes were done behind her back; nobody dared say something like that to her face.

"Get out, Hans," she repeated. When he just stood there with a hangdog look on his face, she hit him over the head with an empty whiskey bottle and laughed.

Everybody got out of the way of flying glass. Hans Diedrich toppled to the sawdust floor. A couple of men carried him to the street before hurrying back inside to resume their card game as if nothing unusual had happened.

Hans had been Kitty's lover for the past few months. He was tall, ruddy-faced, and solid as a post. Her interest in him lasted until she'd gotten eight thousand dollars out of him from his mine. When the vein was played out, so was Hans, as far as Kitty was concerned.

After Hans had been dragged out to the street, Kitty joined Gertie, and leaned against the bar. Brushing her long brown curls away from her flushed cheeks, Kitty flashed a big smile. She did a lot of smiling lately since a reporter from the *Sedalia Bazoo* wrote, "Kitty Le Roy's smile is likened to pearls set in coral." She liked that.

"You have embarrassed poor Hans," Gertie told her.

"He better not come near me again," Kitty said, patting the handle of her bowie knife.

Gertie saw Kitty's eyes sparkle almost as brightly as the big diamonds hanging from her ears. Kitty was one to enjoy a good fight...anything exciting and dangerous which was part of her own attraction. She loved telling the story about how she married her first husband because he was the only man brave enough to allow her to shoot an apple off his head while she galloped, by riding backwards on a horse.

Preacher Burr was in The Mint tonight, sipping a few drops of whiskey Kitty donated to him. Kitty whispered

123

to Gertie, "I don't think that mousy little turd is a real preacher. But he's the only man in Deadwood willing to read a few words at funerals and weddings."

Gertie agreed. Preacher Burr dressed in black, carried a big scuffed Bible, and managed to weasel drinks at The Mint now and again. He got away with it only because Kitty thought him a harmless fool, herself enjoying the sight of a "preacher" whining and scratching for a drink.

"Isn't the music too slow tonight?" Kitty asked Gertie. Before Gertie could answer, Kitty shouted to Sweeny the piano player, "Liven it up! I want to dance a jig!" And she did too, because that is how she got her start in Dallas when she was ten years old. Her family owned a traveling medicine show.

Gertie had to agree the music was getting better now. She clapped her hands and wiggled her shoulders to please Kitty. In fact, it did not pay to disagree with Kitty for any reason.

One of the other girls, Dahlia, carrying a tray of drinks from the bar, said to Kitty, "Burt Armstrong is here tonight." Dahlia nodded toward the lean figure slouched at a table, puffing thoughtfully on a cheroot.

Burt Armstrong was a rugged, tall blond fellow who owned the livery stable in town. He did horseshoeing, which developed his back and arm muscles so much his shirts always looked too tight. He had a black stallion Kitty had been trying to buy. But he would not part with the horse, which had Kitty fuming. After money, men, and guns, a good horse was her next passion.

Kitty sashayed to Burt Armstrong's table. Her bouncy buttocks bobbed up and down under her thin silk dress like two cats fighting inside a bag. She yanked the cigar out of Burt's mouth and took a few puffs on it herself. Then, stuffing it back between his startled lips, she made a lot of sassy remarks to him.

Burt was doing a good job of ignoring her and then, WHACK! Kitty slapped him so hard his chair tipped on its back legs. She challenged him to a duel.

The room got quiet. Everybody watched Burt Armstrong to see what he would do next.

A long minute went by, and then he said in a cool voice, "I won't fight a woman." He turned away, slowly examining his hand of cards.

Kitty exploded. She loved to fight. She had been in enough shoot-outs to have six notches on her gun. Kitty was also carrying a big crush on Burt Armstrong. He was one of the few men in town who ignored her—which made her crazy.

"Coward!" Kitty shrieked.

Armstrong kept looking at his hand of cards, although Gertie, who was watching, could see his small pointed ears turn red.

Gasping, eyes flashing, Kitty ran to the bar and snatched a glass of whiskey right out of the hand of one of the customers. "Pig!" she shouted at Armstrong. After swallowing the whiskey in one gulp, she dashed away to her office in the back room where she had a desk surrounded by wooden whiskey kegs and broken furniture. She slammed the door so hard the picture of galloping white stallions tipped behind the bar.

After that, people got back to the business of gambling and drinking. The ragtime piano music gradually slipped back to a slower pace.

About an hour later the swinging doors made a slow squeak. A handsome stranger walked in wearing a black, long-tailed morning coat, black pants, black gloves and boots, and a black plantation hat.

Usually strangers were not that noticeable around Deadwood, but this one had an enormous drooping brown mustache that he fingered as if he was especially proud of it. Besides that, he carried a pair of glimmering pearl-handled six-shooters that glowed in the kerosene light as he swaggered over to the bar. The stranger ordered one drink that he paid for with a newly minted gold coin. After pulling his hat to his eyebrows, he joined the table of gamblers where Armstrong played cards.

Armstrong ignored the stranger. Armstrong was the sort of man who was proud of himself because he was quick and strong, and handy with a gun. In his own conceit he was not threatened by some showoff.

The stranger sat at the table, puffing cigar smoke right into Armstrong's eyes. This caused Armstrong to light up a fresh cigar and puff right back. That went on for a while, which of course resulted in hostile looks between the two individuals. Others sitting at the table were getting mighty uncomfortable.

It seemed to Gertie, who was still watching, that something bad was going to happen. She glanced at the closed door of Kitty's office, thinking Kitty better come out soon in case there was trouble. Kitty never stayed away long on busy nights. But after the way she left the room following her fight with Armstrong, Gertie thought maybe she needed time by herself, so Gertie decided to stay out of things.

"Gertie! More whiskey here," Burt Armstrong called in that smooth, deep voice of his. Gertie carried a tray full of sloshing glasses to the table. She thought it was funny the stranger played cards with his gloves on, but nobody at the table protested. Usually gamblers were suspicious of something like that. They always worried a cheat would hide cards inside his gloves or up his sleeves. But when the stranger opened his coat to pay for his own drink, Gertie saw the handle of a big bowie knife sticking up from the top of his vest. Maybe that had something to do with why the others were not protesting the gloves.

Little Liza, the bony blonde who worked with Gertie and Dahlia, jabbed Gertie in the hip and said she wanted to talk. Gertie followed her over to the bar where Little Liza whispered, "Do you know where Kitty is? There is a man here who says he owes her a lot of money. He wants to pay his debt."

Gertie looked at a short, squatty, dark-haired man twisting his hat in his hands near the door. She remembered he was one of the miners Kitty grubstaked a few months back. Gertie knew Kitty would be anxious to collect the money.

"I'll take a look in her office," Gertie told Little Liza, because Little Liza would not dare go into Kitty's office. Kitty was strict about her employees going back there. Gertie was the only one Kitty allowed to enter the room only because Gertie had worked there three years, and Kitty knew whom she could trust. "I'll be right back," Gertie said.

Gertie pushed the door open—Kitty's office was empty. Dark. The place smelled like sawdust, cigar smoke and stale beer. Kitty was not around. So Gertie gave Little Liza this news, which Little Liza passed along to the miner, who promised to come back the next day.

Suddenly an argument broke out at the table where Burt Armstrong and the stranger played cards. The stranger accused Burt of cheating. The rest of the players jumped away. The stranger grabbed Burt by the front of his shirt, snarling in a gravelly voice that Burt was a rat, a cheat, a liar, and worse.

Burt grabbed the stranger by his arms and tossed him easily against the wall. Thud!

Gertie was smart to duck behind the bar. Everybody else in the room dove for cover, too. Gertie knew both men were riled enough to draw guns; two shots cracked. The room smelled like sulphur; bluish smoke hung thick in the air. By the time Gertie stood up to see over the bar, Burt Armstrong was sprawled back on the floor—his gun dropped next to him. Blood seeped through his shirt in a big red patch at the center of his chest.

Looking down at Burt Armstrong, the stranger yanked the black plantation hat off his own head, allowing long brown curls to drop down to his shoulders! Next, he ripped his mustache off. It was Kitty!

Kitty threw herself on the floor beside the wounded man, cradling his head in her lap while frantically smoothing his hair. She crooned how much she loved him.

He did not answer.

Kitty saw Preacher Burr peeping from behind an overturned table. "Get over here with that Bible and marry us!" she screamed.

Preacher Burr did as he was told. Turning to a page in his Good Book, he muttered something about what God had put together let no man put to thunder. Or something like that. Kitty glared around the room until she saw Gertie, then she ordered Gertie to be a witness.

And that is the way Burt Armstrong died—with a surprised look on his face.

APACHE MAY

In November, 1895, a small band of Apaches "jumped" the reservation at San Carlos, Arizona. Making their way south toward Mexico, the renegades killed Eliza Merrill and her father, who were traveling to Globe, Arizona. The Apache raiding party stole the Merrills' clothing, horse, and buggy before making their way into the Chiricahua Mountains near Cave Creek. Here they killed a young homesteader named John Hand. Six months later, in May of 1896, a posse led by John Slaughter caught up to the marauders in the Guadalupe Mountains south of the border where the Apaches were either killed or routed. While John Slaughter poked through the Apache camp before burning everything, he discovered a little Apache girl who had been left behind.

John Slaughter sat a horse like a sack of *frijoles,* his stirrup leathers a notch too long. He rode into the yard reeking of stale sweat and cigar smoke, carrying a sleeping Apache child in his arms. It was a hot summer night in 1892. John and his weary gray horse had eaten many miles of trail dust during the past week's Apache hunt.

"John! What is this?" Viola Slaughter cried, rushing down from the wide veranda. She held her long skirts above her slim ankles. Mrs. Slaughter, known as "Aunty Slaughter" by everyone but her closest friends, who called her "Vi," was yet an attractive woman for her 36 years.

John Slaughter gently lifted the dirty bundle over his saddle horn to hand it to his wife, but the baby suddenly awakened. Her small bronze fists curled fiercely while she hissed and spit at Mrs. Slaughter like a mean cat.

"John!" Viola gasped, cringing away in surprise. "Where is the mother?"

John allowed the child to climb around his neck. Even though the Apache was tiny, I guessed her to be at least one year old and extremely agile and alert. Her suspicious black eyes were looking around the yard at everyone and everything.

"I found her abandoned in the Apache camp we raided," John said. "We will have to keep her. The parents are either dead or disappeared in the Sierra Madre."

My own heart fluttered at the mention of Apaches. Being Mexican, I knew first-hand the destruction and terror they had wreaked upon this land since as far back as I could remember. My ancestors had always been enemies of the Apaches.

"We can't keep her, John," Viola protested. "Her family will come looking for her, and we will all be murdered!" She pressed the back of her hand against her mouth. For as many years as Mrs. Slaughter had lived in Arizona, she was still worried about Apaches. While Geronimo had surrendered ten years ago, in 1886, a few renegades were still about. Sometimes a band jumped the reservation, as in the case of the parents of this child John Slaughter held in his arms.

John Slaughter stuttered when he got nervous or annoyed. "I say, I say, Vi, we will keep her! I will not send her back to the reservation." He gave me a stern look, and since I was Mrs. Slaughter's maid, I stepped forward to take the squirming child from his arms. It was apparent from the first moment that this baby was strongly attached to John Slaughter, and would not easily be handled by anyone else.

"Thank you, Lola" he said to me. John Slaughter was always polite to the servants.

Seeing her husband's determination (John Slaughter never gave in once he made up his mind), Mrs. Slaughter wrung her hands while that expression of indulgent surrender crossed her face—an expression she used often around John. "All right, John. But I insist she be given a bath!"

"I say, I say, Vi," he muttered, dismounting stiffly from his horse.

The child's stringy black hair was knotted and tangled around her dirty face. Her body was filthy with dust and grime; the clothing she wore was a mature white woman's dress that had been ripped off at the waist, which allowed the garment to be short enough to fit the child like a dress.

Mrs. Slaughter and I wrestled the squirming creature into a tub of warm soapy water. Mrs. Slaughter eyed the garment the child wore, saying "I wonder if this is all that is left of poor Eliza Merrill."

I only nodded. Eliza Merrill was the murdered white girl who, along with her father, had fallen victim to the Apache raiding party six months ago. The basque had large white buttons, and there was a tattered shawl fitting the description of the clothing worn by Miss Merrill when she was abducted. We dropped these things to the floor, and finally got down to the diaper of sorts fastened around the child's lower body. It was all that was left of an old 1888 Cochise County election banner. Mrs. Slaughter allowed a naughty smile to cross her face. The banner had belonged to the Republican Party, featuring the opponent of John Slaughter who ran against him during the Cochise County sheriff's election of that year.

"At least a good use was found for this banner!" Viola laughed merrily. She was always one to find humor in a situation.

I knew John Slaughter won the election that year. He became Cochise County Sheriff for another two years, serving all together from 1886 to 1890.

132

Women who lived at the Slaughter ranch joined us in the kitchen. They were full of curiosity about the Apache child since word had already circulated among the many residents of the ranch about her arrival. While the Slaughters had no children of their own, John's son and daughter from his first marriage lived on the place, and there were many others whom the Slaughters gathered around themselves over the years because they'd had no other homes. White, black, Indian, and Mexican alike, the color of skin or personal background made no difference to the Slaughters.

I was finally able to get a good grip on the child's arms, while a teenage girl, Mathilde, scrubbed with a bar of soap. Another girl, Edith, combed the tangles out of the little Apache's hair. The child was a great novelty with her spitting and biting, like a cornered bobcat. But for some reason, her vehemence was directed toward Mrs. Slaughter more than anybody else in the room that night.

"I will tend to John's supper," Mrs. Slaughter said, realizing that when she backed away, the baby seemed less agitated. For a moment their eyes locked, and those wary, dark Apache pools blazed like silent tomahawks.

Since this was the month of May, and the child was definitely Apache, the Slaughters decided to name her Apache May, which was soon shortened to Patchy. And while the child continued to show her dislike toward Mrs. Slaughter, Patchy deepened her relationship with John Slaughter, which was both heart-wrenching as well as humorous. She called him "Don Juan" which meant "Mr. John" in Spanish, tagging after him, clinging to his boots, riding with him on his horse, choosing the closest seat beside him at the dinner table, and crawling up on him whenever the occasion allowed.

I knew what a kind and generous person Mrs. Slaughter was, and I grieved, knowing she, too tried to conquer the heart of Apache May, but it was not to be. Words were not necessary—it was plain to see that Patchy was in love with John Slaughter.

The Slaughter ranch was known as the San Bernardino, an oasis for hundreds of people who traversed southern Cochise County in the late 1880s. Cowboys, drifters, military men, prospectors, politicians, lawmen, traders, Indians, Mexicans, and whites alike crossed back and forth, many staying at the ranch. The Slaughters were known all across the territory for their hospitality. The ranch was self-contained with a store, blacksmith forge, school and post office. Thus Patchy had the opportunity to meet many individuals from all walks of life. But her Apache ways were not outgrown, and those dark, brooding eyes stared sullenly. While she quickly learned to chatter in English, Spanish, and Apache, she remained suspicious of most people.

On a summer afternoon in 1898, when Patchy was about four years old, a group of ladies from Bisbee, Arizona visited Mrs. Slaughter at the ranch. She was anxious to please them because the spaces between the ranch and town were great. Visiting with friends was a treat for this gentle lady. Her friends finally arrived in their buggy—having traveled the distance of forty-five miles from Bisbee. They were anxious to sink into chairs inside the cool house and sip fresh lemonade. The party planned to stay the night, so there had been much bustling about in preparation for their arrival.

Mrs. Sloan, the oldest lady in the group, seemed to have the most trouble recovering from the long journey. She sat on the edge of a couch in the corner of the living room, fanning herself. As she reached for her lemonade, little bronze hands darted out from under the couch, clawing Mrs. Sloan's ankles while at the same time a terrifying Indian howl pierced the air!

Thunderstruck, everybody jumped. Mrs. Sloan slumped back into her chair in a dead faint; black-stockinged legs jerked forward spasmodically.

Viola Slaughter tore around the back of the couch, yanking Patchy out from under the ruffles! Patchy's cunning eyes glowed with mischievous delight.

Gasps came from the horrified ladies, who circled around Mrs. Sloan, fanning her face and patting her wrists.

Embarrassed, Mrs. Slaughter shook Patchy, crying, "Naughty! Frightening my guests! Look what you've done to poor Mrs. Sloan!"

Patchy's mouth turned downward. Her eyes slitted dangerously while she pushed Mrs. Slaughter away with her digging fingernails. "I will kill you someday!" Patchy promised, spitting viciously into Mrs. Slaughter's face.

Mrs. Slaughter was mortified in front of her friends, so I rushed up and took Patchy out of her arms and quickly left the room. Patchy hung limply in my embrace. Sullen and wicked, she did not show any dislike toward me, but then, I was not her opponent. It was Mrs. Slaughter who distressed the child—it was Mrs. Slaughter to whom John Slaughter belonged.

On a cold winter morning in 1900, Mrs. Slaughter decided to accompany John to Bisbee. He had business to attend to, and she wanted to go shopping.

"Lola!" Mrs. Slaughter said to me, "please tell Jess Fisher to start a fire and heat rocks to take in the carriage with us this morning. My feet need a toasty nest for the long drive to town."

Jess Fisher was Viola Slaughter's cousin and ranch manager. I gave him Mrs. Slaughter's instructions. A fire was quickly started near the blacksmith shop where several large stones were placed at the bottom of the coals to be heated. Meanwhile, the Slaughters busied themselves for the trip.

Patchy stood bundled in a shawl wrapped around her long cotton dress. Her eyes squinted and accused, as usual. She remained somewhat aloof from the rest of the children who laughed and played in the yard. She watched them through a picket fence that stretched between the blacksmith shop and the school. Her playmates soon began poking sticks at her while she exercised her spitting technique. The game bordered on both fun and cruelty for all participants involved. Patchy was especially sullen this morning. She knew John Slaughter was leaving the ranch for two days... a trip she could not take part in, even though Mrs. Slaughter was going with him.

"I say, I say, Vi," John scolded, impatient with his wife's nervous fussing and last-minute orders to servants.

Mrs. Slaughter had dashed up and down the front steps three times already, back and forth to the buggy, then remembering something else, she leaped out and rushed inside the house with one more instruction for us. I finally stood at the bottom of the steps, hands clasped. "Yes, señora! I will take care of everything! Don't worry. Please go and have a good time!"

They were finally loaded into the buggy after Jess placed the bundle of warm rocks wrapped in an old saddle blanket on the floor for Mrs. Slaughter to warm her feet on. John yielded to her whim, giving her a little hug. "I say, I say, Vi, are you ready?"

Before she could think of something else to detain them, he slapped the lines on the horse's back a little harder than necessary. The buggy lurched forward. It clattered out of the yard while the two people sat warm and close without looking back. John Slaughter was nearly 20 years older than Viola, and it was touching how the couple was so much in love.

Patchy stalked from her place behind the picket fence. Suddenly she ran broken-hearted to the center of the big yard. Keeping her eyes on the buggy, she glowered until it disappeared, a tiny speck in the distance. Her eyes were so full of jealous hatred I shrank from her gaze when I tried to persuade her to come into the house.

She turned abruptly. Joined by the other children for more taunts and rough exchanges, she wandered over to the fire Jess Fisher had built to heat Mrs. Slaughter's foot-warmers.

I saw Patchy holding her little hands in front of the crackling flame, raising her arms and elbows so that the front of her body caught the heat. The other children stood nearby, imitating her expression and movements—everybody sticking their tongues out at one another. Then, with a sudden cry of surprise, Apache May jumped as the hem of her dress glowed in one fiery burst.

"Her dress caught fire!" I screamed, racing down the steps to help her. I knew smothering the flame was her only hope. The other children danced around Patchy, laughing at first, not understanding the danger.

Jess Fisher appeared from the entrance of the blacksmith shop. "By God, don't run!" he shouted at her, big spurs jingling while he tromped across the yard toward her. But Patchy was already dashing down the road in the direction the Slaughters had taken.

"Don Juan! Don Juan!" she shrieked, little arms flailing, legs pumping hard over the ground. Her running only fanned the flames up her dress and around her body until she was enveloped in one luminous ball.

"Patchy!" I gasped, "stop!" But I was no match for her terrified sprint as I tried to catch her.

Jess ran beside me. We finally caught up with Patchy when she fell just beyond the main gate, twisted and moaning; black eyes blazing with shock and pain.

Jess picked her up in his arms and I wrapped her in my shawl. Together we trundled across the yard toward the house.

By now all of the ranch hands, wives, and children had gathered in the yard. One of the women suggested putting cold water on the wounds, so we rushed the child into the house while Jess galloped away on his horse to catch up to the Slaughters.

By the time the Slaughters returned, Patchy's strength was ebbing. When her eyes lit on John Slaughter, she seemed somewhat relieved. The Slaughters had sent Jess on to Bisbee to fetch a doctor when he caught up with them on the road. But many hours passed by the time the doctor arrived at the ranch, and by then it was early evening. The long, terrible night settled upon us.

People tiptoed about, stunned by the event, knowing there was no hope even before the doctor made the announcement. There was nothing he could do but give the child laudanum to ease her suffering, but she was soon unable to swallow. As the hours dragged on, poor Patchy grew weaker. John Slaughter told everybody to get out of the room. He could see she was calmest when they were alone together.

Horrified that her presence caused the child so much torment, Mrs. Slaughter left John alone with Patchy. She walked the living room floor until she finally collapsed just as the first rays of morning light showed in the east.

Meanwhile, John Slaughter spent the long night alone with Patchy. Holding her tiny hand, he gave her wild spirit whatever nourishment it was she craved, for Don Juan belonged to the heart of Apache May.

Apache May's life ended at dawn. Jess Fisher built a small wooden coffin. The following day we stood around the tiny grave. The child was buried quietly without a service on a windy knoll near the ranch house. Her cross was made from cholla cactus that stood with brazen, thorny resilience like the fearless little soul resting below.

CALAMITY JANE

Martha Connarray was born in northern Missouri around 1852. By the time she was 12 years old, her family moved to Virginia City, Nevada. After losing their mother, Martha and her siblings had a rough childhood—she herself dressed in men's clothing, and learned to ride and shoot. By 1875 Martha was living in the Black Hills where she was known as a local character who drank whiskey, drove stagecoaches, and professed her love for Wild Bill Hickok. She had one daughter with a man named Burke; they lived for a time in El Paso, Texas. Nicknamed "Calamity Jane," Martha led a rough, frontier existence until the end of her days. She died in 1903.

The family buried their mother in a weedy, lonely spot behind their shack a week ago. Now the weather turned cold. Hateful November wind stirred cross the Montana plains causing the children to shiver and draw their old clothing around their young bodies. Pa had gone into town for a day of drinking. The big sister, Martha, who was sixteen, decided to make soap.

Sara, the next oldest sister, sensed the project was a tribute to their mother. Ma prided herself in appreciating the nicer things in life that she remembered from her childhood in Missouri. Even though Martha did not come right out and say it, Sara figured that Martha must have been grieving for their mother worse than the rest of the kids.

Their family spent the last year trekking west across the Territories from Missouri to Montana in a wagon train. The six kids were lonely, scared, and confused now that Ma was dead. Their last recollection of her was seeing her withered frame inch around the shack last week. She tried to keep her children's spirits up by talking about how the next day she planned to make perfumed soap....

Yesterday, Martha leached rainwater through a bucket of wood ashes to have lye water necessary to make soap. Sara watched Martha test its strength by dropping a raw potato into the white liquid to see if the potato would sink. When it floated, Martha knew the lye water was strong enough. After heating the lye water, she added rendered pork fat. It would result in hard, dry soap, but it was all that they had. Beef tallow was better for soapmaking, but the family had not seen a piece of beef in months.

The kids stood out in the middle of the front yard— Martha mixed the gray tallow and lye concoction in a big iron pot swinging over a bed of red-hot coals. She stirred the liquid 'round and 'round with a long-handled wooden spoon she had carved from a cottonwood branch. Martha was careful not to splash the scalding liquid on her skin.

The littlest kids hung around, sad-faced and whining on account of the way things were. Martha had been sticking close to home since Ma's burial, and Sara knew it was because she was so concerned about the rest of them. Otherwise Martha was usually out riding her horse, shooting game, or cutting wood. She was kind of a father to them since their own pa spent a lot of time in saloons. When he was home, he was usually in a mean temper.

"Wake up, Sarah!" Martha said, signalling her younger sister. "Bring some of Ma's oil of lavender so we can pour it into this here mix! You know how she always liked the blossomy smell of that stuff in her soap."

Sara shook her head. She held the youngest baby brother in her arms while he squirmed and whimpered. "The lavender oil was used up the last time Ma made soap," Sara said. "The only thing left is the geranium perfume she made before we left Missouri."

"Then bring it!" Martha bawled. She wore a short dress over a pair of bloomers drawn in at the ankles. The outfit was invented by a woman named Amelia Bloomer back in 1851, before Martha was born. Their mother was quick to realize the possibilities of that comfortable garment even though it turned out to be just a fad. Ma said most women went back to wearing long dresses after that. But Ma kept her bloomers, and now they fit Martha. Sara thought they looked kind of funny, but Martha insisted that bloomers made it a lot easier to ride a horse. And anyway, Martha was never one to fret about the way she looked.

One of the middle sisters, Katie, piped, "The geranium perfume is in Ma's old trunk. I'll bring it." She dashed into the shack.

"Don't be getting into Ma's trunk!" Martha called after her, but the door slammed. So they all trooped inside. The wind was whipping up anyhow, and they were glad to find a reason to get out of it.

Besides, they had always been curious about Ma's trunk. Not that it was any big secret. But their mother had been a real lady before she married Pa. There were some things inside her trunk that she did not allow the kids to play with.

The big wooden round-topped trunk stood in a corner under some blankets in the little bedroom that Ma and Pa slept in. The kids slept here and there around the common room. That was all there was to this shanty Pa rented. He said it was temporary until he could raise enough money for them to move on to a better place. He was not happy here in Blackfoot, but then he had not been happy anywhere.

Katie's eyes bugged when she lifted the trunk lid. There were books, shoes, a little box full of earrings, a cloth bag crunchy with dried seeds and flower petal potpourri, a bundle of baby clothes including a white christening dress, and a stack of *Lily* magazines written by Amelia Bloomer dated 1851. Sara later learned these magazines were full of articles about voting rights, equal pay, and sensible clothing for women.

Martha poked through a collection of glass jars filled with colored pastes. Meanwhile, Katie examined sweet-smelling white powder in a faded blue box tied with a silk ribbon. There were bottles of complexion salves, colored oils, and spine-tingling oddities that the children did not know a use for. Their imaginations ran wild.

At the bottom of the trunk, folded inside a cloth sack, was their mother's wedding dress. Musty-smelling, yellowed and creased, nevertheless they recognized its quality when they slipped it out of the bag. The long skirt was made of cotton eyelet. The frilly basque had a high lace collar. Sara petted the leg-of-mutton sleeves. Small cloth-covered buttons were sewn in a long row on the cuffs.

Martha held the dress against herself. It looked like it might fit her. She skittered out of her bloomers and short dress. In a minute the kids had her all hooked up in the wedding gown. They'd never seen their big sister all gussied up before. Everybody stood there staring like cows at a gate.

Katie found a velvet reticule containing mother-of-pearl combs inside the trunk. She handed one to Martha who used it to pin her long, straight hair up off her neck. Martha struggled with a lopsided chignon that made her look swan-necked.

Encouraged by the way the kids gaped at her, Martha swooped around the room. She held the long skirts away from her sides with the tips of her fingers like she was a butterfly. She hummed and showed off like a rooster ready to crow.

"How's this for a fancy lady?" Martha asked, raising one of her thick eyebrows. She had a long nose, small dark eyes that sometimes crossed, and a coarse face usually caked with trail dust.

They giggled, knowing that she was entertaining them, causing them to laugh for the first time since Ma died.

Charles, the ten-year-old brother, stood barefooted on the cold dirt floor, hands shoved into his overall pockets. He sized Martha up. "Your face don't go with that dress," he said dismally. "Fancy dress or no, you got a jaw like a mule. You ain't foolin' nobody."

"Hogwash!" Martha scolded him. She reached into the trunk and found a jar inside one of the storage boxes. She twisted the lid off before patting white powder all over her face with her hand. "This will cover my sunburn. You will see what a grand dame I really am! Today I'm trading my gunpowder for this here face powder…no more freckles, no more dirt! So quit snortin' like a bunch of skittish jackass colts at my new appearance."

They all burst out laughing then, because the powder gobbed in lumps on the end of her nose. She looked more like she'd been baking bread than attending a party.

"Ain't you supposed to use a powder puff?" Sara asked, getting into the spirit of things. She jiggled the baby, who had finally fallen asleep over her shoulder.

"Huh!" Martha grunted, opening another jar and matting pink powder on her cheeks with her thumb this time, making her face look feverish in a mass of rose petals. Sara could tell Martha was play-acting. Martha was usually somber and at odds with their pa. But the kids had been so lost without their mother that they needed one another now to survive their grief. It surprised Sara that Martha was playing the fool, but it was also heartwarming knowing that she would act silly just to entertain the rest of them—ordinarily, being frivolous went against Martha's grain.

Martha's chignon fell apart, so she twisted the end of her loose hair like a thick rope. She ran it through her mouth, batting her eyelashes like she was a Mexican señorita holding a rose between her teeth.

Just then Sara heard the door creak open. Before any of the kids could react, Pa stumbled into the shack. He swayed there in the middle of the floor gawking at Martha like he'd seen a ghost. His eyes were all red and puffy.

Martha quit prancing, while the rest of the kids cringed.

"What in hell are you doing?" Pa yelled.

Martha looked kind of sheepish while spitting the rope of hair out of her mouth. "Nothing, Pa. I just...."

"You just what?" he bellowed. "You dare desecrate your mother's wedding dress! You? Who has never cared to act like a lady! Always riding and shooting. Now you stand there with a face full of powder like a shameless cat! Next you'll be painting your lips red and walking a little dog on a leash like them harlots in town!"

"Martha meant no harm," Sara said to him, wondering what a harlot in town was.

"You shet up! Stay out of this!" he snarled at Sara. His big craggy nose was swollen from whiskey. He clenched and squeezed his fists like he was milking a cow.

It was horrible to be a little girl and useless. Sara felt sick and lonelier than ever. Ma had always known what to do when he came home like this. The kids were usually told to go do chores, or if it was dark they were herded into a corner of the shack while Ma tamed Pa down enough so that he'd fall asleep. But Sara could see that Martha was not good at mollycoddling. She was too much like him to use anything but her own temper in a fight.

"Git that dress off!" He yelled, taking a shaky step toward Martha. Before she could move, he grabbed the front of the dress in his fist and yanked it off her body in one long rip.

Martha gasped in surprise, raising her hand in front of her face. He caught her hair in his right hand, with his left he scooped pink powder from one of the jars and rubbed it all over her cheeks. "I hear them prostitutes use beet juice!" he raved. "And they tweak their cheeks to make 'em blush…has to be red! Bright red! You should know about that!" He brutally pinched her face until he made her cheeks purple.

Till now Martha stood there shaking, defiantly standing up to him by not crying. Martha gritted her teeth, and Sara could see she was mad at herself for getting caught this way.

Then Pa said something that really got Martha's hackles up. "They told me in town today that you have been talking with that young hellion, Bill Hickok! Making big plans about joining the Pony Express?"

"That's right," Martha said, trying to keep her voice from cracking. "I already signed on. The Pony Express pays good money, and I'll be doing what I want to do!"

"You're going to stay home. Here. Tending to woman's work. And these," he said, eyeing the bloomers on the floor, "I'll fix this right now." He let her go and reached for the bloomers. "You will do as you are told. You'll quit acting like a man! You got woman's work right here in the house now your mother is dead." He tore the bloomers into shreds. "Crazy notions your mother put into your brain...a woman don't belong in nothin' but a dress!" His eyes fell on the *Lily* magazines.

Martha tried reaching for them but he grabbed the whole stack, flipping the pamphlets around the room like floundering pigeons. He tossed the magazines against the walls. They even hit the ceiling, the torn pages fluttered like leaves in the wind. "You're a calamity!" Pa raved at Martha. "Nothing but a damned calamity!"

The rest of the children scurried out of his way. Huddling in a corner, they knew he would not hurt them as long as they did not stand up to him. He liked seeing everybody cower until he finally collapsed in a drunken sleep. In the morning he always acted like he could not remember what happened. Afterwards their mother kept the peace by pretending she did not remember anything either.

But Martha was not the mother. Sara could see things were not going Pa's way tonight. When Martha just stood there glaring at him full of resistance, he made a move to grab her again. This time she doubled her fist and swung so hard that her knuckles connected flush against his jaw. He toppled face-first to the floor; out cold after hitting his head on a chair.

147

"Maybe I am a calamity," Martha said, "but he can't make me take up where Ma left off." Watery-eyed, as close as she would ever come to crying, she gathered up the crumpled *Lily* magazines and straightened their pages the best she could. She handed them to Sara. "Hide them. Ma was keeping them for us. I reckon now they're yours."

Next, she picked up the torn wedding dress and the shredded bloomers. Carrying everything out to the yard, she stuffed the bundle of torn material into the hot coals under the bubbling soap cauldron.

Half-naked, in just her underdrawers and camisole, Martha stalked blue and shivering back inside the shanty. She found a pair of Pa's pants and an old cotton shirt that were still folded at the bottom of Ma's mending basket. She put them on. Boots, a dirty felt hat, and her jacket made up the rest of her attire. Lastly, she buckled on the gunbelt that had been hanging from a peg near the door.

Pa stirred, moaning a little. He rolled over on his side. Palms together, he slid his hands under his face like he was praying, and began to snore.

Martha had a sullen look on her face. "He ain't gonna wake up till morning. By then I'll be long gone."

Sara studied her big sister's face, and was sure Martha had forgotten that her cheeks were still plastered with pink rouge. But Sara did not dare say anything about it. Instead, she told Martha, "I don't blame you for leaving." Sara was still patting the back of the sleeping baby; tears ran down her own cheeks. She would miss Martha. With her gone that meant Sara was the one who had to replace Ma. At fourteen, she was the next oldest.

"I'm sorry, Sara," Martha said, putting a rough hand on her sister's shoulder. "If I stay around here now, either me or Pa is going to get shot. Things will be better for everybody without me. Anyhow, he's always been nicer to you little kids."

"You're lucky, you're old enough to go," the eight-year-old brother Henry said. "I'll help you saddle your horse. I wish I was big enough to join up with Bill Hickok and the Pony Express!" He tagged outside after Martha.

Sara and the rest of the kids stood on the sagging porch. They watched while Martha saddled up that big roan gelding of hers, a bronc only she could ride. Then she waved at them one last time and galloped out of the yard.

CHARLIE PANKHURST

During the 1800s many of the stagecoach drivers became legends in their own time. Most of them did their talking to their teams, and the past histories of these men remained their own business. So it was not unusual that a highly-respected stagecoach driver named Charlie Pankhurst kept his business to himself. When Pankhurst died, it was discovered he was really a woman. Eventually some information came out about Charlie—she was originally from New England where she grew up in a poorhouse. As soon as she was old enough to be on her own, she dressed like a boy, learned to handle horses, and found work in a stable owned by Ebenezer Balch in Providence, Rhode Island. Charlie had unusually sensitive hands when driving horses, and she became known as one of the best "whips" on the line. In the 1850s she headed West, and drove her teams over the High Sierras for nearly twenty years. Passengers traveling with Charlie Pankhurst admired her skill and daring. Charlie Pankhurst died in 1879.

The only thing Charlie Pankhurst ever kissed was a horse. That was kind of a joke between us swampers, shotgun guards, and drivers at the Wells Fargo barn in Placerville, California. The year was 1875 when I first met Charlie, and he was by then getting on in years. I was only pushing twenty myself, and full of curiosity about driving the stage-coaches. My name is Constantine Wibbleton; I was big and husky. My friends called me "Coon."

Charlie Pankhurst had a reputation of being one of the best reinsmen on the line. Known as "whips," these men drove the big Concord coaches, considered the finest built. Eight feet high, eight feet long, five feet wide, the Concord had leather upholstery, leather curtains, and bright red paint with yellow trim. The best were made by the Abbot and Downing Company back in Concord, New Hampshire. Up there on those magnificent coaches, we rode in style.

I was happy when the boss assigned me to ride shotgun with an old pro like Charlie. He was some Jehu—that was another name given to the stagecoach drivers—Jehu. One time I asked Charlie where the term Jehu came from, and he said it had something to do with the Bible.

The most exciting ride I ever took with him happened one time about thirty miles out of Placerville on a cold October night. Charlie encouraged the horses, snapping his long whip. It was known as "giving them the silk." Charlie was hunched to his own side of the seat, as usual, paying attention to his horses. Light glowed from the lamps attached to either side of the coach. Those lanterns were fitted with two French plate glass windows. Mounted on each side of the driver's high seat, candles inside those lanterns measured eighteen inches long and two inches thick. They sent a fine yellow glow into the night.

"Get your long legs out of my way," Charlie said, teasing me. I moved my legs over to my own side of the box. I was six feet tall, and Charlie was always kidding me about my height. When we stood on the ground together, the top of his head barely came to my shoulder.

Sitting up there I watched the expert way he "slipped and climbed the reins"—feeding the lines back and forth through his fingers, talking to his horses. I'd ridden with a lot of other drivers, but I never saw anybody handle the lines as good as Charlie. That night we were packing nine passengers, including two women and one teenage girl. The six men were a mix of drummers, (we made fun of them, calling them "lightning rod salesmen") gamblers, businessmen, and a banker.

The Wells Fargo strongbox under our feet had some cash and the usual sacks of nuggets, jewelry, and checks. The box itself was painted green, made of ponderosa pine, and reinforced with oak rims and iron straps and corners. It weighed twenty-four pounds, measuring 20 by 12 by 10

151

inches. Across the top of this one rested Charlie's old sawed-off shotgun.

Feeling the cold and rain, I tightened my coat collar while holding my shotgun between my knees. I rubbed my hands together, mad at myself for leaving my gloves at the last swing station. It was times like these I was happy for my full red beard—it kept my face warm.

I glanced at Charlie's smooth face. He was one of the few men I knew who did not have a mustache or beard. "I bet your face is getting cold," I tried to tease him.

Charlie was hunched, watching his team travel the high ridges along the lonely stretch. Cliffs covered with broken trees and boulders were at our left side. Far below in the canyon to our right I could not see the bottom in the dark, but I felt the thin air and deathly silence—a hollow void that could not be easily described.

Charlie's whip, seven feet long, was stuck in the whip holder. Charlie reached for it, popping it over the horses' heads. The horses were never touched with the whip, it was used only for its sound. On the downgrade, Charlie touched the brake with the tip of his boot toe. I heard the gravelly sound of brake blocks scraping against the wheel rim.

I had given up trying to get Charlie into a conversation about anything but horses. He spent most of his time hunched over those lines, talking to his best friends through their bits. Anyway, Charlie was not one to brag about his exploits away from work. Near as I could tell he never married, nor had a woman in his life. Horses seemed to be Charlie's first and only love. Being a bachelor myself, sometimes I bragged about my adventures with some girl in town—usually a saloon girl. After listening, Charlie would merely stick his elbow in my ribs and laugh, saying, "You big rascal."

That night Charlie slowed the horses for a long uphill grade. The six big grays pulled into their collars, grabbing rocks with their shoes. At the top of the hill a cold burst of rain started coming down hard, a long quiet rain that soaks you to your skin in a few seconds. I tightened my collar again, pulling my hat to my eyes.

Charlie shivered, coughing. He'd been coughing a lot lately, but I did not dare ask him about it. He'd just say he'd choked on tobacco juice. One time when I was really worried, he got ornery and told me to mind my own business.

Charlie had a deeply tanned face, squinty gray eyes, and a falsetto voice. His hair was cut short, and a lot of gray was mixed with the black. He hardly ever took his hat off. His most notable features were his long slender hands and the fine way he handled his horses. He was a slim-legged little man, who walked with a cocky swagger.

At the top of the next grade, horses slowed again as dawn peeped over the eastern ridge. The rain was still coming down so hard it was difficult to see more than a few yards ahead of the leaders. Suddenly a tall figure dressed in black stepped out from the side of the road. "Throw down the box!" The man wore a black derby and a long coat. He waved a pistol over his head.

I looked at Charlie. I knew he had been robbed along this same stretch less than a month ago. I had not been with him on that run. But he said later, when he got back to the barn in Placerville, he'd never let another man rob his coach. Now I could see Charlie feeding line to his horses instead of pulling them in.

"He looks like Black Bart!" I told Charlie in a low whisper. A fellow named Black Bart had been robbing stagecoaches in this area. Everybody was scared of him on account of he was a deadly shot. Wells Fargo detectives had been on his trail for months, but he had so far gotten away.

"Toss the box, it's insured." I whispered.

"My reputation ain't!" Charlie said, pulling a revolver from under his coat. He shot straight ahead right between his horse's ears. The surprised robber stumbled back, arms up, ducking into the bushes.

Screams came from inside the coach. The passengers heard the noise. "What's going on?" somebody yelled.

Charlie grabbed his whip from the socket and gave his horses a loud pop over their heads. They lurched forward in a wild scramble. Chains, harness, and coach squeaked, rattling. We rumbled over the hill, skidding along the trail, zigzagging in the mud.

I grabbed my hat, still holding my gun between my knees. "Jesus, Charlie," was all I could think to say. I looked over at him for some comment, but he was grinning and shaking his head as if he had pulled off something good. I was glad we got away with it, but if that was Black Bart out there, I knew we had taken a mighty big chance. The man had gotten nearly $600 from the Point Arena-Duncan Mills stage at Russia River, and more recently $400 from the Quincy-Orville stage at Berry Creek. He was known to leave notes at the scene of his holdups. One memorable verse had made it to all the California newspapers:

I've labored long for bread
For honor and for riches,
But on my corn's too long you've tread
You fine haired Sons of Bitches.

Wells Fargo detectives were really out to get Black Bart. He had been making fools of every marshal and sheriff's posse for a couple years.

Charlie was grinning to himself, still grabbing and slipping the lines, leaning forward with his horses, eyes on the trail. He chuckled, lost in his thoughts. I could see he was pleased with himself.

Dipping into the next low spot on the mountain trail, warm sunlight suddenly collided with cold rain, and dense fog accumulated. Charlie drove his team into the thick mist. I blinked. It was like swimming through milk. The lead and swing horses had disappeared. Only the rumps of the wheelers showed in the misty-wet atmosphere.

I looked at Charlie. My own hand was clamped to the iron rail behind the seat. "Hadn't you better stop until the fog lifts?"

"What for?" Charlie croaked, leaning still farther forward. "My leaders can see the trail. I trust 'em."

I cleared my throat. "Yeah, but one wrong move and we're over the cliff."

"Naw," Charlie mumbled. "I can tell by the sound of my wheels when we get too close to the edge—kind of hollow, like dancin' on drums. So shut up, and let me listen."

I shut up. Riding behind those gray horses in that soup was like riding atop a ghost train. I kept wondering if we hadn't already been killed. Were we somehow driving a stagecoach in the sky? Black harness glistened through the haze, and the gray horses melted in and out of the atmosphere as if we were traveling through clouds. My heart thumped. I felt that vast chasm to our right—the cold silent air told me an enormous void with an endless drop into the canyon waited if the coach made one wrong move.

Angling still lower along the narrow road, now only the wheelers' rumps could be seen. Traveling back up a steep grade we reached an elevation where the fog cleared a little. All six horses appeared—their heads and necks showing.

In places the sun came through strong enough to burn some fog away. It hung in long flat layers. Just when I thought we'd get some relief, it started drizzling again. The cold hovered with icy stillness in the forest all around us. I tried not to think of the terrible drop-off to our right: a big cold emptiness drawing us near.

The rain came down harder again, washing away some of the fog. We came clattering down a steep grade toward the Tuolumne River. A long wooden bridge spanning the water was the only way across. Holding the horses to a slow walk, Charlie eyed the river up and down. The thing had burst loose, running its banks. Water crashed and swirled in waves of foam.

"Must have rained mighty hard up there in the mountain," I said, looking at Charlie. I had never seen the river this bad. The bridge looked small and dangerous all of a sudden. Behind us the long slippery trail was too narrow for the coach and horses to turn around. We were stuck here.

Pulling the coach to a stop, Charlie pondered to himself. One of the male passengers opened the door. He stepped out, slapping his arms around his body for warmth. "We better wait here till the water goes down," he called up to us.

"Get back inside, and shut up!" Charlie bellowed.

I nodded to the fellow to do as he was told. Charlie was not in the mood for idle conversation—nor taking orders from passengers.

Charlie slapped his lines, talking to his leaders who had braced themselves to refuse taking another step. The horses pawed and snorted, ears back, eyes rolling. They recognized disaster when it stared them in the face.

"Come on boys, come up fellows, steady now," Charlie told his team. All six horses had their ears flicking back and forth, nervous, legs braced to balk. The leaders were already twisting around in their harnesses. The swing team was confused, and quivering, caught between alarmed leaders and frozen wheelers.

Charlie talked to them some more, adjusting his lines, snapping the whip over their heads. Calmed, the leaders went forward with a jump. I heard some folks yelling inside the coach. I leaned over my seat, telling the passengers to keep quiet and let Charlie talk to his horses

Over the bridge we rumbled. Squeaking, the support posts seemed shaky even from where I sat. I tried not to look down at the avalanche of white foam swirling underneath us, carrying broken trees and loosened boulders.

"Easy boys, easy," Charlie kept talking. By the time the leaders hit solid ground, the coach was more than halfway across the bridge. It trembled like a leaf in the wind. Behind us timbers crashed. Support posts caved in like dominos. Bridge swaying and collapsing behind us, Charlie let out a big yell, urging his team forward. The wheelers hit

157

solid ground. The front wheels caught on the road. The back of the coach shuddered, slammed, wheels finally grabbing, horses lunging forward. We were off with a bang.

Charlie merely gave a sigh, saying nothing. I kept my eyes glued to the road. Up the next hill we rumbled, clattering, charging away from the swollen river. Steam rose from the backs of the sweaty horses; warm body heat colliding with cold air.

"Five miles to the next home station," Charlie said, more to himself than to me. "You have to watch around here; there's likely to be another bunch of those robbers about."

I looked at him. "Don't you think we've had enough trouble for one day?"

"Holdup men ain't fussy who they waylay."

I knew Charlie was right. I'd been in enough scrapes riding for the Strawberry-to-Placerville line to know highwaymen made their living holding up the stages. Day or night, all kinds of weather, no matter who drove or who was aboard, everybody was fair game.

Charlie slowed for the next long grade. These were the bad places along the road. Holdup men knew the horses had to slow to a walk to pull the heavy Concords up steep grades. While I was thinking about it, a short figure stepped out of the brush by the side of the road.

"Holdup!" The bandit yelled. He wore a dark hat pulled to his eyes. A red bandanna covered the lower part of his face. A shotgun rested across his arms. A second holdup man stepped out in front of the horses about thirty paces between our leaders and a felled tree across the trail.

"Ain't no running past 'em this time," I told Charlie, eyeing the downed pine.

Without answering, Charlie put his lines down. But at the same time he yanked his sawed-off shotgun he kept resting across the strongbox under our feet. Firing over to his right, he dropped the first highwayman. I raised up enough to get the second man in my own sights. Before I could pull the trigger he bounded away into the bushes. I heard twigs and branches snap.

One of the male passengers gave a yelp, opening the door. He stepped out on the road, looking around, stunned. Two other male passengers got out next to him. All three of them held pistols, but they did not look too sure of themselves.

Charlie looked down, yelling at them to get a move on. "Drag the tree off the trail!" The three passengers hurried along beside the horses, pulling the big sapling out of the way so the coach could get by. All the while I kept my gun trained on the bushes where the second holdup man had disappeared.

"Come on! Get in!" Charlie yelled at the men, while at the same time popping his whip.

The stagecoach door slammed just in time. The horses pulled forward with a clatter of wildly flying hooves. Scared by the gunshots, the six horses threw themselves into their collars, pulling the coach up and away with a wild burst.

Rocking beside Charlie on the seat, I looked back over my shoulder through canvas baggage, leather bundles, hat boxes, and trunks. "Somebody's coming on a horse!" I told Charlie, seeing a rider burst from the timber. "The same robber who was in the road. And it don't look good!"

"Go ahead and shoot the bastard," Charlie yelled to me, rocking with his lines feeding through his fingers. "Eee—hah!"

"A shot's liable to cause a runaway!" I yelled at Charlie.

"What the hell you think we're doing now?" he shouted. "If they run any harder my wheels'll fall off!"

I felt the coach sway kind of bad. We were really rolling. I turned in the seat, and braced my boots against the express box. I aimed over the top of the coach through the piles of luggage. I knew it would be hard to hit the robber what with the coach swaying and rocking, and his horse galloping like a jackrabbit. But I took a shot anyway. The horse ducked, throwing its head. The rider reined back, waving his fist at us. We left him back there on the road. I don't know if I hit him or not.

Turning in the seat, I looked over at Charlie. His expression had not changed—he was still grinning. He finally got his horses under control. An hour later he told me to toot the horn, a signal to let each station know a stage was coming in. It gave the hostlers warning to rustle up hot coffee, and prepare fresh teams. I raised the bugle to my icy lips and let out a half-hearted blast.

The fog had not entirely lifted, and I was not sure where we were. But Charlie knew every inch of the road. A few minutes later we jingled into the home station—the fog was thicker here. The building and corrals looked like black charcoal smudges against an artist's white canvas.

Pulling on their coats, Brewster Jones and Lem Ard met us in the yard. The two friendly hostlers began unhitching the gray team. Passengers filed out, heading stiffly for the building for a cup of hot coffee. A big fire roared inside the home station fireplace.

Later, inside the station, Brewster and Ard were busy getting all the news from me. Meanwhile one of the male passengers jumped all over Charlie for having crossed the swollen Tuolumne, risking all our necks.

"We made it, didn't we?" Charlie said, huddling beside the stove. He held a cup of steaming coffee in his trembling hands. "You rather be stranded back there at the river? No way to turn around on that narrow road? Trapped there with the bridge out, and nobody scheduled to come along for twenty-four hours? Wet and cold, no way to build a fire? With three women along?"

The passenger kept sputtering what a fool thing it was to do, taking the chance of dumping us in that raging river. But Charlie finished his coffee, then walked into the add-on room where he curled up on the cot.

I walked outside talking to Brewster and Ard, giving them all the news of both holdups, and what happened at the river. Brewster laughed, knowing Charlie was right to try to get us safely across. Ard was not so sure. But then I knew he was one of Charlie's critics, always thinking Hank Monk was the best whip on the line. There had always been competition between the dozens of stagecoach drivers —each had his admirers as well as faultfinders.

An hour later the fog lifted for good. The sun felt warm on our hides. The strong odor of wet pine and damp leaves filled the mountain air. I walked back into the station, and called to Charlie. He had fallen sound asleep. I had to rock his shoulder a little to get his attention. I noticed how pale he looked. The wild drive had taken a lot more out of him than he had shown or would ever admit. I was surprised to notice how frail Charlie's shoulder was under his heavy coat when I shook him awake.

"Time to go?" was all Charlie said.

I nodded. "Team is ready. The weather has cleared. I reckon the passengers have simmered down. They are anxious to get to Placerville."

"Me too," Charlie said, following me outside.

Shortly after that Charlie quit working for the stage line. I figured he would miss the Jehu life. After all, he'd done it more than twenty years. And those horses meant everything to him. He never gave anybody a reason for quitting, but I could see he was not feeling good—coughing the way he did. One time I noticed blood when he spit. Later I heard he was working for the Murray Ranch, breaking horses for the widowed Mrs. Murray and her spinster sister, Miss Larkin.

About two years later I was standing in front of the livery stable in Placerville. It was late December, and the weather was mighty cold. It was my day off. While oiling my new bridle with neat's-foot oil, I watched folks ride up and down past the barn. Mrs. Murray clattered into view driving her black buggy. Beside her sat the old maid sister, Miss Larkin. The two always dressed in black. Both prim little ladies, they were known to stick their noses into every local doing.

"Mr. Wibbleton?" Mrs. Murray called.

I grinned at her. "Howdy," I tipped my hat. "Just call me Coon."

"I know you are Charlie Pankhurst's good friend. I wonder if you would ride out to my line shack at the ranch? Mr. Pankhurst has been breaking colts out there for the last year. He comes to the main house for supplies each Saturday. But he did not show up yesterday. A rider from the Broken W came by this morning, saying he'd stopped at the line shack last night, but the place was dark and closed up. The door was locked from the inside. You know, the shack has that big wooden drop bar."

"You want me to check on Charlie?" I asked her.

"Oh, would you please? In case of trouble, my sister and I might not be able to manage."

Getting worried myself, I went into the stables and saddled my big dun. A few minutes later I was riding out of town beside Mrs. Murray's buggy. The ladies seemed content gossiping between themselves. I rode along in silence. Somehow I had a bad feeling. Charlie had not been feeling good for a long time, I knew that. His cough had gotten worse. I had only seen him in town one time this past year since he quit driving stage. He hung around the barn for a few minutes petting the horses. Then he disappeared before I had the chance to talk to him. I had been meaning to ride out to the Murray place and visit with him, but it seems like we too often let important things in life slide by.

Riding into the yard at the line shack, we saw Charlie's old white dog come crawling out from under the building. The mutt looked shy, and scruffy, like he had not eaten for a while. I dismounted, tying up in front of the shack. The ladies pulled the buggy in beside me, and climbed out. They spoke to the dog. It whined, cringing away with its tail between its legs.

I tried the door. Sure enough, it was locked up tight from the inside. I banged on it for a while, but there was no answer. Three nervous horses inside the corral whinnied at us, looking like they had not been fed.

I walked around to the back of the building and looked through the glass window. Cupping my hands beside my eyes, I cut off the shadow. It looked mighty dark in there. Mrs. Murray and her sister had followed me. They stood on tiptoes, trying to peek through the window, too, like a pair of inquisitive little hens.

"You want me to break the window glass, ma'am?" I asked, figuring it was her property.

"Oh, yes, please!"

I found a chunk of firewood and smashed the glass with no trouble. Picking the shards away from the frame, I climbed up, crawling in head-first. Right away I saw Charlie stretched on the cot, covered only with a blanket. His frail white hand dangling off the side of the cot told the whole story. Charlie's clothes were still draped across the back of the wooden kitchen chair. The stove was cold; the fire had gone out long ago.

I hurried to the door and yanked the bar up, allowing the ladies who had run around the shack to come in.

"Oh!" Mrs. Murray said, holding her hands to her face. "Poor Charlie! Dying here alone. How long you think it's been?" She looked at me, averting her eyes away from the corpse.

"Can't say, ma'am." I touched the body. It was mighty stiff. Luckily the cold weather kept it from too much damage.

The ladies looked worried and nervous. "Coon," Mrs. Murray said, "could you please dress the body? It would be indelicate for me and my sister to...uh...Well you know. Him being a man and all...."

I nodded, shooing them outdoors. I told them to clear the back of their buggy to make way for the corpse.

I picked up Charlie's shirt and jeans from the kitchen chair. I was a little nervous about this myself. I'd seen plenty of men shot. I'd even handled a few dead holdup men, but this was different. I minced over to the cot and peeled back the blanket.

Jumpin' Jehova! I blinked. I stood there gawking. Thunderstruck, I dropped Charlie's clothes on the floor and ran outside. "Mrs. Murray! Miss Larkin! I reckon this is a job for you ladies! Charlie Pankhurst ain't no man!"

ELLA EWING

Ella Ewing was born near Gorin, Missouri, in 1872. By the time she reached adulthood, she weighed nearly three hundred pounds, and stood eight feet and four inches tall. Her shoe size was twenty-four. Ella achieved financial independence by earning a living in sideshows with some of the leading circus attractions of the time including Barnum-Bailey, Buffalo Bill's Wild West Show, and Sells-Foto. To throngs of gawking spectators, Ella was merely "the tall lady in the circus," but she managed her handicap with dignity, character, and refinement. Ella Ewing died in 1912.

"Rascals! Get away from that window!" Maude yelled at six little boys who had formed a pyramid in front of Miss Ella Ewing's window. Three on the bottom, two more on their shoulders, and one at the very top, they giggled and hooted. The one on top looked through the window glass, telling the others what he saw inside the house.

When Maude rushed at them, swinging her black umbrella, they toppled over laughing. She continued shouting while the scoundrels darted across the porch and away down the street. Each had a stack of school books tied with a strap and slung over his shoulder.

Jiggling the basket of groceries on her right hip, Maude stormed to the front door. Before she could reach for the doorknob, Ella herself opened the door from the inside. Ella was still snickering, bent over at the waist, gleefully pounding her thigh.

Maude swooped in a huff to the kitchen. She heard Ella's lumbering footsteps follow her through the house. The tallest woman in the world, Ella stood eight feet and four inches tall. Her long silk dress came to the floor, rustling as she walked, the hemline barely covering her size twenty-four shoes.

"Oh, Ella," Maude said, climbing up on a chair to put the grocery basket on the counter, "why do you allow those little ruffians to peek through your windows? They're just laughing at you. Awful brats. I recognized all of those boys. They need to be spanked. I've a mind to visit their parents about it."

"Oh, no, please don't," Ella said. She sat in a wooden chair at her kitchen table. Everything inside the house, an-the house itself, had been built to her enormous proportions. The only thing regular-human sized in the whole place were the dishes and silverware. Ella did not mind handling the tiny teacups and flatware. However, her own dinner plate was the turkey platter.

Her voice, deep and hollow, rumbled as if she spoke through a tube. "Oh, Maude, they are only curious. I don't mind the children staring at me, darling things. I do my slow-rising act and they nearly break their little necks looking up and up and up! It's all right—let them have their fun. My one regret is that I have no children of my own."

Standing there on the chair, looking back at her, Maude felt a lump in her throat. Poor Ella was such a gentle person. Having suffered the indignities of being a freak of nature, she had endured laughter and taunts all of her life. The date was 1912. Maude had taken the job of companion-secretary to Ella a year before when Ella took time off from her job with P.T. Barnum, a job for her that lasted seventeen years. But Ella was feeling worn out, tired of the constant travel. She hoped by resting at her home for a few months in Gorin, Missouri, she might recover her strength.

Maude climbed off the chair, and standing on her tiptoes, placed some apples on the table in front of Ella.

167

Ella reached for one. Her great hand picked it up like a grape. "I was thinking I want to put my scrapbook in order, Maude," she said. "I have a box full of news clippings and photographs that need organizing. I've let it go for such a long time."

Maude merely nodded. The project sounded like a good one. She had always admired Ella Ewing. To Maude, Ella was a great lady in more ways than one.

Nibbling around the apple core like a horse, Ella smacked her lips and reached for another. Ella ate everything in doubles; two sandwiches, two glasses of milk, two steaks. Her black hair was pinned at the back of her head. She had a long nose, wide, deep-set dark eyes, and pale skin. She weighed two hundred and ninety pounds. Her torso was not so gigantic, so that when she sat in a chair she did not seem much different than anybody else. But when she stood up...and up...and up...she was somewhat shocking. The great length of her arms and legs made her look as if she towered on stilts.

Later, Maude dragged a box of mementos off the top shelf of Ella's closet. Maude had to stand on a chair to reach this, too. Ella had built this house years ago from her earnings working at circuses. The place had fifteen-foot ceilings, ten-foot doors, and seven-foot windows. All of the furniture inside was custom-made to suit Ella's great frame; even the piano had elongated legs. Her dresser drawers were built six feet off the ground. Her bed was nine and one-half feet long. Her gigantic closets held an extensive wardrobe. Ella liked finery, something she did not have as a child growing up.

Her poor parents had been hard-pressed to clothe their unusual daughter, and children made fun of her at school. As a child, Ella had been reluctant to attend social functions after she had been humiliated by unthinking individuals. A friend once told her as long as people were going to stare and make fun of her, they might as well pay for the privilege. And they did—Ella eventually joined a circus.

After dragging the box of old photos and clippings off the closet shelf, Maude lugged everything to the living room where Ella sat waiting for her at a favorite place by the big window. Ella looked out across the tree-lined street; that part of Missouri was beautiful in the fall. Gold, orange, and red maple leaves fluttered in the crisp wind.

"Let me see," Ella mused, taking the box in her huge paw. Picking gently through the stacks of papers, she began organizing her life's memories.

Maude looked at her, suddenly wondering why Ella felt the urge to put her memories in sequence. Born in 1872, Ella was now only 40 years old. "Ella, is there some reason you want to do this today?" Having spent so much time with Ella, Maude learned to sense deeper feelings Ella had about life, feelings Ella did not always express with words.

Ella merely looked at Maude, the eyes in her big face rolled only slightly. A flat grin crossed her wide lips. "Maude, you have been a good friend and faithful companion. I value your friendship more than you know. I need somebody to humor me, look after me—nobody really knows or understands the loneliness I have endured. I can't count the times I have simply wanted to put my arms around someone, to lean on someone and cry."

It seemed to Maude that Ella was evading the question about the sudden interest in organizing her scrapbook. Maude's eyes flitted to the window where just moments ago a group of nasty little boys had been spying. Yet, Ella had handled the situation with good humor. Maude was angrier about it than Ella was. *And now this*—Maude thought to herself, *getting her life's memories organized. Was there some reason Ella felt the need to do this now?*

Sorting through the material, Ella began making little piles established by date. "Here, this will go in the book first," she said. "It was my acceptance of an invitation to read the Declaration of Independence at an old-time Fourth of July near Gorin. I was a teenager at the time." Ella sighed, studying the brief newspaper announcement. "Do you know what? Up until that day I really did not know how different I was."

Maude peeked over Ella's arm at the news item, but said nothing. Ella seemed anxious to do the talking, so Maude did not interrupt. Sometimes Ella spent her entire days not saying a word, rambling about the house, reading books, brooding in silence. So if she was in a talkative mood today, Maude was glad for the company.

"Growing up I scampered along with the rest of the children—playing—enjoying life," Ella said. "When I first noticed I was getting bigger than the other girls, I stuffed myself inside the desk at school, hunching my shoulders so that I would not seem so tall. But at the picnic that day, after leaving the podium, a group of strangers followed me away as if mesmerized by the sight of me. It was that moment, that very moment, I realized how different I was. I ran home and promised myself I would never appear in public again!" She smiled sadly.

Maude took the clipping from Ella's hand, putting it face down on the table to begin her pile for the scrapbook. "What's next?"

"Here, look! I took the advice of a friend who persuaded me I should get paid by those who wanted to stare at me.

My parents accompanied me to the county fair that summer, and we went on exhibition. My six-foot two inch father, and my five-foot six inch mother stood beside me. It wasn't so bad. We were nervous of course, but my ability to earn my own money more than made up for the embarrassment. It was the only time my parents ever appeared with me; they were very brave. If they had not come with me that first time, I don't think I would have had the courage to go on."

"You were just a schoolgirl," Maude said, holding up the clipping. "Your first public appearance?"

Ella smiled, looking at the picture. "I was so young. And look at that poor cotton dress! My parents had worked so hard for so little. It made me happy to finally be able to do something for them."

Maude knew that Ella had maintained a loving relationship with her parents, even now, after all these years. Ella had been generous with her earnings, helping them in any way she could. One time her mother came to visit while Ella was asleep. Without disturbing her, Maude saw Mrs. Ewing walk lightly to Ella's bedside, kissing her daughter tenderly on the cheek as if she were still a small child.

Ella's fingers riffled through the box, still sorting, showing Maude clippings from her days with Barnum-Bailey Circus, Buffalo Bill's Wild West Show, and Sells-Foto. Ella earned a whopping $250 dollars a week, enabling her to build this custom house, order custom furniture and clothing, besides helping her parents out of poverty.

The afternoon slipped by. Maude scooted off the couch to start a blaze in the fireplace. The rooms needed to be kept warm. Ella's great size caused her hands and feet always to be cold. Maude supposed that Ella's poor blood

171

circulation was due to her size. Sometimes Ella dragged her great rocking chair in front of the fireplace, where she held her enormous shoes to the flames.

Ella hated her feet. She wore size twenty-four shoes turned on a last especially made for her by a St. Louis shoemaker. For a time he used one of her shoes as a sign over his door. Ella was so sensitive about her feet that she wrote in every circus contract that her feet must never show. Her long dresses usually solved that problem. When alighting from trains she had a short curtain set up alongside the steps. This usually protected the outward thrusts of her big shoes from spying public eyes.

Ella dozed in front of the fire while Maude went into the kitchen to make another pot of tea. There was a cold draft inside the house. Winter was coming on. But more than that, Maude sensed a heaviness about Ella's persona that had her worried about her friend. Maude had grown fond of the giantess. She knew the real Ella was a delicate and sensitive person sentenced to life imprisoned inside a grotesque body she could do nothing about. Acceptance, it had to do with acceptance. Ella had learned long ago to cope.

Maude heard a tap at the front door, and hurried to answer it. Young Mrs. Downing from across the street came over with a freshly-baked peach pie. Maude invited her into the house. Mrs. Downing held in her arms her infant daughter bundled inside a blue blanket.

"Who is it?" Ella called from her place by the fire.

"Mrs. Downing and her new baby," Maude answered. "She has brought us a warm peach pie."

A bubbly roar could be heard—the closest Ella ever came to a chuckle. "Mary Downing! Come in! Let me see your baby."

Mary tiptoed across the vast hardwood floor. She stood at Ella's elbow and looked up. Even though Ella was sitting in a chair, she was still several inches taller than Mary.

Maude took the warm pie to the kitchen where she fixed tea, cut the pie, and carried it all back into the living room. Ella loved snacks; she was never one to fuss about eating anything special at any time of the night or day. Maude guessed it was because of the circus routine Ella had grown accustomed to, eating and sleeping at odd hours.

Mary Downing held her infant daughter, blanket drawn away from the little pink face. The baby was sound asleep.

Ella took the bundle in her gigantic hands, holding the child as if it were a miniature doll. She smiled, rocking the infant back and forth, humming from within her chest. Tears brimmed her eyes. "Here!" she said, handing the baby back to its mother. She gently twisted one of the gold rings off her huge finger, then slid it carefully onto the baby's wrist like a bracelet.

"Ella!" Mary Downing looked genuinely pleased. "Such an expensive ring. For the baby?"

"Now don't allow the ring to stay on there too long!" Ella told Mary. "Her little arm will grow, and you'll have to saw the ring off."

Mary smiled. "Oh, no! I'll take the ring off tonight. I'll put it in a box, and give it to her when she is old enough to appreciate it. I'm sure she can wear it on a chain around her neck. We will treasure it always."

173

Ella smiled, nodding, reaching for her teacup. She tweaked the little handle between her thumb and first finger. Steam rose while she sipped.

Maude crawled back up on the oversized couch. Curled in a corner, she enjoyed a big slice of warm pie and sipped tea. Ella and Mary chatted quietly about baby matters. Ella seemed endlessly fascinated with children. Maude thought it was because Ella would never have one of her own, or perhaps it was her curiosity about things small and "normal." Examining Mrs. Downing's baby, Ella inspected each tiny finger, one by one.

Maude concentrated on the pie. She was nearly fifty years old. An only child, and now a spinster, Maude had never had much to do with babies. She had cared for her elderly parents until they died, and did clerical work until applying for this job with Ella Ewing. So while Maude considered babies rather messy, it was touching to see Ella so intrigued with them.

Later, after Mary Downing left the house, Maude fixed dinner and cleaned the kitchen. Ella returned to her place by the fire to read a favorite book. She was always reading.

When Maude joined her in the parlor, Ella said, "Tomorrow is Sunday. After church, I want to continue organizing my scrapbook."

Maude simply nodded, and went up to bed. She knew that Ella was a highly religious person. Ella rarely missed attending Sunday service at the Harmony Grove Baptist Church in Gorin. Here in northeast Missouri, she was known as the "Saintly Giantess." She had been baptized by immersion in the nearby Fabius river.

The next morning the two women walked the three blocks to church. Ella enjoyed walking, as long as it was not too far. Otherwise she tired. Her great frame seemed to grow weary under too much physical exertion.

Later, after church, they had Sunday dinner and delved back into Ella's box of mementos. She continued stacking and organizing as she sorted by dates. Circus engagements, people she met, places she saw—each held a special memory. It occurred to Maude that, while Ella had suffered greatly because of her extraordinary body, she had nonetheless persevered. Ella Ewing met her challenges, accumulated enough wealth to support herself and build this house, and still remained a dignified lady.

Maude looked at her. "Ella, forgive me if I am being too outspoken, but I am astonished by you. Your lifetime achievements, overcoming adversity, are amazing."

Ella dug to the bottom of the box, finally picking up the last item she had saved. "I only did what I had to do with what God gave me. Strangeness made a strong person of me. In my heart, I am very timid. If I had not grown to this size, I'm sure I would have never left the village of Gorin. Maybe I'd have been a housewife, or a school teacher."

"Both honorable professions," Maude said.

"Yes. And how I would have traded this body for either. But I was forced to accept my fate. Once I understood that, I went on. Believe it or not, I feel blessed. I came to understand being different does not mean defeat."

Maude was still staring at her. As much as Maude liked Ella, and appreciated her, Maude had secretly felt sorry for her. Now Maude felt guilty at having harbored those narrow thoughts. She was suddenly ashamed of the smug twinge in the back of her mind, knowing that she was lucky enough to be "normal," while Ella was not. Maude looked at Ella now, but did not have to say anything. Ella was searching her friend's mind with those deeply penetrating eyes of hers, an all-knowing person who has suffered, and overcome adversity. She acquired a deep understanding of human nature through her own experience. Having been stared at as a freak in a circus for nearly twenty years—Ella Ewing had knowledge and compassion few people ever achieve.

In the morning a warm breeze blew across the land. The sun came out, and Ella wanted to go for a drive. Maude hooked Ella's chestnut mare to the large buggy, and off they went through town. The buggy had custom seats built farther back from the footboard than was standard. Ella wore her long black silk dress, and a flat-crowned felt hat decorated with net, purple ribbon, and silk flowers. With lace gloves, and a new silk shawl, Ella met the world in style. She was careful to cover the tips of her big shoes with her long hemline.

They rattled down Main Street. Folks waved; Maude clucked to the old chestnut mare Ella had owned for most of its life; a gentle horse, trustworthy and anxious to please even though she was getting a bit arthritic. Dust rose up through the shafts. "Get up, Babe!" Maude crooned.

When passing the dentist's office, Ella let out a chuckle. "Each time I visit him, he braces the chair with boxes before he lets me sit down! He will be glad enough after I'm dead—he will not have to worry about my breaking his chair."

Maude had dark thoughts about the dentist. She assumed a medical man would have more sense than to embarrass Ella that way. But Ella seemed to take it in her usual good humor.

Leaning with the jarring buggy, Ella hugged her cape about her shoulders. Even though the weather had warmed, Maude could see Ella was feeling a chill. But Ella's eyes were on the countryside, taking in each tree, each field, each house, each distant hill. "I was raised here," Ella said softly, as if not caring whether Maude heard or not. It was more of a talk with herself. "Here is our old tree where the boys built a hut—and there is the spot Billy Elders fell off his pony and broke his arm."

Two miles out of town, at the long sandy curve near the creek, Ella asked Maude to stop the buggy. She stared far across the rolling hills and into the distant stands of pine and oak. "Pheasants and deer and rabbits used to gambol here," Ella said, pointing. "As a child I played with my friends in these very fields. And way back in the old days, about the time I was born, they say Indians used to come bartering game for sugar and tobacco with the homesteaders."

Maude looked at her, still not saying anything. Maude had passed these places often, never thinking one way or the other what sentiment rested here. Ella was somewhat of a historian, having lived through the eighties, gay nineties and turbulent turn-of-the-century.

"A little farther—one more stop," Ella said, pointing a great finger down the road.

Maude slapped the driving lines against the mare's back, and clucked to her. The mare worked up a smart trot. Her cream-colored mane and tail flipped back in unison with her forward thrust. The mare was beginning to sweat around the flanks and under her tail. Old and well-fed, she was not used often enough by Ella, who rarely ventured outside the house when she was home in Gorin.

"What a great feeling, to simply go on and on," Ella said. "The world is full of adventure. I have no regrets. I loved to travel, I have seen so much. Thank you dear Maude for listening to my prattle! You must be bored."

A lump came into Maude's throat. "Knowing you has been my great pleasure, Ella." Riding beside Ella in the buggy, listening to her voice, seeing her absorb the land, Maude could not shake the awful sense of foreboding. It seemed to Maude that Ella was savoring her childhood memories with particular sentiment this afternoon.

When Ella grew tired, Maude turned the mare around and began the slow trip back to town. The mare let the occupants of the buggy know she had had enough trotting for one day, she slowed to a walk. Ella seemed not in a hurry. After arriving at the house they found a telegram stuck in the doorjamb; Barnum-Bailey wondered when Ella was returning to work.

While reading it, Ella sighed. "It is good to be missed, but I think I will stay home a while longer."

Ella went to bed that night and never woke up. The gentle giant's heart simply gave out. Maude called Ella's family to the house, then helped with preparations for the funeral. Maude was so sad she could hardly speak. In death, as in life, Ella presented some problems to her family that she would not have wished for.

First of all, the undertaker had no coffin large enough. He worked nonstop through the night to construct a nine-foot-long casket. For the trip to the cemetery in the horse-drawn hearse, the casket had to be pushed all the way under the front seat in order to allow the hearse doors to close. Ella was buried in Harmony Grove cemetery. Later, a large gray stone bearing an inscription would mark the place.

Maude stayed at the house for some months afterwards. She organized Ella's scrapbook, and sorted her belongings —some of which wound up in museums. Maude's family found ways to dispose of the peculiar furniture. Eventually the house itself fell into disrepair. It's uniqueness caused it to be an unlikely habitation for "normal-sized" people.

Maude remembered Ella Ewing with great fondness. She never failed to point out that Ella's gentle nature, depth of human understanding, and genuine courage should be an inspiration to all.

ADELITA

During the Mexican Revolution of 1910, some Mexican women followed their men into battle. A much-loved song of the revolution told of a girl named Adelita who went with her lover, a sergeant, where the regiment was camped in the mountains. Adelita and her sergeant were much in love, and even the colonel respected her. She was beautiful, brave, and good with firearms as well as the cooking pot. In a romantic song, it was said, the sergeant told Adelita that if he died in battle, the regiment decimated, and his body was to be buried, he begged his Adelita to cry for him. To the soldiers of the revolution, according to their songs at least, romance and war were closely linked. But to the female camp-followers, the grim realities of gunfire were likely quite different than soft words and strumming guitars.

Women were not the weaker sex in Pancho Villa's army. We carried ammunition, loaded guns, and fought beside the men. If our man was killed, we were expected to take up with another right away. Pancho Villa encouraged women to join the army—if for no other reason than to keep the soldiers happy. We knew all of the jokes they told about us.

The year was 1910. In the hills south of Magdalena, Sonora, the army hunkered down for a fight in the morning against the Federal troops of the government of President Porfirio Diaz. Those of us who rested under a blanket of stars knew that some of us would not survive tomorrow. It was war; *la guerra,* a time of adventure and hope as well as a time for dying. The success of Pancho Villa meant that large land-owners, or *hacendados* as they were called, would no longer be the ruling class. Poor Mexicans like myself might perhaps have a better life. At least that is what we thought.

My sister, Luz, was one year older than I. At seventeen, she was a healthy girl...a little plump around the waist, but always laughing. She squatted next to me at the campfire, our hands worked quickly patting tortillas for the evening meal. Little fires twinkled across the hillside while a soldier strummed *La Cucaracha* on his guitar—the song of the revolution. Other soldiers laughed and hooted around us, for they drank *pulque.* The Centaur of the North did not care if his men enjoyed their nights, after all, any one could be their last.

Pancho Villa himself did not drink alcohol. He preferred strong coffee in his *olla.* He understood only too well the dangers of his own temper and how drinking caused men to lose their wits.

Luz handed a tortilla to her *hombre,* Pedro, who approached our fire. He sat close to her, stroking her back with his stubby fingers—it seemed the men never tired of romance. War and fighting stirred their emotions, passionate desires mingled with killing—perhaps it was nature's way to ensure new life in the face of death. Luz shrugged his hand away. She stirred copper-colored *frijoles* bubbling in an earthen pot over the charcoals. "At least the flies do not bother us after dark," she said.

I agreed, hurrying with my own stack of tortillas. I knew that Lorenzo would arrive at any moment; he was sometimes in a bad temper. I had only known him for two weeks. He took the place of Ernesto who was killed in a volley of artillery near Cananea. Ernesto had not been my husband either. In fact none of us was married. The men had more important things to do, like fighting and killing. A woman was just for the moment—part of the great adventure.

Luz and I joined Villa's army because it was something to do. Life in a dusty hovel on the *hacienda* where we were born offered nothing but work, dirt, and disease. Our parents were *peónes.* Our mother died after the last baby was born, leaving Luz and me to raise our siblings—six more besides ourselves. Everybody more or less grew up. Our father re-married, and his new wife did not like any of us hanging around. So we had no good reason to refuse when we heard Pancho Villa was organizing his army, men and women alike, promising that we would ride for gold and glory.

But an army moves on its belly, we learned soon enough. We *soldaderas,* or female soldiers, who thought we were in for adventure, were really put to work in front of the fires. When not gathering wood, tethering horses, hauling water, carrying supplies, or getting our heads shot off, we were expected to take up with the men.

"Lola," my sister said, looking at me, "perhaps your Lorenzo has sneaked back to the village we passed this morning to visit the *mariposas.* "

Mariposas, or butterflies, were nicknames for women who lived at a *ranchito* on the outskirts of that town. They had no morals, but it was rumored they helped smuggle guns from the United States into Mexico for Pancho Villa. The women strapped firearms to their legs under their dresses before walking across the border.

"They have plenty under their dresses," Pedro laughed, meaning it two ways. Everybody knew the story about the smuggled guns.

Luz poured steaming coffee into his metal cup. "And so do I," she warned jokingly, patting the knife she had sheathed at her thigh under her long skirt.

I carried a knife, too. All of the women used knives, for there were not enough guns to go around. Anyway, what with all of our camp duties, we did not have the capacity to lug guns along with everything else we had to carry.

But there was one woman in camp who carried guns. Adelita! She owned two revolvers she kept stuffed in leather holsters buckled to her hips. She also got to ride a fine chestnut horse. Her evenings were spent in the officers' tents, not huddled around the campfires patting tortillas.

Of course everybody noticed she was a special favorite of Pancho Villa, and there was no question that he liked women. No drinking, no marijuana for him, but plenty of women. If a *soldadera* wanted to stay out of the clutches of the Centaur of the North, it was best that she did not make herself too visible. However, moving with the army made it impossible to stay away from the men, and that is why many of us were disillusioned when we realized we were nothing but servants, attending to the men's needs— day or night.

Lorenzo finally joined us, sprawling in the dirt next to me. His big black boots, taken from a dead Federal, extended toward the fire. *"Caramba!* It will be cold tonight. I look forward to having you join me under my sarape," he laughed, looking at me.

"I join you under your sarape every night," I said dismally. Ernesto had the tiresome habit of running his fingers over his mustache before licking them.

"You sound as if you do not appreciate it," he said in that macho tone, acting as if he were doing me the favor.

"I joined the army to do my part in the fighting. Your sarapes are not what I bargained for," I said, fanning the fire with a piece of straw torn from an old *petate.*

He frowned, drawing a long bronzed finger under his mustache before licking it. "Well, cheer up. Perhaps tomorrow I will die. Then you will be free of me."

"Yes," I muttered. "Free to get stuck with yet another *hombre*."

"Oh, come on now," he bantered, "you know that Pancho Villa says you *soldaderas* must do your part by recruiting more men for the army." He winked at Pedro.

"Recruiting" meant having babies—pregnancy and childbirth was a big joke with them.

Pedro piped, looking at me, "Why don't you tie your legs together above the knees with strips of buckskin like some of the pregnant women do?" He and Lorenzo burst out laughing.

I wanted to slap both their faces. Their jokes about women disgusted me. I could see Luz was not pleased either, but she seemed to make light of things easier than I.

Luz whispered. "Pst! Look who joins us!"

I could hardly believe my eyes. Adelita strolled towards us, swaying lightly under the heavy arm of Pancho Villa.

Villa's dagger eyes sparkled in the firelight when he stopped in front of us. "Simmering tortillas, chiles, and *frijoles!* The best aroma in the world." Pancho Villa's laugh was more like a roar. He had a barrel chest and a large head. Some women thought he was handsome.

I said nothing, for I was too afraid of him. Everybody knew of his wonderful generosity, but at the same time he had a terrible temper. It was simple for him to order anybody shot just to make an example of one of us. Last week

I watched when he ordered his soldiers to rope and drag a young gringo cowboy we met in the desert. The gringo died horribly, only because Pancho Villa was mad at the President of the United States for some reason. After his wild temper cooled, Pancho Villa felt remorse over what he did, but by then it had little effect on the bloody remains of the poor cowboy.

Adelita looked down at us. Even though I looked for hostility in her expression that I could dislike, I found none. Her dark eyes were soft. Her smile hinted of friendship. She allowed the arm of Villa to drape around her slender shoulders, and I noticed she was not carrying her *pistolas* tonight. Perhaps she did not feel the need to protect herself in camp since two guards bristling with guns walked closely behind Villa.

"I have decided that you two will join Adelita for a special assignment," Pancho Villa said, looking roughly at me and Luz. "I have chosen you two above the other *soldaderas* because you look strong and healthy. You have no children hanging on your arms...yet. Besides, you are both *muy guapas,* good looking!" He laughed, winking at Luz and myself.

Both Lorenzo and Pedro jumped to their feet, offering Villa coffee, which he waved away.

"When you are finished feeding your men," Villa told Luz and me, "join me in my tent. There you will learn what I have in mind."

"*Si!* Right away," Lorenzo said. Pedro chimed in, vigorously nodding his head like a pet dog trying to gain attention from his master.

"No, not you *hombres.* Only the women," Villa said. His look was withering, so Lorenzo and Pedro did not dare say another word.

My hands shook so badly I made an oblong tortilla. I could not imagine what Pancho Villa had in store for my sister and me. I had tried to be a good worker, while at the same time avoiding too much contact with the men. I'd held my *rebozo* in front of my face while scurrying to do my duties. How or why Villa had singled us out was a mystery to me, but it was too late now to get out of it. I imagined a tent full of drunken officers at a noisy party was where our "strong and healthy" services were going to be needed.

"Santa Maria! Mother of God!" I cried to Luz. "What is in store for us now?"

Luz was feisty, and braver than me. She made a last taco for herself by rolling a spoonful of beans inside a warm tortilla. "Quit acting like a scared goat. If Villa singled us out for whatever reason, you know we have no say in the matter. We do as we are told unless we want trouble."

Sighing, I followed her across the hillside where soldiers and their *soldaderas* huddled near their own fires. Murmuring voices laughed and talked in the night.

Adelita sat across from Pancho Villa at a wooden table inside his tent. A kerosene lamp cast wavering shadows across the canvas walls and piles of rifles. Her legs were crossed under her long brown riding skirt. She patted the side of her head where her straight black hair was severely pulled into a braid that hung down her back. Adelita watched us carefully with gold-flecked brown eyes.

"I do not like to give speeches," Villa began. "I don't even like to listen to speeches! So I will make this brief.

You three will go back to that village we passed this morning. Look for the *ranchita* of the *mariposas,* and ask for work."

My mouth dropped open. Working as a prostitute in a *ranchita* was worse than death to me. Being handled by filthy drunkards, perhaps winding up with the woman's disease! Villa must have seen the horrified expression on my face because he roared with laughter, adding, "You are on special assignment for our cause. Anyway, you won't stay there longer than you have to."

Adelita broke her silence. "There is a *bandido* named Juan Ochoa who visits the *ranchita.* He has been carrying information about our movements to the Federals stationed in Zacatecas.

"That's right," Villa added. "I got this information just a few hours ago. Your job is to put an end to Juan Ochoa, the sooner the better. Talk to him—get information out of him—then kill him."

"Why don't your soldiers kill him?" I asked.

"Because, " Villa answered, "he's smart enough to stay away from soldiers. Besides, we want to find out who he gets his information from. There is a traitor in this camp. They meet secretly, somehow, and then Ochoa carries the messages to Zacatecas. We know that he stops at the *ranchita* for a little tequila, and perhaps more information-gathering of his own along the way." Villa laughed sarcastically. "He combines business with pleasure."

Adelita's eyes flashed. She spoke to me and Luz. "I offered to do this by myself, but General Villa thinks the three of us will work better together."

Villa grinned slyly at her. "Besides, the three of you can keep an eye on one another—there is safety in numbers."

Somewhere in the night a guitar strummed *Cuatro Milpas,* a song about four little cornfields—the official goodnight song of the revolution.

The next day found us wearing old cotton dresses, ragged underclothing, and carrying poor bundles of provisions over our shoulders. We three *soldaderas* trudged over the dusty hills toward the little village of the *mariposas.* Adelita no longer stood out from my sister and myself, since she, too, was dressed in a bedraggled frock. A faded gray *rebozo* covered her face. She took long strides, puffing and sweating.

We stopped in the shade of a mesquite bush when the sun got high. Huddling under the wispy branches, we drank water we carried in a dented metal flask. Gnats droned around our faces, darting at our eyes for moisture.

Luz rolled a dry tortilla around a smudge of cold beans and chile sauce. "So," she began, looking at Adelita. "My sister and I joined the army because we would have starved anyway, and something is better than nothing. But you look like a lady of class and manners—what is your excuse?"

Adelita took a sip of water. "My widowed aunt owned Hacienda Madraso, just south of Nogales. When the fighting began, she was one of the first to be killed by Villa's revolutionaries. I was away at school in the United States. Her death and the destruction of our property left me poor. Now I am alone in the world."

"If Villa's Dorados ruined your life, why do you take sides with him?" I asked.

Adelita gazed up at a hawk circling slowly in the hot sky. "Life is full of paradoxes," she said, leaving me and Luz scratching our heads because we did not know what a "paradox" was. Before I could ask more questions, she sprang suddenly to her feet, crying, "Let's hurry!"

Late in the afternoon we arrived at the *ranchita* known as Caballo Blanco. The owner, Elena, was a fat, dark-eyed woman with short gray hair. She could have passed for anybody's good little grandmother. She looked at us suspiciously at first. But we finally convinced her that we were refugees from one of the northern villages, our husbands were dead, and that we were willing to work.

Elena smiled, for she was always looking for healthy young recruits that would bring her more *pesos*. She showed us around the *cantina,* explained that we would be expected to encourage customers to buy drinks. And, if necessary, accompany men to the little rooms called "cribs" off a long hallway in the back of the building. More *pesos* were to be earned then, but she of course handled all the money. When not busy with men, we could expect to do household chores around the place.

She gave us an armload of clothes to pick through, newer and gaudy compared to what we had on our backs. We retired that first afternoon to wait out the hot sun, trying to get some rest in a dark room that had three cots and one threadbare handwoven rug on the dirt floor. Adelita poured water for us from the clay pitcher. I could not help but wonder what the night would bring.

Luz, talkative as usual, tried to keep our spirits up by reminding us that we were doing our part for the revolution. I felt better patting the knife strapped to my thigh. Adelita remained silent, although I detected an expression in her eyes that told me she was very worried.

189

"What does Juan Ochoa look like?" I asked Adelita.

"Tall," she said. "Big shoulders, smooth skin, straight teeth, high cheekbones, trim mustache, jangling spurs, tight pants, and greenish-gray eyes. His laugh is musical. And he has beautiful hands."

"You sure he's a *bandido*? He sounds like a dream *hombre*," I said.

She stiffened. "Ah, well, I will point him out to you if he comes in, so do not worry. Your main purpose is to keep your ears open for rumors about Federal troops in this area. Listen to what the *borrachos* have to say. Tequila warms their tongues."

"How did Juan Ochoa become a *bandido?*" I persisted. Her flattering description of him piqued my interest.

"He was a *hacendado's* son. Villa killed his father and brothers. So out of hatred for Villa, Juan Ochoa became a spy for the Federals."

"Everybody in this war has their own tragedy," Luz murmured.

"And this Juan Ochoa," I asked Adelita, "you plan to kill him?"

"Those are my orders," Adelita said. As soon as the sun went down, we heard laughing in the *cantina*. Customers arrived to drink and brag. The place smelled like stale beer and urine. I felt weak as the three of us walked into the barroom wearing gaudy dresses held up by little straps. My feet were stuffed into high-heeled shoes that caused my ankles to wobble. Of course we had to leave our knives hidden under the mattresses of our cots—they would have shown through our thin dresses.

The evening did not start out as bad as I thought because the men were mostly interested in drinking and boasting about themselves. As long as we kept encouraging them to take more *pulque* and tequila, they soon reached a point where they lost interest in doing anything more than a little hugging and drooling. When anybody passed out, Elena's bouncer, a big Indian named Hipolito with yellow teeth and a long handlebar mustache, carried the groggy customers out the front door. They were dumped onto the ground.

With us were several other girls too. They drifted around the room selling drinks. Occasionally one of them disappeared in the back with a customer. But mostly it was drinking and talking. Guitar music came from the corner of the room. A blind man named Kent, a blond, white-skinned German, played beautiful Mexican songs for a few *centavos* that customers plunked into a chipped enamel plate resting on the bench near his knees.

Watching Kent, I realized that my own plight might not be so bad. At least I could see. And see I did! A tall, handsome Mexican strolled into the room, spurs jangling. By the expression on Adelita's face, I could see this must be the celebrated *bandido* we were after. His pale eyes flashed like sparks when he saw Adelita. He even choked a little, smoothing his mustache with the back of his hand.

He leaned against the bar where in a few moments Adelita joined him. The two spoke softly to each other. I saw Luz watching too. I was glad, thinking that we could get this over with and be out of here in one night. When Adelita and Juan Ochoa walked tensely from the room, they headed down the hallway toward the cribs. I raised an eyebrow at Luz, and at the first opportunity, we slipped away to follow Adelita and the man she was about to murder.

We hesitated outside the door, listening....

191

"We must get away together," Juan Ochoa said. "Certainly he suspects you now."

"Yes, I think that is why he chose me. He will kill us both!" she said. "The *soldaderas* who accompanied me here will tell him about us."

Luz and I looked at each other in wonder. There was more to this than we had imagined.

"*Por favor,* Juanito," Adelita begged, "it will be best if you kill me now. Those two *soldaderas* will report to Villa that you got away after murdering me. It is your chance to escape. At least I will not have to face his wrath."

"Kill you? Are you crazy? I would rather stand in front of that pig's firing squad than harm one hair on your head!"

"Do you love me, Juanito? Really love me?"

"But of course! More than life itself! We have done our part here. Now that we have been discovered, let's get away to Spain. My grandfather still has property there."

Adelita did not answer. But Luz and I could hear the lovers sighing and smooching.

"*Ay, Dios,*" I whispered to Luz. "So she is the one who has been passing him the information Villa talked about... she is the spy. The two are lovers!"

Luz looked at me. "When Villa finds out Adelita has betrayed him, he will not hesitate to kill her. And if we go back without her, he will kill us."

"Adelita and her *bandido* must escape," I said. "I'm sick of the killing. Besides, Villa is no better than the Federals." I was thinking of the young gringo who was dragged to death behind a horse until he looked like skinned squirrel.

Luz nodded. "And I have been thinking, too. Traveling with the army just to do the bidding of men is not what we were promised. As a woman, I deserve better!"

While hashing this over, we were surprised when the door flew open. Juan Ochoa and Adelita yanked us into the room.

"What to do with them?" Juan asked furiously.

"We cannot harm them, Juan. They are just poor peasant girls looking for a better life."

"We heard you talking," I said. "But we will not give your secret away, if that is what you are thinking."

"Do you mean that?" Adelita asked with some suspicion.

"Of course! Do you think we are happy in the army? Working like donkeys, getting pawed by a new soldier every night?"

Juan Ochoa raised an eyebrow at me. "I had not thought of it like that. All of you *soldaderas* are said to be faithful to Villa to the last drop of your blood."

"The cause is a good one," Luz interrupted, "but we as women have a cause, too. Men are the ones who love to fight, so let them fight. Take us with you as far as Zacatecas. After that my sister and I will get lost in the city. If we are to work as servants, at least we ought to get paid. We are tired of doing special favors for a whole army. Even a mule gets tired and deserves a rest once in a while."

Juan Ochoa stuck to the hills on his horse. Riding a trail above us, he kept an eye on our horse-drawn *coche,* which he stole from the *ranchita.* Fortunately we met neither Villistas nor Federals on the way to Zacatecas. On the outskirts of the town, Luz and I got out of the buggy. Adelita remained inside, handling the driving lines.

After riding to us on his horse, Juan Ochoa handed Luz a small bag of coins. "Here, you will need this until you get a roof over your heads. And, thank you." His eyes were kind. I could see why Adelita was so happy. I smothered my little pang of jealousy. To be so in love with one man who returned the feeling must have been wonderful.

Adelita slapped the lines against the horse's back and the buggy clattered over the cobblestones; Juan rode away beside her.

We waved at them, feeling neither sorrow, regret, nor guilt. If we were only thought of as means to produce new recruits for the army, well...

BELLE BOYD

Belle Boyd, born in 1844, was a controversial figure of the Civil War. Confederate spy, feisty beauty, friend of Stonewall Jackson, she shot and killed a Union officer for invading her home in Martinsburg, Virginia. Belle spent time in a Union prison for being a spy. After the war she married a Yankee and fled to Europe where he died. Author, actress, once widowed and twice divorced, Belle's last husband had her committed to an insane asylum. After her release, she earned her own living by giving "dramatic readings" about her Civil War experiences to audiences across the United States. She died in Wisconsin while on tour in 1900.

Aveline was only sixteen and had not seen much of life yet, so when she found Belle Boyd's body it was a shock. Aveline had known Belle less than a week, but that was time enough for Belle to make a lasting impression on the girl.

Aveline looked at Belle's face, white in death. Belle's eyes were open, and there was a faint smile on her lips. One corner of the gray and white quilt was held up to Belle's chin by one cold, slender hand. Aveline wanted to thank Belle, and let her know how much she appreciated the kind way Belle had treated her. Even though Aveline was just a Yankee servant girl, she had been wildly impressed by Belle's life story.

Aveline stepped back from the bed, running all those thoughts through her mind, trying to share a last few quiet moments with Belle Boyd. Aveline would have to let her employer, fussy Mrs. Hunt, the owner of the boarding house, know Belle was dead. Aveline knew pandemonium would break loose over that news. Most likely Aveline would not have another chance to be alone with Belle again.

Belle Boyd had arrived at the Wisconsin Dells a week before, and checked in at the boarding house where Aveline worked. Belle earned her living putting on stage performances in theaters all across the United States. Her theme was "Civil War Recollections of the Siren of the Shenandoah." That nickname, "Siren of the Shenandoah," had been given to her during the Civil War when she was a Confederate spy. Belle was proud of it. Belle Boyd was intensely loyal to her native Virginia. Aveline could tell by reading between the lines that Belle had had more than a passing interest in Stonewall Jackson, as well. He had been a lot older than she was, but a spirited man, nevertheless. Belle aided him by prying secrets out of talkative Yankee soldiers, then carrying the information to the Rebels.

All of that happened back in 1861, more than twenty years before Aveline was born. It was 1900 now, and Aveline wondered why people hadn't forgotten that old stuff, but everybody seemed more interested in it now than ever. Elderly men around there talked about battles, military strategy, Abe Lincoln, and reconstruction. They'd go on and on about horses dying in the Tallahatchie, skirmishes with the Fourth Mississippi Cavalry, and fighting in peach orchards. The men even bragged about how their eardrums got punctured from the roar of artillery fire. One time, Aveline saw two old soldiers peel off their shirts to examine each other's scars.

The elderly veterans liked to gather at the boarding house porch to reminisce on warm summer nights. After a while their stories got boring to Aveline, but that was before Belle Boyd showed up at the Dells to pique the girl's interest in the Civil War. Belle's stories were from a woman's point of view.

Belle gave her stage performances while all dressed up in a butternut gray sidesaddle suit decorated with gold braid and fringe. "Confederate States Of America" was engraved on the brass buttons; Belle carried a saber, too. When she propped her boot up on a little wooden stool to rest her elbow on her knee, she looked tough and determined, and the audience got real quiet. Aveline knew people were not used to seeing a woman talking with such passion while waving a saber around her head.

Aveline had never been to the theater before, on account of she never had the seventy-five cents extra for things like that. But Belle must have noticed how much she intrigued the girl. On Wednesday morning, which was Belle's last day in town, she gave Aveline some money out of her own purse and told Aveline to use it to see her show.

"You remind me of the girl I was," Belle said, twisting that thick black hair of hers into a roll at the back of her head.

Aveline was taking her time dusting Belle's bedroom—straightening the quilt on the brass bed—changing water in the blue ceramic pitcher on the dresser, all the while eyeing the long, velvet gown Belle wore. It was black with a white, lace-trimmed bodice. The sleeves hung open from Belle's elbows like the insides of swans' wings.

Aveline gaped at her. "I remind you of yourself?" Aveline was short and plump with red hair and freckles…she did not look anything like the tall, shapely Belle Boyd. Aveline knew Belle was past fifty years old, but that was just one more reason her beauty intrigued the girl.

Belle chuckled, fixing the clasp on her silver necklace while at the same time admiring herself in the mirror. "It has been said that I have an aquiline nose." She turned

197

her face from side to side before spraying perfume on her neck and wrists from one of those little glass bottles with a puffer.

Aveline blushed, not saying anything. She thought Belle had sort of a long, horse nose.

"The reason I compare myself to you," Belle continued, "is that I can see you are a daydreamer. I too romanticized inside my head all the time when I was your age."

"Oh," Aveline said, blushing harder, not realizing her reverie was so easy to spot.

Belle let out a laugh. "You are struck by my clothing, my lifestyle, and the stories you have heard about me. You wonder what it would be like to escape your life as a housemaid! To be your own person—a woman of the world!"

Aveline nodded guiltily. Belle saw right through her. Aveline had never been beyond the outskirts of the Wisconsin Dells. Her folks died of typhoid fever when she was thirteen. Aveline had been working as a servant for Mrs. Hunt ever since, and felt lucky to have the job.

Belle turned away from the mirror to look at Aveline. Her face was broody. "I was born to a well-to-do family in the Shenandoah Valley. Martinsburg, Virginia. I was loved by my parents, educated in a fine school, and had everything to look forward to until the war (she pronounced war, "waah") destroyed us—my family, and our farm. The Yankees ruined everything." She raised her voice as if she were speaking to a large crowd.

Aveline nodded, listening, not daring to interrupt. She knew that Belle had been married three times. Her first husband was a handsome Yankee soldier named Sam Hardinge. He died in England after the lovers ran away together at the end of the war to escape criticism for "consortin'" with one another—considering they were supposed to be enemies. Her other marriages after that were unhappy, ending in divorce. One of her ex-husbands put Belle in an insane asylum because she wanted to write books. Aveline knew these things because she heard Mrs. Hunt and her friends gossiping about Belle over a pot of tea in the kitchen one morning after Belle first arrived at the boarding house.

"Miss Boyd," Aveline said, "I could never do all the things you've done. You are a very brave lady."

Belle smiled before turning away with a swirl of her heavy skirts. She stood in front of the window and looked down on the street. "Horses and carriages and green summer days," she said with a sweep of her hand. "Look down there! A dappled gray. What a smooth haunch. How General Stonewall Jackson would have loved that horse!"

Aveline heard the clip clop of horses' hooves coming from the street below. Belle was always quick to remind people that she had been a personal friend of General Jackson. Aveline asked her, "Did you know him very well?" Aveline did not know what else to talk about, but she figured Stonewall Jackson would get Belle to open up.

Belle raised a thin black eyebrow. It formed a naturally high arch, and when she was impatient, the bow shot nearly to her hairline. "He was the finest gentleman! A great military genius. Impeccably mannered, and my hero. I keep his memory alive through my performances, while at the same time telling the story of our Great Cause."

Aveline could not tell if Belle was really speaking to her, or just using her presence as an excuse to repeat herself. But Aveline's ignorance of detailed Civil War events and personalities precluded a debate with Belle. And anyway,

Aveline felt like every second spent with Belle Boyd brought new excitement into her young life. Aveline had never before met anybody like Belle Boyd.

Just then Mrs. Hunt poked her mob-capped white head through the doorway. She told Aveline to hurry up in Belle's room because she was way behind with her chores. Mrs. Hunt's tone was bossy as usual, and that is when Belle offered Aveline the money if she promised to use it to come to Belle's performance that night.

Aveline grabbed at the chance. Mrs. Hunt stomped away with a sniff.

Aveline arrived early at the theater because she heard it would be packed. She was sitting right in the front row when Belle walked on stage and everybody clapped and cheered. The hometown band struck up "Dixie" before Belle's introduction. Of course Wisconsin had belonged to the Union, and "Dixie" was a southern song, but the war ended almost forty years ago. Everybody there was a good sport about it. Besides, it was agreed they were all Americans, and anyhow the Southerners had fought bravely. Somebody like Belle Boyd just had to be respected. She was somebody special.

Old men wearing Union or Confederate uniforms mingled throughout the crowd. They were the ones who liked to remember the Civil War. These men were not mad at each other now, as near as Aveline could figure. The reasons for the war were not as important as the part they'd played in it. In most cases, fighting in the Civil War was the most exciting thing these men had ever done.

One of the uniformed veterans in the audience was slender, blue-eyed Colonel Avery. A widower who had been a wealthy Virginia plantation owner, he lost everything in the war. After the deaths of his wife and son, at war's end, he moved to Wisconsin where he made his new home. It was said that he had fought alongside Stonewall Jackson, and even took part in the battle of Gettysburg where he'd lost his left arm in a cavalry charge. Colonel Avery was a real southern gentleman. Everybody in town admired him, but there was no woman in his life. He seemed sad and lonely and mostly kept to himself.

When the music and clapping finally died down, Belle began her story with how she shot a Yankee officer who invaded her family home in the Shenandoah—how she was captured three different times for spying—and the harsh way she was treated by the male guards who watched her night and day at Old Capitol Prison in Washington.

Belle told about all the daring and clever ways she devised to get information out of the Yankees. Her escapades were full of how she "waved her bonnet," and how she encouraged the soldiers to "press forward," and how she dashed around at a "rapid pace," and how "shot and shell whistled over my head." Belle used big words and expressions like, "notwithstanding my fatigue," and, "Sir! Give me opportunity to recover my breath!" Her story had the audience sitting on the edges of their chairs.

Aveline got the feeling Belle was leaving a few things out when it came to exact details on how she fooled the Yankee cavalry into giving her all that information. Aveline suspected it was Belle's way of encouraging her listeners to use their imaginations.

When the performance ended, Belle pushed her gray hat bedecked with gold ostrich feathers back on her head. Aveline noticed how flushed Belle was from the exertion of her speech. Her cheeks were red as strawberries; her eyes looked glassy.

Aveline waited for Belle after the performance, hoping that Belle might allow her to walk back to the boarding house with her. But Belle said she had to stay late to sell her autographed books entitled *Belle Boyd in Camp and Prison*, which had been first published in 1865. Aveline was dying to own one of those books, but she could never afford one. Belle was so busy with people milling around her that Aveline slipped away and walked back to the boarding house alone. In awe, she wondered how any woman could be so interesting and independent.

Aveline crawled into her bed in the servants' quarters off the kitchen. Mrs. Hunt left the kerosene lamp burning for her. This was the first time that Aveline had stayed out so late at night by herself. She lay for a long time, trying to stay awake, thinking that she would hear Belle when she got back and Aveline might get another peek at her. After all, Belle planned to leave in the morning.

But Aveline fell asleep. The next thing she knew it was dawn; whitish streaks came through the window. She heard the clip clop and clatter of a horse-drawn carriage pulling up in front of the house.

Jumping out of bed, Aveline looked out the window in time to see Belle with the old southern gentleman, Colonel Avery. He was still wearing his gray Confederate uniform. Suddenly the colonel embraced Belle right there on the buggy seat while giving her a kiss! The left sleeve of his cavalry coat was squarely pinned up, but his right arm was working pretty good. Belle and Colonel Avery hugged and swooned over each other for at least a minute.

He finally said in that soft southern accent, "Thank you, deah Belle, for a glorious…evenin'…full of…reminiscence …of our Great Cause."

"The pleasure was mine, Colonel Avery," Belle said before slipping down from the buggy. She was still wearing her gray Confederate costume, but it looked kind of wrinkled. Looking into the colonel's eyes, Belle put her arm around his neck and kissed him yet again! After that, she sashayed up the steps that led into the boarding house.

The doctor said Belle Boyd died of a heart attack in her sleep. The citizens of the Wisconsin Dells made sure that she got a fine burial. Aveline did not say anything about having seen her with the colonel. But Aveline was happy knowing Belle died for a southern cause, after all.

MATTIE BLAYLOCK

Celia Ann "Mattie" Blaylock was born in Iowa in 1850. An unsophisticated farm girl, she got bored with life on the prairie. She went to work in a gambling saloon in Fort Scott, Kansas where she met and fell in love with Wyatt Earp. The two never married. They lived in Wichita, Kansas for a time, and then she followed him to Tombstone, Arizona, where they lived together as "Mr. and Mrs. Wyatt Earp." Mattie had a drug addiction, and became increasingly jealous of Wyatt, who spent most of his time with his brothers. In Tombstone Wyatt fell in love with a cute little actress who performed at the Bird Cage Theater. When Mattie's possessiveness became an embarrassment to Wyatt, he dumped her without ceremony. Mattie, still professing her love for Wyatt Earp, died a prostitute in 1888. She lies buried in an unmarked pauper's grave in Pinal, Arizona.

Louisa Houston first met Mattie Blaylock when the Earps gathered in Tombstone in 1879. Louisa thought Mattie was a rather pathetic figure, mainly because of her cloying love for Wyatt. Mattie and Wyatt occupied a little house on Fremont Street. Although everybody suspected they were not legally married, the pair was known as "Mr. and Mrs. Wyatt Earp."

Admittedly, Louisa was nobody to criticize unmarried couples. She herself had refused to wed Wyatt's younger brother, Morgan. Morgan and Louisa lived together as husband and wife, even though there had never been a wedding ceremony. But in Louisa's case, she was not sure that she wanted to give up her own name and personal identity. Louisa Houston's father was the illegitimate son of Sam Houston, produced when Sam Houston had an affair with a Cherokee woman. So that made Louisa, Sam Houston's granddaughter. Although she could not lay claim to any inheritance, she was still proud of her lineage.

Louisa's love for Morgan Earp came naturally enough. He was the tallest, gentlest, most handsome of the Earp brothers—an important member of that itinerant family, who dabbled in law enforcement when not themselves gambling, or working in saloons. And Wyatt's association with Doc Holliday, Bat Masterson, and some other characters caused Louisa to be cautious about joining them on a permanent basis. Involvement with the Earps, good or bad, was not with just one of them, but with the whole clan.

Louisa had plenty of time to observe the women. Mattie was an ex-dance hall girl whom Wyatt had found in a saloon in Fort Scott, Kansas. They met soon after his legal wife, Urilla Sutherland, died in childbirth. Next was Allie, another Earp woman crazy in love with Virgil, whom she always called "Virg." She lavished her undying love and loyalty on the man. Allie and Virgil were not legally married either. James, the eldest brother, was the only one who believed in tying knots—his wife, Bessie, bore him one daughter. James was permanently crippled from an injury suffered during the Civil War—perhaps forcing him to be more of a family man than his brothers.

Louisa knew her thoughts about the clan were cynical, but it was impossible for any female to maintain her own identity once she threw in with the Earps. The women were expected to follow in the footsteps of old Mrs. Earp, Virginia Ann, the mother of the boys. She bore eight children for Nicholas Porter Earp, plus raising up a son of his from his first marriage after his first wife died in childbirth. Virginia Ann was the image of the perfect frontier wife and mother—strong, loyal, childbearing, tight-lipped—who stood by her man no matter what. She crisscrossed the territories by wagon train, toiled on a homestead, helped in a grocery store, worked in a garden, cared for the stock, suffered through drought, illness and poverty, bore and nursed baby after baby...with few if any complaints. Once, when Louisa dared suggest to her she was drastically taken for granted, Mother Earp's eyes turned cold as rifle scopes.

In Tombstone, the Earps lived in houses near one another during the eighteen months the family lived there. Louisa understood that the Earps were a clannish lot, and by joining the family she was expected to become all of what they were—even living close together, which Louisa hated. There was never a moment of privacy.

Louisa tried to like Mattie, but found her somewhat tiresome. Mattie loved Wyatt unconditionally. She was always quick to admit he had rescued her from drudgery in a saloon. Mattie had become the doting, affectionate, loyal woman that he expected her to be. Wyatt was a natty dresser, and Mattie scrubbed and ironed his clothing daily, making sure his shirts were glowing white, his hats brushed just so, his boots polished, his pants creased. Sometimes Mattie's own appearance was left badly lacking because she was so busy fussing over him, which may have worked against her in the end.

But even if Mattie had taken better care of herself, Louisa felt that big trouble was on the horizon for the woman. By the time Morgan, Wyatt, Virgil and their friend, Doc Holliday were involved in the gunfight at the O.K. Corral on October 26, 1881, a theatrical troupe from San Francisco had already arrived in Tombstone, and was putting on plays at the Bird Cage Theater. A member of the troupe was a sassy little actress named Josephine Marcus. It was soon rumored around town that Wyatt and the attractive Josephine had fallen for one another. However, Louisa nor any of the other Earp women dared bring the subject to Mattie's attention. Louisa knew Mattie had a drug habit she had acquired while working in Kansas saloons. During times of anger or despair Mattie turned to her old obsession, and none of the Earp women wanted to get caught in the crossfire between Mattie and Wyatt.

On the day of the gunfight, Wyatt and Doc walked away from the uproar without a scratch. But Morgan and Virgil were wounded. They had to be carried to Virgil's house where, in their agonies, they shared the only bed.

Louisa dashed to Virgil's house when she heard the news. The whole family was inside the house together. Louisa was terrified because of wild talk in the streets about a vigilante committee forming to hang the Earps for killing Billy Clanton and the McLaury brothers. What with all the hubbub, Louisa did not at first notice Mattie's reaction to the trouble.

Morgan and Vigil were moaning side by side. A pool of blood collected on the mattress from the wound in Virgil's right leg. Blood dripped to the floor, forming a puddle under the high iron bed. Allie fretted and dashed about, changing bandages, trying to stanch the flow.

Morgan gasped with his own pain. Louisa trembled fearfully because the bullet had entered the point of his right shoulder, before running through his back and passing out his left shoulder. She could only press bandages across his wound and pray until Doctor Goodfellow arrived to take care of both men.

Later, the tall, blond doctor finally announced Virgil and Morgan would live, which was more than he could say for Billy Clanton and the McLaurys "This is a bad day for Tombstone," Goodfellow said, glaring all around.

A terrible silence settled over the little house because of the anxiety. The doctor gathered up his instruments when

207

Mattie, who had been wringing her hands at the foot of the bed, suddenly cried, "Thank God, Wyatt is unharmed!"

To which Wyatt shouted, "Go home, Mattie! Get out of here, damn you!"

Louisa thought his behavior was strange, because he and Mattie should have been in each other's arms. But later, Louisa got the cold feeling it was not from Mattie's arms that Wyatt craved comfort.

Mattie, paling as if he had struck her, gulped back her tears and raced out of the house. She was closely followed by Doctor Goodfellow who announced he would come back tomorrow.

Wyatt spent the next twenty-four hours pacing around the house like a caged cat. He fiddled with his guns, ready to protect the family in case the vigilantes really tried to carry out their threats. But by the following day the town was quiet, and then Wyatt slipped away. Louisa thought he had gone home to see Mattie. But shortly after Wyatt left, Mattie appeared, looking for him. Before any of the women could say anything, Virgil told Mattie that Wyatt had some business downtown, and that he would be back soon. So that was the end of that.

Mattie pouted and squinted, which did not do anything for her already rather coarse features. Her long brown dress looked like she had slept in it. Her dark hair was frizzed and dirty. It seemed to Louisa the poor wretched thing made such a doormat out of herself that Wyatt had grown tired of her. He simply did not know how to handle the matter of separation.

"He has gone to that woman!" Mattie shouted, finally bringing it out in the open. "And you are all in this together!" She impaled everybody with her eyes before whirling out the door, skirts flying.

Later that afternoon Wyatt finally returned to his house. In a few moments Louisa and Allie rushed to the window because they heard Mattie shouting and crying in their yard. She clutched Wyatt's arms, begging him to stay home with her. But he pushed her away, scolding her because she had not gotten his best shirt clean enough. He thumped heavy-booted up the street, back in the direction of the Bird Cage Theater.

The next two months in Tombstone proved to be a nightmare. Both Virgil and Morgan recovered from their bullet wounds, but in December Virgil was ambushed in an alley by friends of the Clantons and McLaurys. He was left for dead. Virgil survived, but poor Allie went through the trauma of another near-killing. This time Virgil permanently lost the use of his left arm.

Meanwhile, Mattie continued to be tormented by the awful truth that Wyatt was involved in a passionate affair with the enchanting Josephine Marcus. Josephine was ten years younger than Mattie, and quite attractive with her slim figure and fetching dark eyes. Josephine was a member of a wealthy San Francisco family. Having some money of her own naturally piqued Wyatt's interest. Between her theatrical performances, she flounced around Tombstone in beautiful dresses with Wyatt prancing behind her. There were more scandalous rumors when Josephine dumped her fiance, Sheriff Johnny Behan. She chose instead the company of Wyatt Earp, and the whole town was talking.

Of course, the rest of the Earp women would have nothing to do with Josephine if they happened to cross paths with the little chit on the street or inside a store. But neither could they side in very much with Mattie because the Earp men closed ranks with Wyatt. When it came to women, none was considered indispensable. They did not dare encourage Mattie if she came to them for sympathy.

Louisa understood Mattie's love for Wyatt, because Louisa had those same feelings for Morgan. And while Morgan and Louisa made a happy couple, she knew that Morgan's first loyalties were, and always would be, to his brothers. The Earps confided in each other about everything, so it was a dangerous matter for anyone to try to influence one of them singularly.

Louisa carefully tried to talk Morgan into going away with her, leaving the family and their difficult ways. She knew that Allie had tried to convince Virgil in the same manner, but both were met with stubborn resistance. It all finally boiled down to the family maintaining strength from its solidarity, which of course became part of the Earp mystique.

Meanwhile, it tore at Louisa's heart to see how Mattie suffered. But there was nothing Louisa could do for her. Louisa hoped that Wyatt would get over fancy Josephine, and that things between him and Mattie might get back to the way they were. But, that was not to be.

Soon it was Louisa's turn to wear widow's weeds. On the night of March 18, 1882, Wyatt and Morgan played their last game of pool at Campbell and Hatch's Saloon. Assassins' bullets ripped through a window facing the alley. Morgan was struck in the back. A bullet shattered his spine. He died in Wyatt's arms before Louisa could be summoned.

The next day Louisa left Arizona forever. The Earp men decided Morgan's body was to be sent to the family plot in Colton, California where Mr. and Mrs. Earp lived. No Earp would ever be buried in Tombstone.

Allie, Virgil, Mattie, and Louisa prepared for the long journey with Morgan's body, first by wagon, and then by train to Colton. Meanwhile, Wyatt and Doc and their gunfighter cronies got ready for their bloody ride of vengeance out of Arizona Territory. They had a score to settle with Morgan's killers.

At the train station the morning of their departure, Louisa could see that Mattie was dreadfully pale. Wyatt gave Mattie a quick hug, simply muttering, "Wait for me in Colton. I will join you there later."

The tone of his voice was not very convincing. Louisa watched his tall, black-coated figure hurry away. Mattie stood on the platform, looking after him. It was Louisa who finally took Mattie's elbow and guided her up the steps into the passenger car.

Morgan's death, the Earps' sudden retreat from Tombstone, the frenzy of the town's citizens, and all that went on seemed a blur to Louisa when she thought about it many years later. She tried to recall the final events, but thinking back on it, she knew that Mattie suspected it was the end for her and Wyatt.

At the time, Louisa herself was in shock with her own grief, and could not worry about Mattie. But when reminiscing, Louisa could still see Mattie sitting ahead of her on the train, pressing her worried face against the window glass to catch one last glimpse of Wyatt Earp. Mattie's eyes were blurry, her lips trembled—she held a black lace hanky (they all wore black in those days in honor of the mourning ritual) as the train ground and clattered out of the Benson station.

After Morgan's funeral, Louisa slipped quietly away from the Earp family. She had no reason to linger. When looking into Mrs. Earp's tormented eyes, Louisa was reminded of how much she herself had loved her son. Losing a son was like a fatal stab in the heart of poor Mother Earp. Sadly, Louisa had been unable to influence him in a way that might have saved his life.

Louisa moved away, living in obscurity on a small sum of money Morgan and she had managed to save. Meanwhile, Mattie clung steadfastly to the Earp family for some months until she was finally told that Wyatt was living in Colorado with Josephine Marcus.

Lonely and broken-hearted, Mattie visited Louisa before leaving California. Mattie planned to join Doc Holliday's woman, Big Nose Kate, who ran a gambling saloon in Globe, Arizona. Mattie was embittered at the thought. "I am middle-aged! And now forced to go back to the only profession I have ever known." She was devastated by the way Wyatt left her...failing to face her...not having enough gumption to speak to her personally... leaving his poor old parents to tell her she was through.

Looking back on it years later, and knowing the depth of Mattie's unreasonable love for Wyatt, Louisa understood that by not facing Mattie, Wyatt likely saved them both the embarrassment of a terrible last scene.

"I am sorry, Mattie," was all Louisa could say to her. Less than one year after Morgan's death, Louisa was still wearing her mourning dress. Seeing Mattie's tortured face and listening to her cries only brought back tragic memories of her own. Louisa was not able to be strong for her. They cried together, embracing each other as they had not been able to do in Tombstone. In their own separate ways, they too were victims of the Earps.

"Goodbye, dear Mattie," Louisa said.

Six years later, in 1888, Louisa read a small article in a newspaper. It said the wife of Wyatt Earp, Celia Ann "Mattie" Blaylock, who worked in a house of ill fame in the mining camp of Pinal, Arizona, had committed suicide. She took an overdose of laudanum mixed with whiskey. Mattie told a friend before she died that Wyatt Earp had deserted her, and that she had no reason to live.

KATE BENDER

In the early 1870s a family named Bender, consisting of Ma, Pa, Kate, and John, opened a sort of wayside inn along a lonely stretch of road outside Cherryvale, Kansas. The Bender tavern offered food, water, and a place to sleep. Neighbors thought the place looked ratty and dirty. The Benders themselves were secretive. Nobody knew where the Benders came from, but in those days, it was considered rude to ask. Travelers heading West stopped along this road, for there was nowhere else for them to go. In the great quiet of the prairies, people helped one another. But here, on this bare flat stretch of land, unsuspecting men, women, and even children would find out too late what lurked at the Bender Inn.

Kate Bender and her clan were murderers, but we did not have an inkling. Spring of 1871, they came rattling into our farmyard in their wagon loaded with rickety furniture, a crate full of chickens, pots and blankets all helter-skelter. The wagon was pulled by two of the skinniest horses I'd ever seen. Tied to the back of the wagon was a staggering, bloated milk cow that looked ready to deliver a calf.

It was springtime. The grass was lush in the fields around our farm in Cherryvale, Kansas. The land in the region had a reputation for fertile soil and good water. Many homesteaders were moving in. The sight of the Benders looking so poorly played a big part in my brother-in-law's feeling sorry for them. Tall and sun-reddened under a battered straw hat, Lester listened to their story from our front porch.

My sister, Arleta, married to Lester, was nearing her time to have her first baby. Arleta studied the Benders with disapproval. While she did not like the people, her eyes kept roving over that pregnant cow as if she understood the poor critter's dilemma.

It was Ma Bender who did the talking. Sitting up there on the wagon seat wearing a long-old, sun-faded brown prairie dress and bonnet, her gnarled hands clasped a tattered Bible on her lap. She was missing both front teeth. When her jaw worked up and down, the white folds under her chin swung like a dewlap. She went on and on about how the good Lord provides, and how we should allow her family to camp for a spell somewhere close to our water. They were hoping to file on a homestead in our district. All the while her slithery blue eyes scanned our yard. She seemed particularly interested in the pair of plump turkeys that were Arleta's favorites.

Sitting next to Ma Bender on the wagon seat was her husband, John. We got to know him later as Old John, and he spoke with a German accent. The couple was in their sixties, and Old John was as gray-haired and leathery-faced as his wife. His baggy overalls were patched at the knees with red wool material that had come from threadbare longjohns.

Riding in the back of the wagon was their dim-witted son, John Junior. He grinned, showing his bad teeth while holding a scrawny hound-dog pup on his lap. John had to be nearly thirty years old, and I did not like the way he watched me. I just looked away. Sitting behind John Junior on a pile of rags and blankets was his sister, Kate. About my age I guessed, Kate was in her late teens. She grinned slyly at Lester. Kate had thick auburn hair, straight white teeth and gray-blue eyes. Her full breasts strained against her pink calico dress that looked to be the only clean garment in the whole wagon. Kate seemed too pretty to belong to the Benders when you considered what the rest of them looked like.

Arleta hesitated about letting the Benders camp down in our pasture. But soft-hearted Lester gave in. I could tell by the way he eyed that old wagon and poor critters he was wondering what he could do for those sorry people. Lester was always the first to help in emergencies, known to give garden vegetables to folks in need, quick to donate to the church and other causes.

Meanwhile, Ma Bender said things about the Lord while making references to the Good Book, and all that. So finally Lester said it was all right if they camped at the very edge of our property where the turn in the road led to Cherryvale. There were big cottonwood trees down there, and a grassy meadow where spring water trickled into a small pond.

Receiving Lester's permission to camp, Ma Bender's darting eye lit up. She smiled and humbled herself. Old John slapped the lines against the team's bony rumps. The wagon squeaked and strained out of the yard.

"I hope you didn't make a mistake letting them camp down there," Arleta told Lester.

"But did you see that poor sufferin' cow and those thin horses?" Lester asked.

"Our livestock would be in trouble too if we drove around the countryside harpin' Good Book themes instead of tending to our land," Arleta said.

"Sometimes poor people need help," Lester answered. "They won't stay too long. After they file on a claim of their own, they'll make good neighbors knowing we gave them a helping hand."

Lester and Arleta walked arm-and-arm into the house. I knotted my bonnet strings under my chin and headed toward the vegetable garden. I had to tow my weight around here. I appreciated the fact my sister and her generous husband let me live with them. I was nineteen years old and still trying to get over the loss of my young husband, Lucas, who had been killed in a fall from a horse the previous summer.

A month went by. I was out in the garden one day pulling weeds which caused my back to hurt after a couple of hours of straining and yanking under that hot Kansas sun. I stopped long enough to press my hands at the small of my back, scanning the lush green fields and pastures full of orange and purple wildflowers. The vegetable plants in the garden were big and leafy too after the good summer rains we'd been having.

I knew it was all right for me to rest a few minutes. I got melancholy sometimes. Arleta had not had the baby yet, but she was getting bigger by the minute, and I tried to stay out of her and Lester's way. Even though they were always nice to me, they were doting newlyweds all caught up in expecting their first baby. While I was glad for them, I could not help but think of Lucas, and how he and I might be in their happy situation if he were still alive.

The farm bordered the road to Cherryvale, and travelers sometimes came through, asking for water and directions. Now and again a late evening rider stopped, looking for a place to spend the night. Lester always sent them on to Cherryvale after we shared news and water. But word soon circulated that the Benders, who had moved off Lester's property, had filed a homestead claim on a piece of land adjacent to ours. They were putting travelers up for the night, so Lester directed folks to the Benders as a kindness to help Benders make a little money.

I was standing in the garden thinking of these things, and how the Bender shack was thrown together of some rough-cut logs and scrap lumber. It was a one-room shanty with some old canvas sheets strung across the inside to make a divider. I looked in one time when I rode to town with Lester. It did not seem like the kind of place I cared to spend the night. Old John liked to stand in the yard waving that battered felt hat shouting, "Welcome brother!" while pretty Kate sat in a wooden chair in front of the shack, smiling kind of sassy. Ma Bender put looney John to hauling water in buckets from the pond. He had worn a deep rut across the yard to a small apple orchard behind the house. Those scraggly little trees, mostly growing from apple parings, seemed to be the only thing tended around that place.

The Benders' horses looked better now that they grazed on good grass. I never did see the pregnant cow or any calf she might have had. But jerked beef strips hanging from a bush in the Bender's front yard suggested what might have terminated her pregnancy.

Toward the end of summer on a warm, mosquitoey night, I ambled down along the pasture fence. Just going for a walk, I listened to crickets and hoot owl sounds. Arleta finally had her baby—a healthy, fat, pink girl. Sometimes I felt I was underfoot because it was time for the little family to have their privacy. That night I wove my way through tall swishing grass. After slipping through the sagging wire gate, I was straightening up when I heard a voice call.

"Tst! Over here! Margaret!"

I jumped, recognizing the voice of Kate Bender. I stared into the woods bordering the pasture. Kate leaned against a tree, holding her dress all bundled up in her arms! Her long auburn hair fell in a big tangle across her face, hanging

218

every which way to her shoulders. She giggled, calling me again. "Margaret? Wanna talk?"

I approached her cautiously. We had never had a real conversation before, so I did not know what to make of this. But finding her down there in the woods not wearing her dress was a curiosity. "Are you all right?" I asked, wondering if somebody had been chasing her.

She laughed. "I come over here a lot. Hanging around here in the woods, I see you down there in your garden. How come you don't stop by and visit me? We could be friends."

"I have lots of work to do," I said. The truth of the matter was the Benders were rather odd, to say the least. Even Lester was beginning to wonder about them. They seemed to take no interest in planting crops, or fixing up their place.

Kate must have seen something in my expression because she crossed her eyes at me and blurted, "Not good enough for you, eh? You're mighty uppity! But I'll tell you something. We Benders have a lot more than you think. You'd be surprised if you knew what we have."

When I did not answer, she turned away, suddenly dashing down the wooded slope, laughing and shrieking. She dropped her dress and tore at her white cotton chemise before finally ripping off her pantaloons! Following warily, I picked up her discarded clothing. I thought she was getting all worked up because I'd snubbed her, so I wanted to let her know that I was sorry. I kept following her until she reached the spring near the Bender shack. She threw herself into the cold water where she trembled and turned blue, cupping handfuls of water over her whole body. She screamed in fits and scrubbed her skin until she left red claw marks as if trying to hurt herself.

Thunderstruck, I saw her wash her breasts, and between her legs and then she slumped into the water until just her head and neck stuck out. The words she cried sounded like animal howls—whining and begging for the Lord to forgive her—screaming things about devils and hell and blood and sledge hammers and people's damned souls. I heard so much craziness that I backed away from her, shocked.

"I'm sorry!" Kate shrieked, "I'm sorry!"

All of a sudden I heard twig-snapping sounds behind me. I whirled to face the rest of the Benders who must have heard Kate's yelling. Ma Bender, glowering, held a shotgun across her arms. Old John studied his daughter while rubbing a dirty hand through his beard. Young John held a sledge hammer in his hand. He leered and laughed at his sister who continued crying out from the middle of the spring.

Ma Bender said to me. "Daughter Kate is having one of her crazy spells. Female trouble. You understand? Just git on home and forget you saw this. And don't never pay attention to nothin' she says."

I was more than happy to get out of there. I dropped Kate's clothing and ran.

Doctor William York of Fort Scott, Kansas had a shy smile and gentle eyes. He rode through our place one evening needing water and a place to spend the night. When he leaned over for a cool drink from the dipper I noticed a gold ring on the little finger of his right hand. He saw me eyeing it, because he quickly explained that it had once belonged to his mother. Some day he would give it to his bride—whenever the time came for him to marry. There was something about the calmness of his voice and the sincerity of his expression that had me blushing right to the roots of my blonde hair.

My attraction to him was so strong that it shocked me to think maybe I was beginning to get over Lucas. Maybe it was time for me to get on with my life. Doctor York said he was on his way to Cherryvale to meet his brother, and that he would pass by here on his way back. Lester told him that the Benders sometimes put people up for the night. Then Doctor York rode out of my life forever.

I watched the road for almost three weeks after that, expecting that tall figure to come riding back like he promised. I was so sure there was something between us—love at first sight? Before that, I didn't believe it could really happen to people, but it happened to me.

And then one morning at dawn a lathered posse led by Colonel A. M. York, a Civil War veteran, and brother of Doctor York, rode into our yard. Colonel York asked if we had ever seen his brother, Doctor William York, who had not arrived in town.

Of course we had seen him! Lester told the colonel everything we knew. I clutched my throat, wondering what on earth might have happened. Lester explained that he had sent Doctor York to the Benders, because they sometimes put people up for the night.

"We just stopped at the Bender place," the colonel said. "They insisted they never met anybody by the name of Doctor York. But there is something funny going on over there. Those people are mighty strange. I think that young halfwit is wearing my brother's boots! Besides, there is a god-

221

awful smell around that place reminding me of the war, when corpses had to be buried in a hurry in shallow graves."

Arleta gasped and ran back into the house.

I felt my face turn to ice as the blood drained out of my head. I sagged to the ground, suddenly remembering what Kate said about blood and sledge hammers, and going to the devil.

Lester picked me up off the ground. The colonel fanned my face with his old cavalry hat. I felt better, and told Lester and the colonel what happened at the spring that night. After listening, the men turned their horses around while Lester said he'd saddle up and go with them.

After everybody rode away, I could not stand the curiosity. I ran across the pasture and down along the old fence line crossing into the woods. In a while I stood up on the ridge watching the posse dig around the Bender shack. The Benders had loaded up their wagon and taken off before the posse got there, so the place was deserted.

I held my nose. Even at that distance I could tell what Colonel York meant about shallow graves. There was a sinister droning of flies all around the yard. The posse eventually dug some bodies out of the Bender's apple orchard—all the skulls had been crushed. Later, the posse mounted their horses and took off trailing the Benders.

Devastated, I went home.

Three days later Lester came back. His hands shook when he unsaddled his horse. He would not look us in the eye. Lester simply told us the Benders got away. For the rest of his life he never spoke of it again.

In the weeks and months to come, the "Hell Benders" as they were called in the newspapers, became the object of much morbid curiosity. Some of the corpses dug up in the Bender's apple orchard were folks known locally, others were unsuspecting travelers never to be identified.

People wondered what became of the Benders, while at the same time souvenir hunters descended on the shack, carrying away every nail and scrap of wood to be sold at auctions all the way to New York. It seemed the ghoulish stories and jokes would never end.

Many years later, in 1910, the year after Lester died, I was rocking contentedly one morning on the front porch. I liked reading the Kansas City newspaper—testing my new eyeglasses. Arleta hummed and puttered around in the kitchen, for we had become recluse in our old age. I never re-married. Arleta's daughter never married either. She moved away long ago to attend college, and now managed a big department store in Topeka.

A small article on the last page of the newspaper caught my attention. I gasped! It was one of those "Weird Tale" stories that sometimes crop up to amaze readers, sort of a believe-it-or-not. Anyway, it said that an old cowboy dying at a New Mexico ranch told how he had ridden with a posse more than 40 years ago, catching and killing a family named Bender who had committed unspeakable atrocities near Cherryvale on the Kansas frontier. He explained how the posse, led by the brother of one of the Benders' victims, went wild and butchered the whole clan before burning the bodies.

The man making the confession said that the Benders deserved everything they got…at the time he had not felt mercy for the two men, or the women. But after almost forty years of pondering on this, the old cowpuncher decided that perhaps the members of the posse should not have taken the law into their own hands. The article went

223

on to say the old cowboy died feeling better that he had confessed.

For a horrible moment the vision of Kate Bender naked and begging forgiveness in the spring that night flashed through my mind. I shuddered. It happened such a long time ago, but I could still see the terror in Kate's eyes.

"What's new in the paper?" Arleta asked, carrying a tray laden with teapot and china. She placed everything on a table near my chair. Before I could answer, she added. "Lester loved these quiet mornings. He was such a gentle, peaceful man. Remember?"

I folded the newspaper, stuffing it under my chair. "Yes, Arleta. I remember."

JANETTE RIKER

Janette Riker was a teenage girl crossing the Montana plains with her father and brothers in 1849. They were on the way to Oregon. They camped in a grassy valley late in September to rest the oxen, and replenish their meat supply. When Janette's father and brothers did not return from their hunting expedition, and a sudden and overwhelming snow, storm descended on the valley, the girl showed unusual strength and determination to survive.

Western meadowlarks, ponderosa pine, blue skies and cool evening wind—Mrs. Riker rolled these thoughts through her mind to ease her dying. She huddled, shivering, hugging herself inside the canvas-topped Conestoga wagon, whose narrow wooden bed held all of their family possessions.

Her daughter Janette threw a long look from her place on the other side of the wagon. Janette was determined to survive their ordeal. Mrs. Riker was willing to lie quietly, ready to allow death to overtake them. She believed in God. But what had she done to deserve this?

"Mother!" Janette shouted. "Open your eyes! Look at me. Don't you dare fall asleep. Hear?"

Mrs. Riker pulled the cold blankets tighter around her own shoulders. "Janette, I am tired. Hush. Leave me alone."

Janette's pale eyes flickered over her mother in the dim moonlight—Janette had that wolfish look about her, just like her father when he was young, a long time ago.

The year was 1849. Mr. Riker sold the meager family homestead in Montana after deciding to make a new home in Oregon. He thought if they started soon enough, they would make Oregon before winter snows closed the mountain passes.

The first part of their trip was uneventful. They had a good yoke of oxen and plenty of provisions. Janette was yet a teenager, but the sons were twenty, and twenty-one. And, Mr. Riker had always been a strong man.

But after six weeks of travel, they arrived in a grassy valley in western Montana where Mr. Riker decided to hunt. He was looking for buffalo to replenish the meat supply. He and his two sons rode away with their guns, leaving Mrs. Riker and Janette at camp for the day. All would have been fine, except that Mr. Riker and his sons did not return.

Three days later, Janette set off on foot to see if she could find them. But she soon lost their trail and came back to tell her mother the bad news. The women knew something terrible must have happened. The thought of Indians had been constantly on their minds.

The women continued to wait, hoping any moment the wonderful sight of three riders returning safely to their campsite would end this nightmare. But still the men did not return.

On the fourth morning the temperature dropped suddenly. The hard hand of winter was descending sooner than expected. Janette's young eyes first saw sinister clouds hovering over the distant peaks. Great brownish swirls collided with blue sky. "Snow," she said, "early this year. The passes are closing." Picking up the axe and gathering her skirts about her knees, she stomped into the woods.

Mrs. Riker sat by the fire, too desolate to think what to do. Their trouble seemed enormous without the men. They were stranded in the mountains, so far from civilization, with no meat and no hope that anybody would stumble upon them, for they were not traveling any known route. These thoughts filled her mind. She could not shake her terrible depression. She was full of sorrow for herself. Life on one poor homestead after another, years of struggle...and now this!

Mrs. Riker heard whacking sounds vibrate through the forest—axe against tree trunk. She hurried up the slope toward the twang of the ringing blade. It sounded just like the way her husband cut trees. She hoped it was him! Instead, she found Janette in the process of felling a stout pine.

"Janette! What on earth? We have plenty of kindling."

Janette sweated, putting her strength into the axe handle, her slim waist shuddering with each blow. "We're going to build a shelter. I need this pole to hold up the roof."

"Shelter? We're not staying here."

"Can't you see the snow moving into the passes? We won't get out until spring. Besides, in case Pa and the boys are all right, they'll know where to find us."

"A shelter? We have the wagon...."

"We need decent protection, more than that canvas tarp. There'll be wolves, and mountain lions, and deep snow...." Janette's face was red, her lower lip pressed in a hard line.

"But, Janette, I..."

Janette put the axe down, leaning on the handle. "Mother, do as I tell you. You've spent your whole life bossed around by Pa. He's not here now. Maybe he won't ever be back. We have to think for ourselves or we'll die."

Janette's words stung like bees. She was right. Mrs. Riker always followed her husband's instructions. Without him making decisions, she felt so lost and afraid. "Let's just sit and pray that your father and brothers will be back soon. We can't make it by ourselves."

"We have to make it, and we will!" Janette gripped the axe with passion and began thrusting the blade into the tree trunk again. After making a large chink in the downhill side, she went around to the back of the tree and chopped again. "Go back to camp and gather wood on the way," she told her mother. "Keep busy!" The blade continued to chop and twang—hunks of wood flying.

Mrs. Riker stumbled back to camp, trying to adjust to the unsettling thought her daughter was suddenly in charge. Janette was doing all the things Mrs. Riker never thought her capable of. Janette was just a girl. Girls fetched and carried and weeded and hoed, but they did not make decisions. Mrs. Riker had been taught that girls had little worth, and the proof was that she herself always felt so inadequate. Her father, an Ohio minister, believed that girls should learn to read, but mainly a woman's place was to be an obedient wife and good mother. She had been content to allow her father, and later her husband, to make all the important decisions for her. Why not?

They were camped beside a wide stream. Mrs. Riker gathered wood before bringing a bucket of water to the fire where she put coffee to boil. They had a fair amount of provisions, except for meat. Meat! If only her husband and sons had not decided to go hunting, the family would be many miles from there—halfway to Fort Walla Walla by now.

Mrs. Riker heard swishing sounds come from the toppling tree, followed by chopping noises telling her Janette was trimming off the branches. The woman scanned the peaks —dark clouds loomed closer to camp. Falling snow made the mountains look much whiter than they'd looked earlier in the day.

Janette joined her mother at the fire where they shared a cup of coffee for the first time that morning. Instinctively, Mrs. Riker knew to ration things. She cooked only a cupful of cornmeal mush.

After this, the women finished trimming the tree. Later, they lugged the pole back to camp where Janette propped it against a hillside between a boulder and the crotch of another large tree. Lesser branches and small logs made crude walls. Together, the women stuffed the cracks with mud from the stream bank, adding rocks and dry grass.

Using the camp shovel, Mrs. Riker banked earth around the outside walls, the way she'd seen her husband do when he built a soddy they lived in one winter in the Dakotas. Finally, Janette tied the wagon canvas over the whole thing, fastening it to stakes driven into the ground.

Meanwhile, Mrs. Riker dragged the little iron camp stove and the rest of their possessions from the wagon, fitting everything inside the dugout.

"Tomorrow," Janette said, huddling over the stove, "we'll gather firewood and pile it close to the entrance where it will be handy during storms. We can store some of the wood right inside the dugout—at the back, so wolves and badgers can't dig their way in."

Mrs. Riker looked at her, shocked. "You really think we will survive the winter here, don't you?"

Janette rubbed her hands over the heat from the stove. "Snow will likely sprinkle our beds, and we'll have to melt ice for drinking water, but we're going to make it. The cornmeal and preserves we brought from home will help, but tomorrow I'll kill one of the oxen for meat."

"Kill one of your father's oxen! How will we get out of here without the oxen to pull the wagon?"

"They won't survive the winter. I might as well butcher one before something else does."

It was at that very moment that their plight dawned on Mrs. Riker with full impact. Until now her mind pretended that this ordeal would soon end. Her husband would be back. The boys would suddenly appear. They'd hook up the oxen and be on their way.

"Mother!" Janette glared. "Stop simpering like a goose. We have to work fast before the blizzard closes in on us."

At dawn they took inventory. Their possessions included a camp shovel, one hatchet, one axe, several blankets, a small keg of salt, a large keg of cornmeal, several dozen jars of fruit and vegetable preserves, odds and ends of clothing, a box of dishes and pans, coffee, a jar of seed corn, several knives and the revolver.

"Pa left six bullets," Janette said before walking stiffly toward the creek bank where the oxen grazed. The gentle roan team faithfully stuck close to the wagon, because they considered it to be home. The Rikers had always provided them food and protection.

"Poor trusting creatures," Mrs. Riker said, standing beside the lonely skeleton of a wagon—metal ribs arched against the dark sky. "Soon the oxen ribs will join the wagon ribs for all eternity." She could not help herself. All her life she'd found verse comforting during crisis. She'd made up wonderful poems for the days her children were born.

Janette stopped, and tossed a look over her shoulder. "Why do you always get poetic when we're in trouble, Mother? A lot of good that does."

Mrs. Riker burst into tears. "I want only peace. Certainly there must be a reason for the dreadful things that happen in this world. Why can't I find beauty?"

Janette trudged away shaking her head. "We're stranded in the mountains with winter coming on. Starving to death won't be beautiful. Get a knife and help cut meat."

They struggled all through the day. Janette did the killing. Together they skinned and gutted and finally cut all the meat that they could pack in the salt they had. The rest was hung in strips over the stove to make jerked beef. While the women carried the last pieces of meat to the back of the dugout, the first drifting snowflakes settled on their noses and eyelashes. The great white wall blew in from the east.

The lowing of the poor confused ox that was still alive tormented Mrs. Riker. The animal was frightened and confused by the day's events. With large eyes, it scanned the bloodied spot where its partner had been butchered. Mrs. Riker knew that even in its poor, dull oxen brain it understood that something horrible had happened to its mate. And somehow, something worse than death happened—a betrayal had occurred.

"Come on! Hurry!" Ever practical, Janette waved her mother into the dugout as the full blast of the storm settled over the lonely camp. Janette fed wood chips into the stove. Later, rolling themselves into every bit of clothing and blankets available, the women settled in for the long winter.

Each morning, Janette peered out the little doorway behind the stove, scanning the sky to see what the weather was like. Later, each woman in turn took a walk around camp, dragged in more wood, hauled clean snow for melting, and answered nature's call.

Fearful of Indians and wild animals, Mrs. Riker carried the hatchet with her wherever she went. Janette had the pistol and the axe. They cooked a small piece of meat each day, carefully rationing the supply of coffee, cornmeal, and preserves. Meanwhile, they endlessly concerned themselves about the weather. What else was there to talk about?

Nights were long and frightening with wind howling across the valley, usually heralding more snow in its wake. Often the sounds of prowling animals scratching at the walls of the dugout kept the women awake. They debated over using the gun, but Janette was determined to save the last five bullets until an absolute emergency should arise.

One terrible night a wolf pack brought the other ox down. The women listened to the howling and groaning, and finally the snapping of teeth amid terrified bellows that were soon quelled by fiendish yips of delight. Snarls and threats were heard as the carcass was torn apart. In the morning, only bloodstains remained on the snow; bones, hooves and hide were scattered in every direction.

Janette and her mother slunk about camp that day, hurrying back into the dugout without speaking to each other. The fearful aura of the pack seemed to hang in the air. There was nothing they could say to ease the feeling that they, too, had become part of the wilderness.

"The sound is deafening," Mrs. Riker said one night, shivering with her arms crossed under her blanket. Orange

232

flickers from the coals inside the stove made the shadows dance and waver around the pine bough ceiling.

"I don't hear anything," Janette said.

"You are always missing the point. I meant there is no sound. There is nothing lonelier or quieter than an endless forest. It's oppressive in its void. It is as if the world we know does not exist anymore. We could be the last creatures on earth," Mrs. Riker whispered.

"Tell that to the badger that's been sniffing around outside for the past hour. If that critter don't get away soon, I'll club it to death."

"You have become as primitive as the beasts around here," Mrs. Riker said.

"If I sat around spouting poetry like you do, we'd be dead by now."

"Oh, Janette. Just because I crave peace and beauty, you don't have to make me seem like a worthless idiot."

"We're getting on each other's nerves, Ma. Cramped inside this dugout under a ton of snow—critters howling around outside—not knowing if our food supply will last, or how we're going to get out of here after the snow melts."

Mrs. Riker gaped at her daughter. She hadn't thought of that. Both oxen were dead, and the fort at Walla Walla was hundreds of miles away. After the snow melted, they would have to walk, but could they find their way? "Better yet," Mrs. Riker cried, "let's stay here! We have the seed corn. We'll plant corn in the spring." She found the jar of seed corn and drew it inside her blanket to hold against her body. It was a comfort to her, representing hope. Staying here seemed better than trekking into more of the unknown.

233

"We can't stay here after the snow melts," Janette said. "This is not a place for farming. If we hang around long enough, maybe trappers, or another wagon party will stumble across us. But we can't count on that. If Indians find us, I don't know what will happen."

"Indians!" Mrs. Riker remembered stories she'd heard about the atrocities captured white women were forced to endure. She hugged her blanket harder so that the seed corn pressed against her ribs.

"At least we have five bullets left," Janette said. "If the worst happens, I'll shoot you, and then myself. I'd let you handle the gun, but you probably wouldn't have the nerve."

Mrs. Riker thought to herself, *She's right.*

They kept track of time by scratching a notch each evening into one of the logs inside the dugout. But soon the women were both too confused about dates They argued constantly over when they had actually left home, how long they had been on the trail before getting stranded, and whether in fact there were 30 or 31 days in which months. During a fit of temper one morning, Janette grabbed her axe and thrashed all of the markings made on the log so that the crude calendar was turned into a pile of wood chips at her feet.

"I hope you are happy now," Mrs. Riker said, while angrily tying strips of cloth around her leather high-top shoes to keep them from falling off her feet. Months of trudging through the wet snow before warming her feet in front of the hot fire had grotesquely curled the leather until the shoes were painful to wear. The stiff toes pointed up and backward like the shoes worn by Christmas elves she'd once seen in a painting.

"I'm sick of arguing with you over how long we've been here," Janette said. She wrapped what was left of her scorched skirt around her knees. At the same time, she kicked a piece of kindling aside with her gnarled boot.

"Tie up your hair," Mrs. Riker ordered. "It looks like horse's mane hanging all over your body. I can hardly tell where your face is. You look like you're walking backward most of the time."

"It keeps me warm," Janette barked, thrusting a jagged hank over her shoulder. "Your own hair ain't as prim and slick as you think it is." With that she waded outside, dragging her axe behind her in the snow.

Janette's harsh words startled her mother. Of course they had no mirror to see themselves, so they depended on one another's observations. But still, Mrs. Riker had not stopped to think that her own hair had become quite shaggy and unruly. However, she did notice that their charcoal-smeared faces, hands, and clothing reeked of rancid cooking grease and woodsmoke.

Hugging her jar of seed corn, she peeked from the dugout and watched her daughter struggle away through the snow toward the forest. It occurred to Mrs. Riker how brave Janette was, and she felt guilty for scolding her about her hair. Mrs. Riker suddenly remembered she herself was middle-aged, probably a widow, so her own appearance did not matter anymore. But Janette, being young, must have been discouraged by her thin body and how motley she had become. Her hands were red and swollen from scraping and lugging snow. Her face was wind-burned, her complexion blotched from poor diet. Janette's lower lip was perpetually cracked and bleeding. Mrs. Riker ached to hug her, but she was afraid of provoking Janette again.

235

They sensed spring was near because the days were longer. The terrible biting cold had eased somewhat. The sun felt warmer on their chapped faces when the women made morning trips around camp.

"The meat is sour," Janette said one evening, nibbling. "The weather is warming up. Too bad we did not have enough salt to pack more of the meat."

"Perhaps the stream will melt, and we can catch some fish," Mrs. Riker said.

"Not a bad idea," Janette answered. "Meanwhile, we better cook the meat longer so it don't make us sick. Good thing we've still got cornmeal left. There's elk and deer tracks in the snow. I might get close enough to shoot one."

Mrs. Riker did not want to discourage Janette from hunting. However, they both knew it was unlikely that she could get close enough to any game to use the handgun with accuracy.

The warm weather caused the snow to begin melting, while each day Mrs. Riker noticed the distant peaks losing more and more of their whiteness. When the thick snows disintegrated into icy puddles, the dugout lost its insulation. So while the weather warmed up during the day, the occupants were colder at night.

As the ground at camp began to clear of snow, Mrs. Riker saw the scattered oxen bones strewn across the meadow where the wild animals had dragged each piece. She thought perhaps the two creatures, who had been so fond of one another in life, would be comforted if together again. She began dragging the bones back to higher ground near the wagon to assemble the skeletons near one another.

"Ma? What are you doing?" Janette asked, frowning, holding her father's threadbare coat across her chest. All of the buttons had long since fallen off. Mrs. Riker had no way to replace them. There was sewing thread, but somehow she had lost the needle. Janette clawed a strand of dirty hair away from her red-rimmed eyes.

"Bim and Patches gave their lives here for us," Mrs. Riker said. "I hate to see them strewn about." She adjusted the skull that had the bullet hole in it against the other skull, making it look as if the two animals were conversing.

Janette shook her head. "If it makes you happy, Ma. Next you'll be talking to trees." She walked away.

Each morning Mrs. Riker looked out to make sure Bim and Patches were still there. In case some animal dragged a bone away during the night, she retrieved it to complete the skeletons who faced each other; white against the gray hillside. She would have liked to have them placed side by side, facing the same direction as their team in life. But it all got too confusing as to which bone went where. She had trouble discerning between front legs, back legs, and correct locations of the various ribs and vertebrae. Of course she took into consideration they no longer had all their bones. Some had been totally eaten by animals, and others the women had ruined during their own cooking. She spent many hours pondering this puzzle while Janette suggested they make soup.

One terrible morning while Mrs. Riker fretted over bones, Janette pointed to the jar of seed corn held under Mrs. Riker's arm. "Ma! The corn is growing! You warmed up the seeds holding them like that all winter!"

Mrs. Riker jerked the jar up to her face. Sure enough, the kernels had sprouted. Moisture must have gotten into them. Long white roots oozed mold among miniature green spears all tangled in a ball inside the jar. "No! It's too early for planting! Everything is ruined!" she gasped.

"It's all right, Ma. We can't stay here anyway."

Mrs. Riker sank weeping to the ground. Opening the jar, she set it between the lower edges of the oxen skulls near the teeth. "Here Bim, here Patches. At least you will have a green meal."

That night a thunderstorm lashed the valley, and great streams of floodwater drove the women from the dugout. They ran to the Conestoga, which had staunchly survived the winter on its high knoll. They dragged what was left of their supplies into the wagon. Icy water gushed from the sky, swirling over them, dribbling down their sleeves as they fought with the tarp, securing it onto the wagon.

Having completed the task, cold, wet, and shivering, the women clung together while the deluge roared below the wagon. On high ground, they were safe and somewhat sheltered from the storm. For the first time since this ordeal began, Janette and her mother put their arms around each other.

In the morning they peeped out of the canvas to check the destruction the night's floodwaters had wreaked on their little valley. Janette let out a yelp!

Mrs. Riker grabbed the hatchet, fearing the worst. Three Indians sat on shaggy horses near the muddy spot where the women had built the dugout. The visitors scanned the area—eyes particularly drawn to the skeletal oxen facing each other on the high ground beside the wagon.

The leader urged his chestnut horse forward while signalling his wary companions to wait at the edge of the woods. He held a tight rein on his spotted pony, and all the while his right hand gripped the handle of a knife tucked in his waistband.

Janette and her mother hopped down from the wagon, fearful these people meant harm. However, the Indians looked more astonished than anything else.

"I am of the Bannock," the rider said when he drew his horse to a halt in front of the wagon. There were furs tied behind his saddle. He wore long leather leggings and a heavy buckskin shirt. His dark eyes flashed nervously around camp. "You have men?"

Mrs. Riker cringed. Now they would have to admit that they were alone.

But Janette stood right up to him, leaning casually against her axe. "No men," she answered. Her voice was flinty.

The Indian squinted, eyes clinging to Bim and Patches, who nosed the jar of seed corn.

"We are going to Walla Walla!" Mrs. Riker found the courage to blurt.

The Indian's eyebrows shot up. "Walla Walla!" He pointed west while signalling his companions to join him. By using a few words in English and many hand signals, the Indians conveyed to the women that they would take them to Walla Walla.

The women left the valley that day, carrying what few things they could on their backs. The guides treated the women cautiously. Mrs. Riker later learned the Indians were intrigued because they thought she and Janette were insane. One month later they arrived safely at Walla Walla. It was never determined what happened to Mr. Riker and his sons.

ANNA SURRATT

On April 14, 1865, President Abraham Lincoln was assassinated in Washington, D.C. at Ford's Theater while he watched a play. The world was stunned. The assassin, John Wilkes Booth, was hunted and killed by a posse within the next few days. It was determined, however, that Booth had co-conspirators. Soon three men and a woman named Mary Surratt were arrested for their part in the plot. Tried, convicted, sentenced to be hanged, the four were executed. Mary Surratt went to her death professing innocence. Her part in the assassination was never sufficiently proven. Her teenage daughter, Anna Surratt, tried desperately to appeal to President Johnson to show mercy. But Anna was kept from seeing the President by Preston King of New York, and Senator James H. Lane of Kansas. Six months after the execution of Mrs. Surratt, King tied a bag of shot around his neck and jumped off the Hoboken ferry. Eight months later, Senator Lane shot himself.

My execution is tomorrow. I am accused of taking part in a conspiracy to assassinate President Lincoln. My teenage daughter, Anna Surratt, has promised to speak with President Johnson on my behalf. Surely this government will not hang a poor innocent widow. My Anna will find a way to rescue her own mother. Won't she? When last I saw her two days ago, her face seemed so drawn, her lips set in pain.

Tonight is July 6, 1865. I think of Anna. A pretty girl. Dark hair, eyes blue like my own. She has suffered horribly these past three months. First President Lincoln was assassinated by John Wilkes Booth on Good Friday in April. Next, soldiers rushed onto my property, arresting me along with three men who roomed at my boardinghouse—Lewis Paine, David Herold, and George Atzerodt. We were all friendly with Booth, and we were accused of plotting with him to kill the President. Booth himself was soon caught and killed after the assassination—leaving me and the others to face the brunt of Yankee wrath. Cringing in the darkness inside my prison cell, I touch my face. I have no mirror. The newspapers after my arrest called me a handsome widow. Handsome? At age 47 perhaps the word "beautiful" no longer applies. I am of average build. My straight black hair is parted down the middle and tied in a chignon at the back of my neck. I have large, deep-set eyes. Straight mouth. Anna? Have you spoken to President Johnson yet? I beg to hear Anna's footsteps in the corridor outside my prison cell. She will bring the guards to set me free. When last we spoke she was bewildered, so innocent. The tragedy is her youth. How could I have raised such a mild girl? Anna? She is my only hope.

For three months I have been inside this filthy prison cell. Oh God, to think I ran the cleanest boardinghouse in Washington. Here I am defiled and alone. I see myself a pariah scorned by an entire nation.

I must be whining again. The guard peeks through the little barred window at me. He has unquiet black hair; rat-toothed. He is so skinny it seems his ribs undulate inside his shirt like the bones of a hungry dog. Am I losing my mind? Perhaps I only imagine it. Cries in the night, moans and shrieks of caged men awaiting dawn. Old Washington Penitentiary. Inside this dreadful place the dust is so thick it smells. My nostrils are filled with the stink of urine. My ankles are chained. Thank God at least the guards have not placed a hood over my head as they have done to the other conspirators. I understand poor Herold, Paine, and Atzerodt are hooded night and day. What do our tormentors think we are to see? Or do? General Frederick Hartranft is officer in charge of the prison. Has he no pity?

I am but a poor widow, having worked hard all of my life. I raised three children. Men took financial advantage of me after my husband died. Some still owe money for land bought from him—and never paid. How unchivalrous. Those pigs. Forget them.

Anna! Where is Anna? My beautiful girl, how will she stand up to President Johnson? A seventeen-year-old child, giggling with her friends. A coquettish girl not to be relied upon. Anna! My only hope. My heart breaks thinking of her trying to see the President on my behalf. But she is a shy, silly thing. Pasting pictures of John Wilkes Booth behind a mirror in her room! To this witless child I have pinned my hopes of getting a last-minute reprieve? This girl who has done little more in her life than clean house, and simper at Yankee soldiers?

Oh, Mary Surratt! I laugh out loud at myself. I think I am getting hysterical. But the sound of my own voice seems welcome. Can anybody else hear it? Doesn't anybody else know Mary Surratt is a good person who would not murder a President?

And those judges at the hearing. Holt, Foster, Burnett, and Tompkins. Those hanging faces, staring with empty eyes—determined to make an example of we four—calling us "conspirators." Hours and hours of testimony spouted against us—some lies were even told by men who boarded at my house. How they have betrayed me. Only Lewis Paine has repeated over and over that I am innocent. But to what avail? He himself condemned, who will listen to him? It seems after Booth was killed the whole country turned its fury on us. Was it not enough Booth was shot, dying horribly—killed inside a burning barn? Still these Northerners were sorry they had not the chance to hang him up. In one short summer my life has become an unbearable nightmare of worry and fear. *Hanged!* I am to be hanged? Who would have thought such a thing? Hanging is for criminals. Execution is for murdering brutes who

242

show no mercy. But me? A widow from Surrattsville in southern Maryland? A simple woman struggling to survive by running a boardinghouse on H Street in Washington City? Anna? Have you spoken to President Johnson yet? Where is Anna? Where are my children now? Two sons and a daughter who cannot come to their own mother's rescue? I should have strangled them all at birth. And my husband out there drinking in the tool-shed.

Oh Mary Surratt, stop blaming others for your predicament. But really, I knew nothing of this so-called plot I am accused of. Men coming and going from my boarding house, whispering war and kidnap and conspiracy. Everybody is guilty of that! We have all whispered war and kidnap and conspiracy for nearly five years. And Lincoln! Murdered. Killed by Booth. Booth, a man I trusted, a man who had entry to my home. But people like myself who knew Booth were not necessarily involved in his wickedness. Were we? How could he have implicated me? Drag me into his scheme?

Oh, how my mind whirls about, night and day...night and day. Who could sleep on this disgusting cot? I am filthy in my clothing, confounded by my middle-age curse —prison guards bring cloth sacking for me to stuff between my legs. It is all so embarrassing and dreary. How God has punished me for being an innocent woman, a poor dupe too stupid to run away while I had the chance. I should have gone south, to Richmond. Anywhere. Opening a boardinghouse in Washington was inviting trouble. Why couldn't I see it? One of my sons a Confederate soldier, the other a Confederate courier. That did not bode well for me during my so-called trial.

I cannot sleep. Through the barred window is a dull night-sky devoid of stars. The heat is oppressive. The humidity. And the smell.

Feeling sorry for myself will not do. I must remain calm. Anna will appear any minute with the good news President Johnson has pardoned me. Tomorrow is July 7. I have been in this hideous place nearly three months. I have brushed shoulders with the devil. It seems a hopeless journey. My mind does not rest. Sleep. Sleep. If only I could sleep. And wake up in a peaceful country place—even Surrattsville would be a welcome sight again. Under a shady tree—perhaps my husband would stop to talk a while, discuss with me our children and our plans and what we will do with the land and the tavern.

My husband. Gone. Deserted me in death long ago.

I feel this ugly wetness between my legs. More embarrassment when the guards come back. Oh God, if only You will let me fall asleep and take me quickly, while I am dozing. *Won't you please?* What have I done to deserve this calamity? Morning. It is Friday, July 7, 1865. In the dawn I hear footsteps moving about in the corridor. No point in my standing on tiptoes to look out the small barred opening of my iron door. There is nothing different, day or night, except a bowl of bland soup and the exchange of chamber pot. And in my case, a bundle of clean rags.

There is some noisy discussion this morning, a sinister excitement has settled over the place, even more suffocating than usual. I keep waiting for the welcome sound of a guard coming with jangling keys to announce Anna has gotten through to President Johnson. But no. Only a soup bowl passed into my cell, the chamber pots exchanged, the new rags tossed in.

The guard looks at me with some wonderment today, half-frightened. Behind his eyes I see chiseled the dread of one who observes another's misfortune. Like looking at calves going to the slaughterhouse.

Head lowered, I try to take soup, but it has no taste for me. My stomach has been in knots. Anna has not appeared. And I have given up long ago the hope of seeing either of my sons again. Isaac is who-knows-where since the war ended. A Southern patriot, he is understandably fearful of showing up at his mother's execution. And John has run away to Canada. I don't blame him. There was some suspicion he was involved in the plot to assassinate Lincoln, too. Northern authorities were looking for him. Of course he was not involved. But then neither was I.

I keep thinking the dreaded day has finally arrived. July 7, 1865. I had some idea it would be drizzling today. But no. The heat is oppressive. And the sky blue and clear. The sun came up this morning, shiny as a new gold coin. How is it I have not taken the time to notice such details before?

The priest arrives. He soon scurries away without making eye contact with me. His excuse is having to visit the other condemned conspirators. But I suspect Paine and Herold and Atzerodt would sooner stand in the rain than give a confession to a priest. I myself had little to confess. What? Being proud and sometimes willful? I paid my debts. Avoided drink. Attended church. Have had no man in my life since my husband died. What is there to confess? That my great sin is having been stupid? That I will be remembered as a foolish woman who blundered into her own grave?

When I stand on my cot, I look down into the courtyard behind the prison. I shrink from the sight. Soldiers have lined the high brick wall behind the prison yard. The long wooden gallows was erected days ago—big enough to hold the four of us at once. The hammering and sawing was awful to hear. I survived it by closing my eyes, pretending the sounds were of my husband building a new house for me.

It bothers me I am not allowed a mirror. I cannot see my face. Is it clean? Is my hair smooth? Am I smudged with prison filth? I shove the soup bowl to the door. I change the rags—how awful—how embarrassing—male guards knowing my most personal trouble.

It is close to noon. Footsteps echo in the concrete corridor. Cell doors squeaking on rusty hinges are opened along the hall. I hear Paine still muttering in that defensive tone of his. He is quite a handsome man—thick neck and shoulders. But a bully. How I admire him for being strong under these circumstances. Neither he, Herold, nor Atzerodt had a hand in actually killing Abraham Lincoln. But they are accused of the attack on Secretary Seward and some other members of Lincoln's cabinet the night Lincoln was shot. Oh, I suppose they would have killed Lincoln too, had they an opportunity. Booth reserved that for himself. But me? Why me? I get sick killing a mouse.

The guard has opened my cell door at last. Two guards have come in. Without speaking, they remove my shoes. One more violation I must endure. Part of me says, *Scream, claw, fight.* Another part of me says, *It is no use, the best thing you can do is be brave. Mary Surratt, retain your dignity. It is all you have left.* Anna! Have you spoken to President Johnson yet? One guard at each arm, they steer me into the corridor to follow my fellow-condemned outside. We walk slowly, very slowly. Each step closer and closer to the end. I search the corridors for Anna. Where is Anna? Oh, foolish girl, she was not able to see the President after all. But maybe—just maybe there is still time. I have been a good Catholic. If you save me, God, I promise to do Thy will for the rest of my days. Anything. I'll open an orphanage. I'll scrub floors and give all the money to the church. I'll join a convent.

It is twelve-thirty. We are held inside the building for some reason. The word is General Hancock is waiting for a last-minute reprieve. The heat is suffocating. We hear the gallows trap doors being tested outside—thud—a hollow roar. Again. Like distant thunder.

No reprieve has come. Our procession begins. Outdoors the heat and bright sun and milling crowd unnerves me. I begin to weep, not because I am a coward. It is because I am shaky and embarrassed and angry that I have been made a scapegoat. I see myself a loathsome image hanging black-draped; what will be remembered of me? *Remain steadfast, Mary Surratt.* I tell myself. Stare back at them. There are hundreds of them—soldiers, government officials, newsmen, and one woman—Miss Major Walker, a surgeon. Northerners seething for one last chance at revenge. All the years of fighting and killing, and then Lincoln's death, have finally come down to this. Who would have dreamed I, along with three other poor fools, was destined to be the grand finale?

George Atzerodt is pushed up the scaffold steps first, then David Herold. Lewis Paine is just ahead of me, and I have come last. I can see the looks on the condemned men's faces, wild-eyed, breathing hard, struggling within their shackles. It is so high, fifteen long steps. Why so high? The hideous thing sways. Lined up, I look to my left only once to meet the gaze of Lewis Paine, the one man who continues to stress my innocence. Even now he is speaking to the guard holding him—it is as if keeping his mind on me, his thoughts are off himself.

There are nearly twenty people up here on the scaffold—soldiers, prison guards, clergymen, and the executioner. At my elbow is Hartranft in a long white coat and flat-brimmed straw hat. He looks away from me. Scanning the prison yard, my eyes rest on four pine boxes stacked on top of one another. East of the gallows close to the wall, four rough graves have been dug side by side. I can't take my eyes off those black holes.

I search one last time for Anna, but the frightening crowd is pushing and rumbling like a hungry monster ready to eat us all. The guards wrap our legs together with white cloth; the material looks torn from bed sheets. This is to keep us from kicking—it would be unsightly and unnerving to the spectators if we showed ourselves to be in stress while choking to death.

One of the guards is holding a black parasol over me. To protect my face from the sun! I look hard into his eyes for some reaction. Is this a joke? Is he making fun of my womanhood? Or is this a gesture of some kindness? What? Like giving Jesus a sip of water while he dangled from the cross? But I see the guard's face is like stone; eyes glazed. I cannot read his intention. Anyway, I think to hell with the parasol. I want to see the sun. Let me see the sun!

My heart thumps. I am suddenly anxious to get this over with. My lower body is tied round and round with muslin, my long black skirts folded in like an umbrella. Our shoes having been removed, I can see the white stockings of the condemned men. My own feet are covered by my hemline. At least these morbid thrill-seekers will not see my feet. And then the noose. We are each fitted with a noose.

Careful hands behind me draw wisps of hair gently from the back of my neck—why so tender? I suppress the urge to burst out laughing. Instead, I stifle a long moan. The noose. I feel hemp bristles stabbing my jaw. The dreaded hangman's knot is secured beside my left ear.

Anna? God help me! It is not too late. I count thirty armed soldiers slouched on the red brick wall behind us. They watch with no emotion, hardened faces immune to death after four years in the field.

I was told soldiers waiting under the scaffold will knock out the support posts. The gallows floor will drop with a sickening clatter. We four will tumble in unison. Oh God, don't let me fall!

White hoods are placed over our heads. This is not for our benefit. This is to protect the crowd from seeing our eyes bug, and our ghastly faces turn purple. I close my eyes, envisioning a plunge downward; knees doing an involuntary jerk. My ears pick up the sounds I had not previously noticed—somebody in the crowd laughing, others whispering—a paperboy outside the prison gate yells, "Mrs. Surratt is executed!" Anna! Have you spoken to President Johnson yet? The warrant is being read. A voice drones on in monotonous tones, accusing us of our part in a conspiracy to assassinate President Abraham Lincoln—we have been found guilty—we are sentenced to hang by our necks —until dead. It is black. The sack covering my face smells faintly of boiled cotton. I listen for the sound of a sledge hammer against the support posts. My whole world seems confined within the cloth hood pressing against my face. Men speak in hushed tones. Oh God, don't let me fall. Anna? Have...